# Revenge
## AND THE
# Wild

# Revenge
### AND THE
# Wild

## MICHELLE MODESTO

BALZER + BRAY

*An Imprint of* HarperCollins*Publishers*

Balzer + Bray is an imprint of HarperCollins Publishers.

Revenge and the Wild

Copyright © 2016 by Michelle Modesto

For information address HarperCollins Children's Books, a division of HarperCollins
Publishers, 195 Broadway, New York, NY 10007.

www.epicreads.com

Library of Congress Cataloging-in-Publication Data

Modesto, Michelle.

Revenge and the wild / Michelle Modesto. — First edition.

pages    cm

Summary: Seventeen-year-old foul-mouthed Westie, the notorious adopted daughter
of local inventor Nigel Butler, lives in the lawless western town of Rogue City, where she
sets out to prove the wealthy investors in a magical technology that will save her city are the
cannibals that killed her family and took her arm when she was a child.

ISBN 978-0-06-236615-3 (hardback)

[1. Fantasy.   2. Revenge—Fiction.   3. Magic—Fiction.   4. Cannibalism—Fiction.
5. People with disabilities—Fiction.   6. West (U.S.)—Fiction.]   I. Title.

PZ7.1.M637Re   2016                                                          2015015885

[Fic]—dc23                                                                        CIP

                                                                                      AC

Typography by Jenna Stempel

15 16 17 18 19  PC/RRDH  10 9 8 7 6 5 4 3 2 1

❖

First Edition

To my children, Donkey and Butters, for always being there . . . even when I'm trying to write

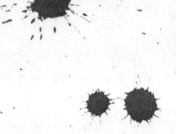

# One

Westie had left the valley at dawn to head home. The sun had risen soon after and followed her throughout the day. By four it just felt spiteful. Though her skin was burned and blistered, she preferred the sun over darkness during her travels. The road between the valley and Rogue City was a long, perilous one with dense woods on either side.

She tried to push away any thoughts of danger. They'd taken up too much space in her head on her journey. All she wanted to think about was home. Only a mile now stood between her and a hot meal that didn't consist of canned beans—she'd be home in plenty of time for supper.

Twigs snapped behind her like breaking bones, and Westie twisted in her saddle. There were plenty of harmless things that lived in the forest, but there were plenty of other things too. For the last hour she'd heard cracks and creaks, too uniform to be commonplace.

Ahead of her the road was barely wide enough to fit a stagecoach. The idea of trying to run her horse over its deep wagon ruts to escape made her nerves hum.

Another branch cracked, this time on her right. She gripped her reins tighter as she gazed out into the forest, searching for unlikely shapes or movement, too absorbed in finding the thing that stalked her to notice the dark figure on her left until it was right beside her.

Her muscles stiffened and she held her breath. Slowly turning, she saw the familiar hunched figure sitting atop a painted horse, looking at her with a smudge of a grin.

"Dammit, Bena, you scared the shit out of me," Westie said, her entire body sighing.

She slid from her saddle and reached for her horse's reins with the copper clockwork machine that had replaced her missing right arm. A labyrinth of brass gears and cogs moved when she flexed her metal fingers around the leather.

Bena Water-Dancer, named for the way she glided through the water while fishing, was a hunter in the Wintu tribe and moved like a shadow. She'd tried teaching Westie the technique once, but as birds scattered from trees and rabbits darted back into their holes, it became obvious Westie was more battering ram than cougar.

"If I'd been a creature, you'd be dead by now," Bena said, her accent dull in comparison to the beautifully fluid tongue of her native Wintu language. She too jumped down from her horse. Her long black hair was pulled away from her broad face into a braid as thick as her wrist. Though Bena was thirty, she still moved like a girl half her age and looked no older than when Westie had met her seven years ago.

Westie shrugged. "Creatures don't bother me none." It was common for creatures to attack travelers, but Westie had never run into any problems. She assumed it had something to do with the strangeness of her metal arm, or the creatures' fear of what she could do with it.

Bena scanned Westie's unwashed hair and her filthy clothes. Disapproval seemed the final judgment.

"It's no wonder. I could smell you from across the cow pastures. Let's get you home and in the bath before someone uses you as a weapon." Bena's eyes were crushed between her low forehead and high cheekbones when she smiled.

Westie grinned back and climbed onto her horse, cringing from saddle burn.

Ten minutes later they reached Rogue City. The tension that had been building up over the last two months melted from Westie's shoulders. She pulled at Henry's reins to stop him before crossing the shimmering dome of magic that surrounded the city. Like a soap bubble, it glistened with color and was near invisible if one wasn't looking for it. Westie was watching the last of the sunlight glitter across its surface when the dome suddenly vanished.

She gasped. "Did you see that?"

Bena looked around. "See what?"

"The dome—it disappeared."

It was only gone for a moment before it flickered back into place.

Had she blinked, she would've missed it. She stared in stunned disbelief, wanting to make sure it didn't happen again.

Bena squinted up at the sky even though Westie knew the woman's eyesight was better than any creature's. "It's still there. You have been on the road too long. Perhaps you are seeing things."

"Perhaps," Westie said, becoming suspicious when Bena didn't make eye contact. It wasn't like Bena to dismiss anything when it came to the protection of her people.

They passed through the watery-looking membrane. When Westie had first crossed paths with the dome on her way to live with Nigel as a child, she'd thought her clothes would get wet with the way it sparkled like water, or that she'd feel somehow changed when entering a place of magic, but it was the same as being on the other side.

The road cut between the parallel storefronts of Rogue City, each painted a different shade of ordinary. Ahead of them on the right was the Tight Ship saloon, a squalid hole in the wall with piano music and cigar smoke rolling out of the open windows. Westie's horse reared up as an elf and a young man crashed through the swinging doors into the street, a twisting ball of fists and foul language. Westie grabbed the horn of her saddle before she could be dumped off and glared down at the pair.

An ogre and a dwarf (or what Westie thought was a dwarf; she was always getting them confused with the bakhtak—stocky little creatures blamed for causing nightmares) stepped out of the saloon behind them to watch the fisticuffs. As soon as the dwarf saw Westie and Bena, he crossed his arms protectively in front of himself and went back inside.

The elf, nimble and rather beautiful with his long, fair hair and soft features, was fast, avoiding the brunt of the young man's advances. But the human was quicker with his feet, kicking the elf's legs out from under him each time he tried to stand.

Each seemed too drunk to get the best of the other until the young man noticed Westie and Bena nearby. His eyes went wide, mouth falling open as he looked at Westie. The distraction allowed the elf to gain the upper hand and pin the human against a hitching post.

"You're strong for a girl," the young man said to the elf, a cocky grin moving his lips. He couldn't have been older than sixteen, an aristocrat from the looks of his clothes, with skin that looked as smooth as the petals of a spring magnolia.

The elf's prominent forehead was even more so when he frowned. "I'm a male." He spit out another word in a language Westie couldn't understand.

The young man's brows rose high on his forehead. "You are?"

With a growl, the elf pushed the young man into the ogre's waiting arms.

"Hello, beautiful," the young man said in a strangled voice. The ogre squeezed him in a vise grip around his torso and then flipped him upside down. Coins fell from the young man's pockets onto the ground.

The ogre, built like the trunk of a redwood with boils and warts covering its greenish skin, released a noxious odor—reminiscent of a polecat—that nearly knocked Westie out of the saddle.

She pulled her kerchief over her nose and laughed as Bena shook her head. Most creatures kept to the wilds, but those who wanted luxuries only humans could provide, and chose to live under the dome, behaved just like any other fool. Though Westie couldn't say she liked them much, at least they were entertaining.

"That's enough," Westie said, her laughter trailing off as the ogre exposed jagged, bloodstained teeth. The boy was no match for a creature. "Put him down."

When the ogre didn't let go of the boy right away, what remained of Westie's smile slid from her face. "Go on now. Let him go before this gets ugly."

A vein protruded from the young man's forehead, his face red and swollen from being hung upside down. "I think this got ugly five minutes ago," he said with a not-so-subtle nod toward the ogre.

Westie rolled her eyes. Clearly he had no idea of the danger he was in. The Wintu might have cast a spell over the town making it impossible for creatures to kill humans without giving up their own lives, but there were things worse than death.

The ogre looked from the young man to Westie's mechanical arm, then dropped him to the ground.

On the opposite side of the road, at the blood brothel, a group of vampires cheered for the fight to continue, only a glimpse of pale faces and the glint of dark-lensed goggles visible under the awning that protected them from the sun.

The young man stood up, brushed the dust from his clothes, and ran a hand over his dark, oiled hair, never taking his eyes off Westie. The color came back to his face, leaving a beautiful flush in his cheeks.

Frowning, Westie covered her chin with her hand, wondering if there was a blemish worth all his attention. She was used to people staring, but it was usually at her mechanical arm.

"Are you some kind of dummy?" she said.

He blinked up at her. "Pardon me?"

She pointed a metal finger toward the elf and the ogre as they receded back into the saloon. "Picking a fight with creatures like that." She didn't like getting mixed up with creatures—not only because of their penchant for violence, but also because they were known for holding grudges.

"I didn't start that fight. . . ." He tilted his head in thought, a smile spreading across his face. "Actually, I suppose I did. You see, the elf had been killing me at cards all afternoon. I tried flirting to throw her—er, *him,* I should say—off his game. I don't think he liked me running my hands through his hair, but how was I supposed to know he was a male? I thought all the hitting was some sort of creature foreplay."

Bena snorted behind her.

Westie shook her head. "The ears," she said, exasperated. "Males have longer, pointier ears."

"I see." He chuckled, looking around, up at the dome. "What a strange place, this Rogue City."

"You new in town?"

Of course he was. Westie knew everyone in their small town.

Not too many humans liked the idea of cohabiting with creatures, and the ones who did were often hiding from something.

He pulled a flask from his hip pocket. "Just arrived today."

Westie watched him take a drink and felt her mouth begin to water. "You'll be lucky to survive the night at the rate you're making enemies."

He had the kind of slick smile that could turn sharp girls into simpletons. "Luckily, I have you here to protect me."

Bena cleared her throat. "We should get you home. It's getting late."

"Perhaps I'll see you again," the young man said.

"Let's hope not." Westie tugged at her horse's reins, urging him in the opposite direction. "You seem like the kind of trouble I want no part of."

His laughter came easily. There was something oddly familiar about the sound of it that put her at ease. She wondered what a dandy like him was doing in a place like Rogue City but didn't want to give him the wrong idea by asking such a personal question.

Past the east side of town there were few creatures to be seen. No laws had been set in place or lines drawn in the sand, but creatures kept to the east side of town and humans kept to the west for the most part in order to avoid one another.

Westie slowed her horse, and they strolled at an easy pace through the center of town. The buildings looked a century old even though Rogue City had been only in its infancy when Westie had first gone to live with Nigel seven years ago. Two traveling men stood outside the Roaming Inn, their heads bent in discussion. When they looked up and saw Westie and Bena, their hands eased toward the weapons at their belts. Curious townsfolk looked out from their shop windows to catch a glimpse of the pair.

Westie wasn't concerned for herself. It was Bena the townspeople had eyes for. They didn't trust the natives. They didn't trust the creatures either, but all the creatures had were teeth and claws—natives had magic. No matter that Wintu magic was the only thing that kept the teeth and claws of creatures from tearing out human throats.

Bena ignored the fear in the eyes of those watching. Westie raised her arm to them, sun beaming off her metal hand as she made a rude gesture with her fingers. The corner of her mouth hooked into a smile when she heard the yelps of women and disapproving grumbles of men before they scattered back into their holes like cockroaches.

# Two

Bena didn't want to get between Nigel and Westie if he started in—yet again—about Westie being gone too long, so they parted ways at the border of Nigel's property, and Westie headed down the long path alone.

Opening the door and seeing that the foyer was empty, she walked inside. The familiar smell of exotic spices brought her back to a happier place. Nigel's house was something to behold, a two-tiered kingdom of baubles picked up during his travels around the world. The place had a cluttered, lived-in quality that Westie loved.

Hearing the tick-tack of claws on hardwood, Westie turned and saw Jezebel, their pet chupacabra, stalking toward her. Westie braced herself, but it was no use. Jezebel pounced, knocking Westie into a flock of metal telegraph birds hanging on strings from the ceiling before falling to the floor.

Despite her aching tailbone, Westie laughed, wrapping her arms around Jezebel's neck. Nigel had saved the young beast from Mexican poachers, who'd had her hung up in one of their traps and were about to cut off her paws for good luck charms.

"Hello, big girl. I've missed you," Westie said as the beast nuzzled against her hand. Jezebel was nearly five hundred pounds, the size of a lion.

Westie had never seen a chupacabra before moving to California and had thought they were just myths, like most of the creatures native to the West that she'd never seen in Kansas. Hunched like bears, with a thick, wiry coat and bone-like spikes that started from the neck and rode down the back to the base of the tail, they weren't pretty. Their fur was black as obsidian, and their faces were elongated, with tufts of hair on the cheeks and chin like a werewolf midtransition.

Westie scratched the beast behind one pointed ear and listened to the deep chuffing sound she made, almost like a purr. She'd wanted to take Jezebel hunting with her—chupacabras were excellent hunters and could easily have tracked a cannibal—but, alas, Nigel never would have allowed it. "You're just an overgrown pup, ain'tcha? You really are a lovely beast when you're happy—"

"Just like someone else I know," said a voice behind her.

Nigel stood in the doorway of the main sitting room. He was from Africa but had lived most of his life in England before moving to America at twenty. He had a handsome face and wore a handlebar mustache waxed to points at the ends.

"Seems a little empty around here," Westie said as she brushed

Jezebel's fur from her trousers. Though the house was full of souvenirs, she could see bare spots where some of his inventions used to be. Instead of the display case full of mechanical limbs, there was a rectangle stamped out of the clutter, showing the green-and-gold damask wallpaper behind it. In a corner, the chest of nonsensical inventions he liked to tinker with was missing.

"I needed the copper," Nigel said.

She looked curiously at him. He rarely recycled copper and found it difficult to part with any of his inventions, even the ones that never worked.

"For Emma?" she asked.

In his younger years, Nigel's inventions had been transportation-inspired because of his love for travel: airships and land engines, mostly. After he took Westie and Alistair into his charge, his creations became more prosthetic and medically geared.

But something had changed recently. All he'd worked on for the last year was a heaping pile of copper parts that seemed to have no function other than taking up space in the great room. He called it Emma—Earth-Magic Mechanical Amplifier.

Westie didn't know much about his new invention. He had told her once what the machine did, something about pulling magic from gold or some such nonsense, but she hadn't cared enough to pay attention.

"Of course," he said.

Westie looked toward the hallway just as Alistair walked around the corner. Paying attention to Westie instead of where he was walking, he bumped into a wall, knocking down a shelf of novels. She would've laughed had her heart not seized at the sight of him. He wore a mask that enabled him to speak, made of clockwork bits that rotated when he breathed. It was lined with leather to keep the metal from touching his skin, and it covered his face from the bridge of his nose to the bottom of his chin. His high-collared shirt hid scars on his neck. Every inch of him was covered except for the top half of his face.

As he looked at Westie with large eyes as blue as a broken heart, a dormant ember stirred within her.

"Hello, Alley," Westie said, hoping her dirty face would conceal the blaze in her cheeks.

He nodded without speaking.

"How did it go?" Nigel asked Westie.

She'd been looking for the cannibals who'd killed her family since she was fourteen. In the beginning Nigel didn't approve of her leaving for weeks without knowing how to use weapons properly or fight, but he never stopped her—even after he'd taught her those things, he still didn't like her being gone. When he looked at her this time, there was hope in his gaze, like maybe she'd finally given up.

"Could've gone better," she said. "Maybe next time."

Nigel released the breath he'd been holding. "I see. Well, anyway, we've missed you around here. You've been gone too long. The road is no place for a teenage girl."

After two months away, Westie had forgotten what it was like to have someone worry over her. It came as both a relief and an annoyance.

"I'm no girl. Women my age are married and sprouting children."

Nigel shrugged his lips and shoulders together like a ventriloquist dummy with one string for all motions. "Perhaps you should be doing the same."

Westie glared at him. "Maybe you're right. I reckon I ought to stop turning down the suitors lining up, waiting to take my copper hand in marriage. Imagine the wedding night." She grabbed two walnuts from a decorative glass tray on the table beside the door and crushed them together into a fine powder with a gentle flex of her metal fingers.

Nigel gave her a thoughtful look and sighed. "I fear I've done you a great disservice by letting you run wild all these years. It'll be difficult finding proper suitors for you with those manners."

She let the walnut dust slide from her fingers onto a Turkish rug and looked at her copper machine. "Manners don't have a thing to do with it."

"Have you been keeping up with your lessons?" he asked.

She patted the leather satchel slung across her chest. "Right here." Ever since she'd gotten kicked out of school, Nigel had been her teacher—a rather relentless one at that.

"Wonderful." Westie pretended not to notice Nigel holding his breath and leaning away from her. It had been some time since her last bath. "Then I suppose you've earned your prize." He turned to his assistant. "Alistair, would you be a saint and fetch Westie's reward? It's in my study. Oh, and some drinks, if you will."

With a nod Alistair disappeared.

A gray-haired Chinese woman wearing a maid's uniform walked in holding a broom and pushed Westie to the side to sweep up the dust at her feet. Confusion twisted Westie's features as more and more servants buzzed in and out of the room. The only time Nigel hired anyone to clean was on special occasions.

"What's with the help?" she asked.

Nigel looked down, brushing some invisible thing off his shirt. "I've invited a guest for supper. He'll be here shortly; the rest of his family will be traveling from Sacramento via airship tomorrow morning with Mayor Chambers. They're possible investors for Emma."

"But you detest the mayor."

"No . . . I dislike the mayor's charging-bull approach to politics, but he's bringing me investors, so for now I find him quite agreeable."

Alistair walked into the room holding a jug, two glasses, and a parasol of fine antique lace and pearls tucked under his arm. Seeing tea in the jug instead of wine, Westie frowned. Her disappointment deepened when Alistair handed Nigel the parasol. It was beautiful, no doubt. All the gifts he gave her were beautiful, but they were usually swords, or daggers. Westie had never been the type of girl to sit in front of picnic baskets or stroll down city streets with a handsome man on one arm and a parasol on the other.

"Thank you, Nigel. It's, uh, something, but . . ."

Nigel ran a long finger down the length of it before gripping the end of the parasol and giving it a sharp yank to unsheathe a gleaming sword made of Japanese steel.

Westie immediately reached for it. "Now *that's* something."

Nigel made a tsking sound, holding it just out of her reach. "You must be careful."

He pointed to the umbrella tip of the parasol. Westie noticed the opening of a barrel, and just above it, a bolt and trigger.

"Oh!"

A gun. Nigel carried a weapon just like it himself, hidden beneath the dark wood of his cane. He took it everywhere and used it to aid the limp he'd acquired from an orc bite during the creature war, when man and creature had been fighting over territory in the West.

Westie smiled down at her gift. Not even an outlaw would take a lady's parasol from her. She liked the idea of never being without a weapon.

She threw herself into Nigel's arms for a hug. He tensed beneath her. Nigel was not affectionate in a physical sense, nor was Westie, usually, but she was thrilled with her gift and he was getting a hug whether he liked it or not. Her mechanical arm with the power of a hundred horses was there to see he didn't argue.

"All right, that's quite enough," he said, pushing her away with a smile in his voice. "Go on, clean up. Supper is in two hours."

# Three

After a bath and a short attempt at a nap, Westie entered the dining room. The servants were still in the house. They prepared the meal and set the table. The food smelled far better than any of Nigel's concoctions.

Nigel and Alistair had already taken their seats. Alistair had an empty place where his plate of food should've been. It was no surprise, for he never ate with them, not since he'd stopped taking off his mask. There were two other settings, one for Westie and one for the mystery guest. Westie sat down next to Nigel and watched a young servant girl haul a stack of linens up the stairs.

"Did someone piss the bed?" Westie asked.

Nigel coughed into his hand. "Honestly, Westie, at the table?"

"Well," she said, noticing Alistair's eyes squint the way they did when he smiled, "why are the servants changing all the sheets in the house?"

Nigel said, "I told you the mayor's friends will be in town tomorrow."

"You mean they're staying *here*?"

"I'm not about to let them stay at that flea-infested inn."

"How long will they be staying?"

"However long it takes to convince them that Emma, when it's complete, will be worth the money they invest and then some."

Westie meant to ask Nigel more about the investors but was distracted by movement in the corner of the room as a man—no, a boy—peeked in from the hall.

"You?" she said, twisting in her seat to look at the young aristocrat from the saloon. Her knife fell off the table with a clatter.

He smiled with his entire face. "Hello again." He'd cleaned up and had changed his clothes since the last time she'd seen him, wearing a crisp white shirt beneath a leather vest. "Sorry I'm late."

Alistair and Nigel rose from their seats. When Westie tried to stand, she stepped on the hem of her gown, teetering before righting herself. She hardly ever wore dresses while on the road. It would take some getting used to again.

"You two know each other?" Nigel asked.

The young man exposed a trellis of brilliant white teeth when he opened his mouth. "She saved me from a troll this afternoon."

Nigel's face was electric with joy when he looked at Westie. "You did?"

"It was an ogre, actually," Westie said, enjoying Nigel's smile for the moment. If tradition held, it was only a matter of time before she disappointed him again.

"Wonderful!" Nigel said, turning to his guest. "James, this is my daughter, Westie, and my assistant, Alistair. Westie, Alistair, I'd like to present James Lovett Junior, the son of our former mayor and nephew of the investors."

"Pleased to meet you," James said.

"Why didn't you travel with the rest of your family?" Alistair asked. His words were monotone, part of the mask he wore. There was a sharp grinding noise as he spoke, like the gears were starting to seize. It was the sound her own mechanical device made when it needed to be oiled.

James leaned away from Alistair, clearly not used to the quirks of prosthetic machines.

"I'm terrified of air travel, actually. I prefer my horse," James said.

His easy admission of fear was somewhat endearing to Westie, but she was still uncertain what to think of him. At a glance he appeared good-looking, wealthy, and well bred—a stark contrast to the tipsy boy she'd seen fighting with creatures in front of the saloon.

They sat down to their meal. James took his seat across from Westie and tucked his napkin neatly into his collar, pressing it down. One of the servants set a steaming plate in front of him.

"This looks delicious," he said.

He used the tips of his fingers on his fork and knife to slice off dainty pieces of meat. When he chewed, his jaw barely moved. It looked tiresome.

When Westie bent to grab her knife off the floor, Nigel shot her a look that said, *Don't even think about it.* On the road, dirt and manners had been the least of her worries. She rolled her eyes, sat back up, and began to eat.

James watched the twisted fork in Westie's metal hand as she scooped heaping loads of food into her mouth and smacked her lips. Nigel tapped his fork against his plate, a reminder for her to chew with her mouth closed.

Westie pressed her lips together, breathing heavily through her nose.

James continued to watch her. It wasn't just her machine he studied—*that* she could handle; she was used to it. When James looked at her, he looked at all of her. She felt exposed, as if he could look inside her head and see all her secrets.

She dropped her fork on her plate, startling the servants refreshing their drinks.

"Anyone ever tell you it's not polite to stare?" she said.

"Westie!" Nigel stuck a sharp elbow into her rib. She winced, grabbing her side. He turned to James. "I'm so very sorry—she didn't mean it. She's just a bit cantankerous from traveling." Nigel's eyes bulged when he looked back at her. "Isn't that right?"

Not wanting to upset Nigel on her first day back, she submitted, sagging in her chair. "Sorry," she said, not sounding sorry at all. "I'm just tired from being on the road, is all." That part was true. Her eyelids and limbs felt heavy, and a yawn waited at the back of her throat. When she was traveling alone, it wasn't safe to close her eyes more than a few minutes. The lack of sleep was finally catching up with her. "If you'll excuse me, I think I'll turn in for the night."

All three men stood when she did. She kicked at the hem of her gown to get it out of her way so she didn't trip over it and make a fool of herself. She walked away, unaware that a piece of the tablecloth was stuck between the copper joints of her mechanical elbow. It wasn't until dishes crashed to the floor behind her and servants shrieked like loons that she realized what she'd done.

"Sonofabitch." She closed her eyes and groaned.

Westie heard the buzz of Alistair's mechanical laughter. When she opened her eyes, she saw James biting his lip to keep from smiling. Nigel's mouth was agape as he took in the destruction around him.

"Nigel, I'm sorry—" she tried to say before he cut her off.

"Go to bed, Westie."

She sighed and, with a nod, went upstairs to her room.


Westie was brushing her hair in front of the vanity when there was a knock at her door.

"It's open," she said.

She watched Nigel in the mirror as he limped across the room and took a seat in the chair beside her bed. He still dressed like a chap in the London fog, wearing a jacket the color of strong tea, just a shade lighter than his skin.

"I need to tell you something," he said.

"This isn't one of your stories, is it?"

When she was young, he used to sit in that very chair, crossing his legs just like he was doing right then. His stories were always about the things she loved: castles and dragons, slaying evil with broadswords. Though she loved the medieval subjects, Nigel was a terrible storyteller. His characters were flat—the maidens were always beautiful, helpless half-wits, and the heroes handsome and perfect, when she knew darn well that after traveling for days to rescue the princess from her tower, they probably stank like pigs and were in need of a good shit.

"Not this time, I'm afraid." He tapped his cane on the edge of her bed. "Come on over—let's talk."

She placed her brush on the vanity, lay down on the bed, and settled in beneath her covers.

The puffy skin beneath Nigel's eyes made him look like he'd been in a fight. "I've given you freedom to do what you want and be who you are, which I'll never regret, but I do wish, for your own good, that I had contained the wildness just a bit."

Embarrassed, she asked, "Is this about what happened during supper? I swear I didn't mean to do that."

"Yes and no. Please, just listen."

She nodded.

Nigel continued, wringing his hands as he went. "The thing is, I need you to rein in that wildness of yours if only a little. It is of the utmost importance."

She didn't like the sound of that.

He said, "I'd like you to be nice to James—and the investors when they arrive. Emma isn't just some silly little contraption to give us more leisure time. It is my most important work yet, and their money is my last hope to finish it."

Westie leaned her head back and let out a loud breath. Nigel thought all of his inventions were important. "Emma is the silliest thing you've made, if you ask me. It takes gold and turns it into magic. It's not like you can do anything with the magic once you make it. Only the Indians know how to use it."

"It doesn't turn gold into magic—it pulls magic from the gold and amplifies it. Gold is to magic like quartz is to sound. It conducts"—Nigel shook his head, looking and sounding worn out—"oh, never mind. That's not important, but what I'm about to tell you is. It is paramount that you keep what I'm about to tell you confidential."

She didn't like the sound of that either. Keeping secrets wasn't something she'd ever win a blue ribbon for.

"Well, what is it?"

He took a deep breath and let it sift out through his teeth before saying, "I don't know exactly how to put this. The thing is . . . well . . ."

Westie had never seen Nigel struggle to say anything before. She sat up in bed, thinking whatever it was must be worse than she'd imagined.

"Go on, spit it out."

He puffed his cheeks and blew the words out. "Magic is disappearing."

"Disappearing?" Westie pushed out a breath of laughter. "When did you grow such a warped sense of humor?"

Nigel frowned. The only other time Westie had seen Nigel look so sad was the first day she'd met him at the Wintu camp, when Bena had told him how Westie had lost her arm. "I'm afraid it's no joke."

"But magic doesn't just get up and leave—" Westie's words caught like a hook in her throat and she was yanked from the water, unable to breathe. A fragmented memory flashed before her eyes: earlier that day she'd been standing in front of the dome, the last of the sun's light clinging to its shimmering membrane . . . and then it was gone.

"The dome," she said, her face drawn. "I saw it disappear for just a moment before it fell back into place. I thought I was just tired and was seeing things, but I wasn't, was I?"

He rubbed his nose as he sometimes did when he was upset. "No, you weren't seeing things."

She didn't know the consequences of no magic. She didn't understand how magic worked at all, really. Nigel told her once that it belonged solely to the American continent. She knew Native Americans, through some evolutionary process, were the only ones able to use the magic because they came from this land. Creatures were magic too, but unlike the Indians, the magic was born *into* the creatures. It was in their blood, muscle, tissue, where they themselves had changed. Because of magic, a vampire could live for four thousand years, a werewolf could transition from human to beast during a full moon, a banshee could see the future, and so forth. The Wintu controlled magic, therefore the Wintu could control creatures. It was how the Wintu could cast a spell that protected humans from creatures and not creatures from humans. Those protection spells were how the two groups had lived in harmony on the continent for thousands of years.

"How do you know it's disappearing?" Westie asked.

"Big Fish told me the earth wasn't responding to her commands. And now the dome is fading. I've been going out to the Wintu village to take care of the injured and ill now that their healing spells aren't working. They'd only ask for my help if things were dire."

"If magic dies, does that mean Rogue City won't be protected from creatures anymore?" Westie asked. It was a scary thought. There was rarely a kind word passed between her and a creature. She'd made plenty of enemies over the years.

"Technically, yes. There will be no protection for us against creatures, but it won't matter because it also means there will be no creatures. Magic lives within the creatures. If magic dies, they die with it."

A sinking feeling settled in her gut. "Does that mean the Wintu will die too?" She thought of Bena and Big Fish, and the rest of the Wintu tribe, who had taken care of her after she'd lost her arm. Losing Bena would be like losing family.

"No. The Wintu are human. They just won't have magic to control. They'll be like the rest of us."

The sinking feeling dissipated instantly. "Well, why didn't you say so? I don't see the problem. No creatures means no need for magic."

Nigel shook his head, disappointment warping his kind features. "The Wintu's control of magic is far superior to most tribes. Settlers stay away from the tribe for the most part because of their fear of magic. It's what has kept the Wintu safe all these years after so many other tribes were slaughtered. Not only that, but killing off creatures is not a small thing either. They have a right to this land and to their survival just as much as the Wintu."

She knew better than to argue with Nigel when it came to the importance of creatures. He'd been a die-hard advocate for their rights ever since he was a soldier during the creature war, when a faery had saved his life after he was bitten—even though her kind was the enemy.

Westie picked at her nails with the tips of her copper fingers. There was a long, awkward pause before she said, "I get why you want to save magic now, but unless these investors of yours are creatures, there's no way they'll want to put money into that machine. They'll see a way to get rid of creatures and Indians alike."

"That's where you're wrong."

"How in blazes do you plan to get folks to buy this machine?"

"Simple. Only the Wintu, Alistair, and the two of us know that magic is disappearing and that when it does, the creatures will die with it. All I have to do is tell people I've built a machine that will produce enough magic with one nugget of gold to protect a town the size of Rogue City from creature attacks for years. Of course, only certain native tribes can use the magic the machine harvests to cast the protection spell." He raised a brow, watching her to see if she understood.

Westie's lips tilted into a knowing grin. "Thus ensuring the safety of the Wintu people, while keeping magic alive for the creatures."

He smiled. "If I can just get these people to invest the money I need to finish the machine, they can in turn sell the technology to other towns and be richer than any tycoon."

Westie glanced back down at her hands and tugged at the sheet stuck between the gears at her wrist. She said, "I take it the moral of this story is not to scare away investors with my rotten manners."

He tapped her knee with a gentle hand. "Don't forget the cussing."

She grumbled. It would be a hard task to pull off, for she rarely thought about such things. "Don't worry. I'll be on my best behavior."

"Thank you," he said as he stood up. "Now get some sleep. We have a big day ahead of us tomorrow."

# Four

The next morning Alistair walked into Westie's room holding a silver tray with a cup and kettle on it. Her heart thumped like a cart with a loose wheel when she saw him standing there in his mechanical mask, dark hair in anarchy around his face. His eyes settled on her, two glowing blue moons behind thick lashes.

"Hope you don't mind me barging in. Nigel sent me to bring you some tea," he said.

There were aches and pains all over her body from the long ride home, but it was the stiffness in her shoulder that stood out most. She tried to move her arm but realized her machine was stuck to her head.

Her face warmed with embarrassment. "Can I get a little help here?"

The skin around Alistair's eyes creased when he smiled under his mask. He placed the tray on the bedside table and sat down beside her. Westie stared down at their touching knees.

"You were gone longer than usual," Alistair said, gently unwinding her hair from the exposed gears of her arm.

"I was closer to them than usual."

The fresh smell of soap wafted from his skin each time he moved. She'd missed that scent so much while she was away.

He kept glancing at her face to make sure he wasn't hurting her. Each time their eyes met, he stole a little piece of her that she'd been trying to take back from him for the last three years.

"Nigel was worried," he said. The voice emanating from his mask was metallic and without emotion, like talking through a fan. But his eyes, they were full of life and sharp as daggers. They could cut a hole in a heart and stay there long after he had looked away. No one knew that better than Westie.

"Oh." She made a huffing sound. "*Nigel* was worried."

He hesitated. "I was worried too. It's dangerous for you to be out searching alone. It's a fool's errand."

Her voice climbed an octave. "A fool's errand?"

Her hair was a knot on the side of her head by the time he was done.

"I know you want justice, Westie, but you've become obsessed."

He always said such things, but she couldn't understand why. As loyal as Alistair was, Westie knew if it was the other way around and the killers of his family were never caught, he would go after them no matter what it took or how foolish it seemed.

With her hands free, she took the kettle from the tray on the table. "You don't understand anything." She blew into her cup, steam wetting her cheeks. "The cannibals who killed your family and took your voice are dead. The ones who killed mine are still out there."

"You don't know that—"

"I do know that!" she snapped. "I feel it in my gut."

Alistair of all people should've understood her need to catch the cannibals. It had been only six years since they'd found him on the wagon trail. Westie was just eleven years old when she and Nigel came upon two men hunched over Alistair like they were praying over their dead. When Westie had asked if they were in need, both men looked up with blood on their faces and flesh between their teeth. Bodies had been scattered across the forest floor, their faces chewed to a pulp. Alistair was the last one left of his entire family too. The two of them were made of the same leather.

The thought of Alistair's close call with death brought forth memories of Westie's own family: her mother and father tied up on the floor of the old hunting cabin, waiting to be slaughtered; her younger brother murdered and made into a stew. There was a throbbing sensation in the stump of her arm. Looking down, she half expected to see her bloody limb hanging on by a tendon. When she saw her machine instead, she took a slow breath and lifted her gaze.

Alistair looked out the window, eyes sparkling like sea glass in the light. She could tell by the crease on his forehead that there was a frown beneath his mask. She didn't need to see his expression to know that. Her memories of him were enough.

"You should get dressed," he said. "We leave for the airdocks in an hour."

He started to walk away and was halfway to the door when he stopped and looked back at her. The crease on his forehead softened. "I'm glad you're back," he said, and left the room.

# Five

Using strategy and some acrobatics, Westie managed to figure out all the different straps and ties of the dress Nigel had brought back for her when he'd traveled to France last year. A visit from the investors was the perfect excuse to wear it. It was white silk with a gold-colored fabric bustle and matching buttons on the front of her bodice like those on a military coat. She liked the masculine way it squared off her shoulders. It even came with a leather jacket like men wore, though it was too hot out to wear it.

On her way downstairs she noticed Bena standing in the foyer beside a dracaena. Westie stopped, watching Bena touch the brown leaves of the dying plant. Nigel had plenty of greenery in the house. He thought the foliage would balance out all the metal, but neither of his thumbs were green, so he left their care to Bena.

All Wintu had a special relationship to the earth and the things that came from it. Westie remembered playing with the Wintu children when she was younger, in awe of their abilities. They'd whisper to a branch high in a tree, and it would bend so they could reach it. Once, while Bena and Westie had been caught in a storm and needed to cross a flooded creek, Bena whispered to the water, her fingers dancing in the air, and rocks began to pile on top of one another, making a path for them to walk.

"Aren't you going to heal it?" Westie said.

Bena turned around, a glimmer of unshed tears in her eyes. Westie had been kicked in the chest once by Alistair's horse, and it didn't feel as crushing as the look on Bena's face. If Bena couldn't heal a sad little houseplant, the earth's magic must be in worse shape than Westie had thought.

"Not right now," Bena said. As she let go of the leaf, it fluttered to the ground at her feet. "We don't want to be late."

After breakfast they left for the airdocks. It was early, but already the day was sweltering. Westie fidgeted. She hated riding sidesaddle, but it was the only way she was able to fit on her horse in the dress she wore. Her skin was slick with sweat, and James and Alistair looked just as uncomfortable in their long boots and trousers—James more so with all the decorative metal pieces covering his sack coat. Bena was the only one who didn't seem affected by the heat. She wore a long buckskin dress with different-colored fire beads in the zigzag pattern that identified her as Wintu. It was also adorned with hundreds of polished deer teeth that let others know she was a great hunter.

While Westie and the others rode horses, Nigel drove a wagon made of brass and wood that looked like a simple box. It had two smokestacks, and he had to continually feed coal to the fire while trying to steer at the same time. He had pulled out all his special inventions in hopes of impressing the investors. Westie had to ride upwind to keep from getting an eyeful of soot from the belching stacks.

When they reached the town, there was a herd of people plodding around, their carts and horses weighed down with mining gear.

"Who are all these folks?" Westie asked.

Typically there were equal numbers of humans and creatures in Rogue City—though there had been times when creatures would overpopulate the wilds after a rigorous mating season and find their way into town by the dozens—but she'd never seen so many humans in town before.

"Walter Cowley struck gold up on Devil's Crag a few weeks ago," Nigel said. "When word got out, people from all over the north valley made the pilgrimage. An airship landed this morning with a flood of prospectors."

Westie's eyes narrowed at a man who bumped into her horse without apologizing. "That's Wintu land. He can't mine up there."

The look on Bena's face grew dark, but she didn't speak. Her tribe wasn't far from that stretch of rock. It was a sacred place used by her people for various ceremonies.

Nigel sniffed and flexed his jaw. "I tried everything I could to stop it. No one will listen. They know the gold will do wonders for the town's economy."

Westie turned to Bena. "Why aren't you saying anything about this? That's your land."

Bena's face remained unmoved, but there was tenaciousness in her eyes when she looked at Westie. "Without the tribe, Emma will not work. If people want their towns protected, they will need our help. It will come at a price. We will get our land back, just not today."

Westie smiled. She'd thought Bena had come along to support Nigel, but it seemed she had her own agenda.

A horde had gathered at the pier where the airship was to dock. James parted ways from the group and headed for the Tight Ship.

Alistair fiddled with his horse's reins, eyes twitching as people stared and whispered. He had always been wary of gatherings and rarely went into town unless it was to assist Nigel in the surgical rooms. He was the ghost of Rogue City. People knew of him, but rarely had he been seen—unlike Westie, who waved her mechanical arm in people's faces for no other reason than to make them squirm. Folks spread rumors about Alistair. They called him a vampire because he only traveled into town under the cloak of night and never removed his mask. Some said it hid fangs, while others claimed there was nothing but bone underneath.

Westie remembered his face beneath the mask quite differently. He had scars on his cheeks and throat, nothing creaturely. If anything, his scars gave him a rugged, outlaw look that she thought made him more handsome. His lips were soft, his teeth white and perfectly crooked. His smile was his most endearing feature, the way it swayed to the side. Before he stopped taking off his mask in front of her, she used to stare at his lips, watch the way he moved them to form words when he'd communicate through sign language even without a voice.

Alistair turned abruptly, catching her watching him. His metal sound box crackled inside his mask before he spoke. "Everything all right?" he asked.

She shifted her eyes beyond him, toward the crowd. "Not really. All these folks shuffling around remind me of the Undying."

The Undying were just that—people who'd died of poisoning after eating creatures of magic but didn't stay dead. When they rose again, they were evil, their skin moldy gray and covered in pustules, killing anyone unfortunate enough to cross their path.

Westie shivered at the thought and backed her horse away from a hunched, arthritic-looking woman tottering by, half expecting her to lunge and start biting.

"I'm not too fond of them myself," Alistair said.

Hired hands came by to take their horses to the livery yard. After she dismounted, Westie heard someone call her name in a shrill voice.

"Westie, yoo-hoo!"

Isabelle Johansson maneuvered through the crowd, holding her skirts in her good hand. Being just an itty-bitty thing, she had to bully her way with elbows and knees. By the time she reached Westie, she was out of breath, chest heaving beneath her low-cut bodice.

"Westie, you are positively radiant in that dress." She touched the fine silk. "It looks expensive." With Isabelle, everything was about money.

She bounced on her toes, making her perfect chestnut ringlets bob. Her parents owned the apothecary between Doc Flannigan's office and Nigel's surgical rooms. They were well-to-do by Rogue City standards, and Isabelle made sure everyone knew it by wearing the latest fashions. The two girls were still friends, but not as close as they'd been when they were eleven years old, before Westie was kicked out of school for breaking every finger in Isabelle's left hand during a game of ring-around-the-rosie while Westie was still learning to use her mechanical arm. Isabelle, whose fingers were bent and slightly deformed from the break, was quick to forgive—the others at school, not so much, thus ending Westie's community schooling.

"I reckon it was expensive," Westie said, though she'd never thought to ask Nigel the price, which made her feel ashamed for wearing the dress in the dirt.

"You must wear it to your coming-out party."

Westie cocked her head. "My what?"

"The coming-out party Nigel has planned for you in ten days, silly. He was telling my father about it just yesterday. All proper ladies come out into society when they turn sixteen. Hasn't Nigel told you anything?"

"I'm seventeen." Westie was sure Nigel knew better than to surprise her with a party. She looked at Alistair, finding her answer in the way he turned his head to avoid her. "You knew about this?" she said.

"I told Nigel it was a bad idea," Alistair said.

Isabelle started to cry. "Shoot. I bet it was a surprise, and I ruined the whole thing."

"Don't worry, Isabelle—nothing's been given away," Westie said. "There's not going to be any party."

Isabelle blinked up at her, slack-mouthed. "But there are to be shellfish, caviar, and snails to eat like they do in France. I hear a brass combo from San Francisco is to play, and there will be candy and confections." Isabelle grabbed Westie's metal hand and promptly let go when she felt the hot copper that had been sitting in the sun. "Oh, you must come out, Westie, you must!"

Alistair lifted his hands in protest. "No, she mustn't," he said. Isabelle shrank away from Alistair when she heard the droning hum of his tin voice. "She should stay in. A closet, perhaps, something soundproofed, preferably."

Isabelle looked appalled. Alistair's humor was hard to comprehend with his mechanics. Without the fluctuation of tones, it was near impossible to pick up on his cues. Westie knew, though. It was the first time he'd teased anyone since—well, she couldn't remember when.

"That's a dreadful thing to say, Alistair," Isabelle said.

Alistair took another step toward the girl. Each time he moved forward, she took a step back.

"You clearly haven't heard Westie complain."

"Ignore him," Westie said.

Isabelle was on the other side of Westie, hiding behind the taller girl's skirts. "Well, anyway, do think about it—"

Isabelle's words were cut off by a rumble in the distance. At first Westie thought it was the airship coming in, until she saw a black cloud of smoke gather over the buildings in town.

Whispers scurried through the folks at the docks like wind through a field of weeds. A black metal land engine fashioned in the shape of a horse came into view. Smoke billowed from the two holes of the terrible face designed to look like nostrils. The engine pulled a stagecoach behind it, made from black squares of metal riveted together like a devil's quilt. Its enormous metal wheels, with spikes as long as shin bones, tore at the earth beneath it.

"Is that Costin's coach?" Isabelle asked, trying to peek around taller spectators.

"Why on earth would a vampire be at the docks in the middle of the day?" Westie heard Nigel say.

He looked from his precarious brass contraption to the vampire's hulking stagecoach and huffed, jealousy showing in every crease of his face. The vampires were brilliant tinkerers themselves and were neck and neck with Nigel when it came to inventing ground transportation—though Nigel still owned the sky—but when it came to style, the bloodsuckers were far ahead in the race.

"I know what he's doing here." Isabelle gave Westie a conspiratorial smile.

Alistair leaned in to better hear their conversation.

"He's not here for me," Westie said.

"Of course he is. He's in love with you. I'd give anything to have a vampire in love with me. And not for the same reasons I love lobster and butter sauce—I mean true love. You're so lucky."

"Costin doesn't love me. There's no room for anyone else with an ego like that. He just wants what he can't have."

Isabelle's lids looked heavy. "He can have me," she said dreamily.

"You just like his money."

Isabelle smiled. "You don't like his money enough."

"I don't care about money."

"She doesn't care about money," Alistair mimicked over her shoulder.

Westie looked back at him with a scowl.

The stagecoach stopped in front of the crowd. A tall, lithe figure clad in a black duster and top hat stepped out of the coach. He wore a black lace veil over his face like a grieving widow. Westie couldn't see much of his features other than his white skin through the holes of the lace. His head swiveled and stopped when he saw her. Two of his guards stepped out of the coach behind him.

"He's endlessly fascinating, don't you think?" Isabelle whispered this time to keep Alistair out of the conversation. "He reminds me of the princes in those European love stories I like so much."

Costin cut a path through the crowd, ignoring the whispers around him.

Westie cleared her throat and straightened her back when he stopped in front of her.

"Westie," Costin said. He had a smooth voice, easy on the ears. "You look stunning as always."

Goose bumps rose on her arm when he took her flesh hand. It disappeared beneath his veil, soft, cold lips touching her knuckles. Blood rushed to her cheeks. When he gave her hand back, she was glad to have scrubbed beneath her nails that morning.

"What brings you out into the sun?" she asked. "Don't you have a brothel to run and listless human bloodsacks to drain?"

A faint rumble of laughter came from his veil. "You make it sound so barbaric. Our patrons feel nothing but pleasure when we open their veins." His voice was like a purr. "I could show you sometime."

Alistair stepped between Costin and Westie. "She's not one of your blood whores."

Nigel had been ignoring the conversation for the most part until Costin's guards moved in. Nigel took Alistair by the shoulders and pulled him back away from the vampire.

"What are you doing here, Costin? This is a gathering for the mayor," Nigel said.

Westie had never heard Nigel speak ill of a creature until Costin came along two years ago. He'd called him a home wrecker and tempter. It was because of the brothel. A brothel, human or vampire, brought the riffraff to town.

"I know what this is." Though Westie couldn't see Costin's eyes, she felt them on her. "I too am here to see the mayor, as the ambassador for the vampires."

"If that's the case, where are the ambassadors for the other creatures?" Nigel asked. Costin ignored him. "There's no such thing."

While Nigel and Costin talked, Westie slipped away with Isabelle and Alistair in tow.

"That was exciting," Isabelle said, stealing glances at Costin through the crowd Westie had put between them. When they were on the other side of the docks, Isabelle snuck back to the subject of Westie's party. "Before Costin arrived, you'd said you would think about the party."

Westie knew she'd said nothing of the kind but didn't feel like arguing with Isabelle, so she said, "I'll think about it," even though she had no intention of allowing a ball in her honor to happen.

Isabelle clapped her hands. "Wonderful. I bet Costin will be invited. I'm going to go find my parents and tell them all about it. I'll need a new dress!"

"I can't wait to see it," Alistair said, taking Isabelle's hand as if he might kiss it the way Costin had kissed Westie's, teasing her like he used to tease Westie when they were still close. Westie felt a pinch in her chest at the sight of it.

Isabelle paled and shook him off her. She stumbled on her words. "I . . . I . . . need to go. I'll see you soon, Westie," she said before fleeing.

"Finally," Alistair grumbled.

Westie just stared at him.

"What?" Alistair asked.

"Aren't you a chatty thing lately."

He gave her a curious look that shrank his eyes. "What do you mean?"

"I haven't heard you say but a handful of words to anyone except for Nigel in the last three years, and now you're suddenly cutting jokes with Isabelle?"

"I talk to all sorts of people." His eyes brightened. "If I didn't know better, I'd say you were jealous."

Westie felt heat creeping up her neck and looked away from him. "Good thing you know better," she said.

The thunder of engines in the sky cut their conversation short. The airship blotted out the sun, casting a wide shadow over the land. Westie's mouth hung open. She'd never seen anything like it. Normally balloons and aeroskiffs were the only things moored at the small docks in Rogue City. She'd seen the blueprints for the airships Nigel had invented, but she'd never imagined them being as grand as this one was. It looked like a flying pirate ship, elaborately decorated in gold-and-red trimming. Six engines breathed black smoke into the air. There were three on each side, controlling spiral propellers, much like the ones on the ornithopter in the da Vinci drawings, only on a much larger scale. Beneath the ship were bags that let out small amounts of air for a lazy descent.

Dockworkers rushed to grab the lines and pull the ship to the ground. When two of those workers were lifted up into the air by a gust, Alistair sprinted to help.

James joined Westie after Alistair was gone. He was the only thing more decorated than the airship. He looked like a poodle among a pack of mutts next to the Rogue City populace.

They faced the airship. James tucked his hands into his pockets and lost the straight posture he used around Nigel.

"I apologize for always staring at you," he said. Westie looked sideways at him. "It's just I don't think most girls could pull off having a machine for an arm. It's not very feminine"—Westie gave him a withering glare, but he seemed not to notice—"and yet it suits you so perfectly. I almost feel like you're more beautiful with it. Either way . . . you're extraordinary." She turned away so he wouldn't see her blush. "But that's no excuse. It's rude of me to stare. I am an asshole."

Westie shut her mouth to keep from smiling. For an aristocrat, James sure had a foul mouth. She liked that about him.

"I won't argue with you on that one," she said. Nigel had told her to play nice, and she fully meant to, but James said it first, and wasn't it polite to agree with a guest? Westie sighed. "I'm sorry for snapping at you during supper last night." She spit out the apology and screwed up her face as if it were earwax on her tongue.

James's lips split into a grin. "That's very touching. Thank you." She shrugged.

"Why don't you let me buy you a drink at the tavern tonight? We can start over."

She took slow breaths as a familiar craving wakened in the pit of her stomach. It had been two years since Westie had had a drink, but every day was a struggle to keep sober. She'd started drinking when she was fourteen, to numb the pain of the nightmares of her past and Alistair's rejection. It started with just a shot of whiskey in the morning, and then one more before bed to get to sleep. At some point, without her even realizing, her drinking had turned into a habit.

Alcohol had made everything seem more fun, and it disrupted her thoughts of Alistair, so she drank a lot. One night, after she and Isabelle had gone to a barn dance and Westie had woken the next morning nearly drowned after passing out in a pig's wallowing hole,

Nigel made a deal with her. If she continued her school lessons and promised never to take another drink, he would provide her with the weapons and training she needed to hunt the killers of her family, something she'd been begging him to do for some time. She'd made that deal with him and fully intended to keep it.

"I don't drink," she said.

Westie watched as Alistair took the rope and was lifted into the air with the other men.

"Looks like your friend could use some help," James said.

Westie laughed, but the sound was lost in engine noise. She ran—as much as one could run beneath the weight of all that fabric—and stood below them. Reaching up with her machine, she took hold of the knot at the end of the rope, pulling the men to safety.

The airship sank toward the earth and bounced to a stop. She cringed at the wail of the engines shutting down. Nigel was a genius, she knew, but she'd never imagined him capable of inventing something so immense.

Westie joined her family to watch the people on the airship emerge from their cabins onto the deck.

"There he is," Nigel said warily as the mayor climbed down the companionway and descended the gangplank.

Westie had never seen the mayor before. Though he was in charge of all the territories in the Sacramento Valley, he rarely, if ever, came to town. He was soft pink and nearly bald, pushing fifty if not already there. He wore a green paisley suit, rattlesnake-skin boots, and a bolo tie adorned with turquoise even though it was an Indian stone, and, according to Nigel, he'd fought diligently to keep the natives out of the city.

The mayor talked around a cigar clamped between his teeth. "Nigel, my good man." He patted Nigel on the shoulder with a pudgy hand. He had a hearty laugh. Pearls of sweat hung from his upper lip. "These must be your automatons I've heard so much about."

Westie's hackles rose. She doubted the insult was intended, but that didn't stop her from wanting to shove her machine up the fat man's—

"Alistair Butler, at your service." Alistair stepped forward, offering his hand. Though Nigel had never officially adopted him, Alistair used his surname.

The mayor gave it a quick tug.

"How do you do?" Westie extended her copper hand for the mayor to kiss or shake, it didn't matter which—either way she meant it to be an introduction he wouldn't forget. Nigel had warned her to behave around the investors, but he hadn't said anything about the mayor.

Nigel stepped in before she could make contact. He put his arm around her shoulder and gave her a painful squeeze. Wincing, she smiled at the mayor.

"And this beauty is Miss Westie," Nigel said.

"A beauty indeed." The mayor was full of smiles until his gaze wavered on her copper arm. "Indeed," he said again with less enthusiasm.

"How was your flight, Mayor?" Nigel asked.

The mayor patted his ample belly, where the buttons of his shirt stretched holes into the fabric, showing the sweaty hair matted beneath. "Just fine, thank you, but please call me Ben. There's no point in using formalities when we're in wild country surrounded by creatures and Indians, wouldn't you say?"

He glared at Bena, who stood beside Nigel looking unimpressed by the mayor, the airship, and the people getting off it.

"Where are the investors?" Westie asked. It was a hundred and hell out, and it felt like swampland beneath her skirts.

"They should be coming." The mayor looked toward the ship. "Yes, there they are."

Westie followed his line of sight toward the passengers on the ship. It was as if someone had reached into her chest and pulled out her lungs. Suddenly the air around her disappeared, stolen by the couple walking down the gangplank.

# Six

The woman stepping off the ship was a wraith from the past clad in flashy red traveling skirts, expensive city fashions with matching hat and gloves. Her dark hair fell in waves over one shoulder and bounced with each step. Her attire hid the fact that she had a plain face with pockets beneath her eyes and irises like two brown scabs. She was short and thin, and the severity of her features gave her a raptor-like quality.

Westie couldn't move, couldn't speak, her thoughts spinning in violent circles between past and present. Beside her, someone was talking. Whether to her or to someone else, she didn't know, for she couldn't think beyond the sight before her. Next to the woman stood a man, a head taller than those around him, stout of chest, with arms as thick as smokestacks and a pocked face. He too was finely dressed, wearing a high-collared shirt, tan sack coat, and breeches. He wasn't ugly, but he also wasn't someone anyone would think twice about after he'd walked away. The couple stood within a group, all vying to get off the ship first.

Westie's throat tightened. She'd imagined catching the cannibals who'd killed her family a million times, but never like this, never caught off her guard.

The sight of them conjured a fear so powerful it threatened to shake her world apart. Her head felt loose, like it would float away if it weren't for her spine. She tried squeezing her eyes closed again, pressing her hands against her lids to block out any light. When she opened them, she was sure the couple would be gone, and in their place would be nice people who looked nothing like the cannibals from her past.

That wasn't the case.

Confusion held her tongue. The people she remembered from the cabin in the woods were vile, dirty things, not society folks. It had to be a mistake.

Alistair was beside her. He said, "Didn't you hear me?"

She didn't dare take her eyes off the man and woman. "What?"

"I said you don't look well." He worried over her like a persistent mother, wiping her brow with his pocket square.

"It's the heat," she said, swatting his hands away.

"I'm getting you something to drink."

After he left, Westie continued to study the couple. A young man joined them, squinting against the sun, rodent-like, with his eyes, nose, and tiny mouth all pushed into the center of his face. His hair was the color of wet sand, worn long and pulled into a tail. He peeled off his gloves one finger at a time.

She dug her nails into her palm until it bled, wondering if he could be their son. There had been four people taking shelter in the hunting cabin when her folks had stumbled upon it: a man, his wife, and two children. Westie didn't remember the boy as much as she did the mother and father, but his age, the color of his hair, it all fit.

The similarities were remarkable, but there had been a daughter too. Where was she? She would've been nine by now, nearly the same age as Westie had been when she'd escaped the cabin. It was possible the girl had died. The wagon trail was no place for children.

Alistair came back with a cup of lemonade and handed it to Westie. She dropped it back in one shot but was still thirsty after, only her appetite required something stronger, with proof. Her mouth had gone as dry as the hot clay beneath her feet.

The rest of Westie's resolve shattered as she watched the mayor and James join the family on the dock.

"Those folks are the investors?" she said.

Nigel gave her an inquisitive look. "Yes, those are the Fairfields."

The cup shattered beneath the grip of her machine.

"Is something wrong?" Nigel said. "Are you ill?"

Westie hesitated, the words stuck in her throat. Her voice was thick with fear when she finally spoke. "I think those folks are the ones who killed my family."

The admission felt dangerous. It had just been a notion before. Saying the words made it real.

Nigel stared at her without expression. When Bena reached for the knife tucked into her belt, he stopped her.

"There won't be any need for that," he said. "I'm sure Westie is mistaken."

Westie looked back at the Fairfields, their attire, their smiles as they conversed with the mayor and James. She wondered if her desire to find the family of cannibals had been so strong that her judgment was impaired. It wouldn't have been the first time she'd gotten it wrong.

A young girl of nine or ten years slipped through the forest of legs crowding her path. She held a rainbow-colored lollipop in one hand and a doll in the other. She reached up, taking hold of the woman's hand.

Westie swayed in the breeze. Alistair gripped her arm to keep her up.

"It's them." Her throat felt as though she were talking through shards of glass. "I need to alert the sheriff."

Her eyes darted around like bugs trapped in mason jars, looking for him.

"Like hell you will," Nigel said, gripping her flesh arm.

She gazed up at him, eyes charred by the screaming sun. "It's them, Nigel. I know this woman's face like I know my own." Westie caught a glimpse of a tan Stetson over Nigel's shoulder. "There he is," she said when the sheriff came into view.

Her hand trembled, stomach coiled with nerves. She shook off Nigel's grip and made her way toward the sheriff. Nigel lunged at her and Alistair followed. Their first attempt to take Westie down before she reached him didn't go well. Alistair received a copper blow to the chest that knocked the air out of him. Nigel's strength was no match, and he soon found the seat of his trousers dusted with red clay when she pushed him down.

"Stop her!" Nigel cried out to Bena, but Bena had seen the aftermath of what the cannibals had done to Westie's family and made no move to help in the effort.

Westie cussed as the hem of her skirt caught on a broken hitching post. Struggling to get free without stripping down to her bloomers, she failed to notice Costin at her side until he tackled her.

She flailed her arms for something to grab hold of. It was no use. Her head hit the dirt with a blunt sound. The pain it caused wasn't as dull. It rippled through her like a rock being dropped into a sleeping pond. Costin straddled her waist while Nigel pinned her metal arm to disable her strength. A tendon in her shoulder was the key to her machine, a shutoff switch. The arm was useless when enough pressure was applied. Nigel knew exactly where to push, and there was no doubt in Westie's mind that he'd planned it exactly that way when attaching the machine to her arm. If it hadn't been for that vulnerability, there would've been nothing to stop her strength.

A choking veil of red dirt rose around them as the pair worked to contain her. She fought like a feral cat. Tears filled her eyes. She let out a howl that caused the women who'd gathered around to step back, and their children to take shelter behind their skirts.

"What's happening to her?" she heard Costin ask.

"She's having a seizure," Nigel said to Costin and the crowd, "a long-standing medical condition. Please stand back and give the poor girl some air."

Costin started to stand. Nigel stopped him. "No, not you. I need help keeping her down." Costin hesitated. Eventually his weight settled on her again.

He looked down at her. His face was hidden by his veil, but she saw his throat move when he swallowed. "Do you need my blood to heal her?" he said.

The onlookers gasped. It was an astonishing thing to ask. The consumption of vampire blood by humans and creatures alike was illegal. It certainly had its healing qualities, but it could give a powerful deadly creature even more strength. It could give humans an unnaturally long life span, or it could give them a horrible death and even turn them into the Undying, if someone were to consume too much. It was poison, after all. Only a vampire knew the right dosage, and vampires couldn't be trusted.

Nigel whipped his head to face Costin and answered with an enthusiastic "*No!*"

He leaned into Westie's ear so only she could hear his words. "Stop this at once," he demanded.

Slobber frothed from her lips. "They'll pay for what they did," she said through gritted teeth.

"I'm not releasing you until you calm down."

Clay stuck to her cheeks, turning tears to mud. "But it's them," she said, hating how meek she sounded.

Nigel's expression battled between anger and sorrow. "Are you sure?"

"Yes."

"How do you know? Where's your proof?"

Her forehead wrinkled. "I don't have any."

Nigel pinched her face between his fingers and forced her to look at the woman in red and the family walking toward them. "Look at them," he said. Westie blinked the dust from her eyes. "Those are people of society with a fortune in their pockets. Money means power. Do you honestly think anyone will believe they are cannibals? And do you think the sheriff will just take your word for it like he did the last time?" He didn't wait for her to answer. "I assure you he will not. If you go off spouting accusations and the Fairfields catch wind of it, they will get spooked and leave."

No, that wasn't at all what she wanted. She hadn't thought of it that way. If the sheriff didn't believe her, the Fairfields would be gone, and by the looks of it they had enough money to take themselves far out of her reach.

"You need to forget about this, at least until we can get home and discuss it rationally," Nigel said. He let go of her face. "Now, pull yourself together."

She wanted to curl into a ball and hide from everyone watching her. "I don't think I can."

"You must try." He glanced to his side. "And be quick about it."

The faces of the mayor and the woman in red appeared above her like air balloons hiding the sun.

"Is everything all right?" the mayor asked with less concern than curiosity.

Costin climbed off Westie and helped her to stand. Her dress was filthy and the hem was ripped. She dusted the clay off the best she could and smoothed her unruly hair. Alistair stood several feet away covered in dirt, steam blasting from his mechanical mask as he struggled to catch his breath. She was glad to see she hadn't hurt him too badly.

Clearing the dirt from her throat, she said, "I have these spells. An affliction from a sickly childhood."

"Oh, you poor dear," the red huntress told her.

Her voice, Westie noticed, was the same as she remembered. Kind, like when the woman had welcomed her family to sup with them. She remembered, too, how quickly that voice had turned to shrieks as Westie ran through the cabin trying to escape.

When the woman touched her, the stump of Westie's arm began to throb beneath her machine, and her skin prickled as though it were trying to shrivel away from her.

The mayor sighed. "If we're done with this, I'd like to introduce my guests."

A pig. That's what the mayor reminded her of, with his sun-tender skin and the curly wisps of hair on his head. So why hadn't the cannibals turned him into bacon already? *Unless he's one of them*, she thought.

"Nigel, my good man, I'd like you to meet Mrs. Lavina Fairfield," the mayor said.

Lavina Fairfield. Was that her real name? They had never mentioned their names in the cabin. Westie needed something definitive. Something that made her certain, that she could put in Nigel's face and say *I told you so.*

"This here is Hubbard, the head of the Fairfield clan and a fine cook, I might add." Westie put a fist in front of her mouth, silently belched acidic fumes, and hoped she wouldn't vomit. "This strapping young lad is their son, Cain." Cain's rat eyes studied Westie's mechanical arm, his mouth puckered in disgust. "Of course you already met their nephew, James Lovett Junior."

And then there was James. Westie was unsure where he played into the whole picture. He hadn't been with the family at the cabin. His presence stirred more doubt within her, a feeling she wasn't too fond of.

"And here is the youngest of the clan," the mayor said.

The little girl lifted her face. She wore a pink ruffled dress, with her flaxen ringlets sticking out of her bonnet. When she smiled, Westie felt unease wrap around her like a smothering embrace.

"This little spitfire is Miss Olivia, but folks call her Olive."

All the names swirled around in Westie's head like too much whiskey. She would never remember them all. She could hardly remember seconds after they were announced.

Olive looked at her mother, who was staring curiously at Westie. The little girl frowned and strangled her doll. It was handmade, similar to the dolls Westie's mother used to make her, and had a pink dress with a crisscross pattern all over it. The girl twisted its head until it popped off.

"Oh no, Olive, look what you've done," her mother scolded. "How many times must I sew this head back on?"

"Don't worry about that ragged old thing. We'll get you a proper doll. I hear the general store here has a collection of lovely dolls made of porcelain with eyes that blink," the mayor said.

Olive threw the toy to the ground. "I don't want a proper doll. I want you to fix this one!"

The girl's voice grated at Westie's ears. It was all too much to handle. She needed to escape. She turned to Alistair, who had already recovered.

"Fetch my horse, Alley. I'm not feeling so good."

Only when Alistair returned with her gelding and his mare did her stomach settle. Just as she was about to mount her horse, she felt a gentle tap on her shoulder. When she turned, she came face-to-face with Lavina Fairfield.

Westie took a deep breath and tried to keep the fear raging inside her from showing on her face.

White powder settled into the crow's-feet around Lavina's eyes and the frown lines of her mouth. The powder was meant to make her look young and fresh but had the opposite effect. The scent of rose water coming off her skin reminded Westie of old people.

"I hope this isn't terribly intrusive, but may I ask how you lost your arm?" Lavina said.

Westie hadn't expected such a blunt question. It was rude of Lavina to ask. It would've been even ruder for Westie not to answer. Everyone around them watched, waiting for the answer.

"It was a steamboat accident," Nigel answered for her. The

tendon in Westie's jaw relaxed. Nigel stood behind Bena, holding her shoulders. Whether it was for comfort or to hold her back, Westie wasn't sure. "A sad story, really. You see, during my travels back East years ago, I was on a barge heading down the Mississippi when my crew and I came upon a sinking vessel. Westie was drowning, her arm caught in the spinning paddle. I couldn't save her family, who'd also been aboard, so I took the child into my charge."

Lavina's shifty eyes settled, seeming convinced of the story. After all, Nigel's word was as good as gold in Rogue City and its surrounding sister towns. The rest of the onlookers believed him as well.

Only Nigel, Alistair, the Wintu, and the old sheriff—who was dead now—knew how she'd really lost her arm. All everyone else knew was that one day Nigel went into the woods with Bena and came back weeks later with an armless white child. A great mystery had been solved. Some looked disappointed that it hadn't been a more thrilling tale.

"How very generous of you," Lavina said to Nigel.

Nigel smiled and bowed his head. "If you'll excuse us," he said, "I must get Westie home for her treatment."

# Seven

When they got back to the mansion, Westie went straight to her room and locked her door. Nigel's muffled words came from the other side. "Westie, we need to talk about this."

Ignoring him, she went to her desk, crushing several pieces of graphite between her metal fingers before she finally managed to scribble a note for Bena. She attached it to a telegraph bird and sent it on its way.

Nigel continued. "James and the Fairfields are staying at the Roaming Inn. I told them you weren't up for guests after your episode at the docks. They were very understanding." There was a long pause. "Please, Westie. Talk to me."

She shut him out until he finally gave up. Beneath her bed was a loose floorboard with a groove just big enough to get her fingernail into. Inside the nook was a silver flask. It was empty, of course.

Having booze so close would've been far too tempting. Instead she kept it as a reminder of all she could lose. But on that day it reminded her of what she was missing.

She sat against the wall, knees pulled to her chest, twisting it in her hand until the sun went down. Her eyes and cheeks had gone raw from wiping them.

"I need a drink," she said to the empty room.

She knew if she drank again she'd regret it the next morning—and possibly all the mornings that came after—but she found it difficult to care about that at the moment.

Changing out of her ruined dress, she put on a lace blouse beneath a striped vest, brown knee trousers, white spats over her boots, a leather holster that went over her shoulders and crossed her back to carry her parasol, as well as a leg holster for her knife. She'd learned long ago to pack heavy and never wear a dress in the Tight Ship saloon.

The saloon was anything but the tight ship it claimed to be. The floors, made from the rotted hulls of wrecked steamboats, were stained with blood and vomit. Bullet holes peppered the walls and pointed dirty fingers of light at the tables from the lamps outisde. It was a stinking tomb made worse by the sweat and bad breath that thickened the air during the last week of summer.

Westie took a seat at the table with the fewest gamblers and placed her bet, her gaze sweeping the room. A pack of werewolves in human form sat at the table beside her. They took turns pissing on chairs, marking their territory each time one would get up to buy a drink. A banshee cancanned on top of the bar, giggling as a drunken goblin sang off-key and an old sprite sitting on a rickety stool looked up her skirt. It was a rowdy bunch of patrons that evening.

Westie held a tumbler of whiskey in her copper hand. The amber pool sparkled in the muted light as she swirled it in the glass. It seemed the pact she'd made with Nigel two years ago to stop drinking was void now that the cannibals she'd been hunting were down the road staying at the inn. She no longer needed Nigel's training, money, or weapons.

But the thought of disappointing Nigel made her hesitate. She'd given him her word, and that was supposed to mean something. With her elbow on the table, she put her head in her flesh hand and tried talking herself into leaving, thinking about all the horrible—and downright stupid—things she'd done while drinking. Like how she'd earned the nickname Wrong Way Westie, because after a few drinks she couldn't find her way home.

Only the memories of her drinking days weren't all bad: the burn, the courage, and eventually feeling nothing at all. She wanted to feel nothing again. History told her that particular feeling was addictive, that she'd need to drink more and more each time to sustain it. Stepping off that wagon was easy, but getting back on was nearly impossible.

She stared into her glass, eyes burning. She'd love nothing more than to throw the tumbler across the room, but the idea of taking her pain home with her, sitting with it the rest of the evening, was too much.

Putting her lips to the glass, she tossed her head back, the whiskey warming her all over like a hug. She winced, shook her head, and stuck her tongue out.

Several hours, and tumblers, later Westie blinked. Hazy light flashed before her as if she were watching the landscape through the spokes of a moving wagon wheel. Two gamblers sat at the table with her. Both were leprechauns. The *T* scars on their wrists were thievery brandings, letting honest folk know they were fugitives.

Another gambler put his coins on the table to join the game. Westie looked up, spit whiskey all over her cards, and nearly fell off her seat when she saw James.

"Are you all right?" he asked as she coughed.

"I'm fine," she said in a strangled voice, throat feeling like she'd swallowed a wasps' nest.

He sat beside her with a drink in hand. He had an educated thirst, sipping bourbon from the top shelf. She snuck glances at him as he smiled at the dealer and placed his bet. He didn't look like a monster—he didn't look anything like the Fairfields at all. With full lips, a straight nose, and a spattering of light freckles across his cheeks, he was downright handsome. She couldn't imagine him being a killer like his family.

Westie tried to put the Fairfields out of her head. She'd come to the saloon to forget about them, after all.

"I thought you didn't drink," James said to her.

She picked the cards in front of her up off the table and fanned them in her mechanical hand. "I do now."

Westie tossed her coins onto the pile in the middle of the table.

One of the leprechauns, an old buzzard with jaundiced eyes, watched her. He ran a filthy hand through his yellow beard, his face more hair than flesh with the exception of a knobby potato of a nose and plump red lips.

"What?" Westie said, crushing her face into a glower. "Haven't you ever seen a girl before?"

He looked back down at his cards, sitting so long in silence that Westie feared he'd gone and died until he piped up, voice loud enough to belong behind a Sunday pulpit.

"Aye," he said in a charred voice, "too rich for this old bag o' bones," and tossed his tobacco-smeared cards facedown on the table.

The other leprechaun was much younger than his companion. He continued to glance between his cards and Westie's mechanical arm. His sour stench reached across the table and rustled the hot whiskey stewing in her guts. He pointed at her arm.

"How do you move that thing?" he asked.

Westie's vision twinned. She wasn't sure which one of him to look at. "Wintu magic."

Both leprechauns bristled at the mention of the natives.

It wasn't true. Her machine was just a prosthetic attached to bone and nerves.

"The tart's trying to distract you, fool. She's taking all your money," the old leprechaun said to the young one with amusement in his voice.

Westie looked at James through tricky eyes and a blue curtain of smoke. "You fixing to play or not?" she said.

He smiled, tossing his offering to the table.

The smoke in the room, the smell of piss, and the drink that had gone to her head made Westie's eyes water. The pungent sweetness of cigar smoke and the earthy smell of spittoons made her tongue feel thick and brought a salty taste to the back of her throat.

She yawned to keep back the vomit and moved her cards into her flesh hand, balling her mechanical one into a fist. The brass gears turned without sound, and clusters of thick copper wire moved like tendons.

The young leprechaun pulled at his flaking bottom lip, took a deep breath, and eased it out before laying his cards on the table and sliding his chair back in defeat. Westie fumbled with the coins, her clockwork fingers not as agile as the flesh and bone of her left hand.

"Hold on one moment, please," James said. There was something about the way he talked, a slight drawl lingering behind certain vowels, that made Westie think all the prim talk was just an act. "You haven't won yet."

He splayed his cards on the table for her to see: queens.

Westie tossed her sevens onto the table and wiped at her eyes.

"Sevens?" James said with a skewed grin. There was a little white scar across his bottom lip, only visible when he smiled. "That's brilliant. I was almost ready to fold. You have an excellent poker face."

"Wait one blamed minute," the young leprechaun said. He climbed onto his chair but even then couldn't match James's sitting height. He took hold of the starched lapels of the boy's coat. "You been cheatin', boy?"

"Certainly not," James said with a stubborn incline of his chin. "I play at the gentlemen's club in the city." He pulled his expensive coat out of the young leprechaun's grip, smoothing the wrinkled fabric. "I have had adequate practice."

Westie tapped a copper finger against the table. Another drink and another game were what the doctor ordered. She wasn't drunk enough to feel nothing yet, and there was more coin to lose.

"Stop your bitching and play the damn game," she said.

The young leprechaun snarled, revealing crumbling teeth and fiery gum disease beneath his pointed nose.

Westie rolled her eyes.

"Take off that fine coat and show me the cards you been hiding up them sleeves," the young leprechaun said, tugging at James's cuff.

"I don't cheat," James said, tugging back. "You're just a shit card player."

The leprechaun's nostrils flared. "What did you say to me?"

"You heard me," James said.

The music stopped as the young leprechaun slid a trapper knife from his boot. A crowd gathered. James froze in place. The dancing banshee shrieked as banshees often did, and ran from the room. Westie was on her feet and around the table before anyone had the chance to notice. The creature thrust his knife toward James's face, but Westie was faster despite her drunkenness. She reached out, gripping the blade with her machine and twisting it until it

65

snapped. The leprechaun dropped what was left of his weapon and tried to flee, but she grabbed his wrist and hugged it in her copper grip. Her innards growled and she had to piss something fierce, but she held on. She stared at him a long stretch, noticed the muscles of his face twitch.

"Know what happens to creatures when they kill humans under the protection of Wintu magic?" she asked.

His chin quivered. He shook his head.

"First the skin bubbles and melts like hot wax. There's a whole lot of screaming, a lot of pain." She waved that part off. "Though there are laws against it, humans can kill creatures at their discretion. We're not affected by magic, you see?"

The young leprechaun soaked up the bleakness of his predicament, and his eyes bloated with fear. He let out a whimper as she tightened her grip.

"I weren't gonna kill him. I was just gonna cut up his pretty face is all," the young leprechaun said.

Westie thought about breaking his arm to show it was no idle threat, but she had seen more than her share of brutality while she was out on the road. She dropped his arm and plucked a silver coin from James's winnings.

"Of all the bets you make this evening, your best would be to walk away," she said.

The leprechaun massaged the raw skin of his wrist and put his scowl on exhibit as he watched her roll the coin over the knuckles of her mechanical fingers. To drive home her point, she pinched the silver coin between her thumb and finger and folded the piece into fourths as though it were a pocket square. The leprechaun's flush started at his neck and rose to fill his face.

Westie glanced between the old and young leprechauns, then placed the folded coin on the table. "I reckon you fellows ought to be on your way," she said.

They were gone before she'd finished speaking.

*Now, about that drink,* she thought. She stumbled toward the bar and found an empty stool.

James followed behind her. "I don't think the creatures around here like me much."

She lifted a brow. "You don't say."

Westie let loose the belch that'd been stalking up her throat and reached down the front of her sweaty shirt to scratch an itch between her breasts.

"Thank you for saving me. Again," James said.

"Maybe you ought to be the one wearing skirts."

James grinned. If her jab bothered him at all, he didn't show it.

"Another red-eye," she called out.

Heck, the barkeep, walked over to her with his strange, bouncing gait. He was an abarimon, a rare creature to see in Rogue City, as they were typically found high in the mountains. They were difficult to distinguish from humans except for their faun-like legs and their jaguar speed. He poured thick black liquid into a cup and placed it in front of her.

She glared into the cup. "What's this?"

He hooked his thumbs around his suspenders. "Coffee."

"I didn't order coffee. I want whiskey."

There was a pulse behind her eyes. She pinched the bridge of her nose between her fingers. Coffee wasn't strong enough to stop her headache, and it sure as hell wouldn't wash away her memories.

Heck planted his feet. Sweat dotted his bald pate. He looked afraid, like most did when Westie was in a mood. If she wanted her way, she could get it with one squeeze of her machine, and she had a reputation around Rogue City for being all horns and stingers.

"Look, Westie," he said with the demeanor of someone skilled in the art of drunken negotiation, "Nigel does my daughter a great service with his medical inventions. He won't be pleased to find I served you in the state you're in."

The reason for Heck's descent from Shasta Mountain was to seek Nigel's help for his ailing daughter when she could no longer breathe the thin air.

"Nigel and his damn inventions," Westie mumbled, knocking her copper fist on the bar three times, cracking the oak, and spilling her coffee. "I don't care. I want another drink."

"Sorry," he said before he walked away.

She let out a growl that sent the patrons next to her scuttling to the other side of the bar. When she stood from the bar stool, her eyes began to float and the wood planks of the saloon floor rose up in front of her. James reached out, catching her before she fell. His arms were strong for a skinny aristocrat.

"Let me help you home," he said. Their faces were close enough for her to smell alcohol on his breath and notice that his eyes were a pale shade of green.

"I don't need help." She pushed his hands off her and stumbled away.

# Eight

It was midnight by the time Westie left the saloon. Ten or so vampires walked the streets, dressed like they were ready for a funeral. Ornate copper gasoliers hung from poles lining the wood planks of the sidewalk, casting enough light to see without a moon. She wondered why they were even lit. The vamps didn't need light, and no human in their right mind would be roaming around town at such a late hour. After nearly an entire bottle of whiskey to herself, Westie was definitely not in her right mind.

She snuck around the back of the saloon to relieve her bladder, and when she came back, Costin was standing out front with her horse.

"What are you doing here?" she said, taking hold of the horn on her saddle to steady the carousel town.

"You've been in there awhile. I thought you might need some help getting home."

The soft light of the gasoliers gave him an ethereal glow. Long black hair shimmered around his face. He had skin without a single pore, like an eggshell, eyes black, pupils blown, lips stained pink with blood. Looking at him took the breath right out of her. He was perfect. Too perfect. Inhuman. That perfection reminded her that he was a creature, and that she couldn't allow herself to get caught up in his charm.

"I can kill twenty men with my machine and not even break a sweat," she said. "I don't need anyone's help."

Westie climbed up into the saddle. Once mounted, she promptly slid down the other side with a yelp. Pain stomped a trail up her back as she hit the ground.

Costin smiled, making no effort to help her. "Clearly," he said.

She heard the cackle of vampires from the top deck of the blood brothel across the street. She glared back at them.

"Damned bloodsuckers," she mumbled.

The ache in Westie's head was enough to keep her on her knees, but she managed to get to her feet, standing on the precipice of ugly drunk crying. After she made several unsuccessful attempts to get back onto her horse, Costin grabbed her by the waist and hoisted her into the saddle. He then climbed up and sat behind her, taking hold of the reins.

She was surprised when her horse didn't protest. Henry was a picky beast when it came to his riders and had never let anyone but Westie onto his back.

*Traitor*, she thought, and gave him a loving pat on his neck.

She didn't have the strength to fight Costin, and once she felt the chill emanating from his skin, she didn't want to.

He clicked his tongue and sent Henry on the path home. Once they were away from the lights of town, everything became suffocated by darkness.

Westie had started to doze off when Costin said, "Do you remember when we first met?" Westie kept silent, afraid if she opened her mouth, more than words would come out. "It happened just over there, beyond those trees." He pointed into the distance, but she couldn't see a thing. "It was two years ago," Costin continued, voice soft, breath cold against her ear. "I had just moved to Rogue City and had decided to take a walk in the woods, not knowing there was an infestation of rebellious young werewolves with a hankering for vampire blood."

She remembered that night. After a fight with Nigel—she couldn't remember now what that fight had been about—she'd stormed out of the house and gone to her favorite spot in the woods. She'd been pouting up in a tree when she heard the cries for help.

"I was cornered by a lone wolf," Costin said. "I had no weapon, and my speed and fangs were no match for a wolf who had already transitioned. I'd lived more lifetimes than I could count and yet there I was, about to meet my end as a meal for some ravenous dog."

He leaned in, lips brushing against her cheek. Closing her eyes, she reveled in the softness of those lips against her skin. It was hard to believe he was over a thousand years old when he looked barely twenty.

"Then suddenly you were there," he said, hand touching her stomach, moving in slow, intimate circles. Her skin tingled.

"Moonlight made a red halo of the hair tangled around your face. With your copper machine you looked like a goddess of war. I'd never seen anything like you. You pulled that werewolf's tail and spun it in the air like a child's toy and tossed it over the trees."

"I know," she said, trying to catch her breath. "I was there."

She was thankful when she saw the porch lamps of Nigel's house ahead. It made her nervous how comfortable she felt being so close to Costin, his lips so close to hers. The alcohol buzzing through her veins, lowering her inhibitions, wasn't helping matters either.

The lamps lit their path and the forest around them. It was still hot out despite the darkness. Westie had felt fine until she saw the trees swaying in the breeze, or maybe that was her. Everything seemed to be spinning.

She leaned against Costin to share in the coldness of his skin. His breathing quickened, legs tightening around her, almost painfully so, but she didn't care. His cold body was the only thing keeping the nausea back.

She closed her eyes and felt some relief as the chill of his lips settled against the side of her neck.

When his mouth opened and his fangs grazed her skin, the muscles in her shoulders tensed.

"Don't you bite me," she said like she would to a frisky pup.

Laughter rumbled in his chest and he closed his mouth, but left his lips lingering. When they approached the house, he sat back. Westie opened her eyes and saw Alistair sitting in a rocking chair on the porch.

Westie grumbled. She'd locked her bedroom door when

sneaking out and had hoped she'd be able to sneak back in without anyone noticing she'd been missing.

Alistair stood. "Costin?" He didn't seem to like the vampire much and had many of the same opinions as Nigel. They were always talking about the brothel, as well as Costin, being the bane of Rogue City. Westie didn't care about the brothel, though. A person had a right to make a living and do with their body as they pleased, in her opinion. "What are you doing with Westie?" His mask made it impossible for him to sound upset, but Westie could tell. He always breathed heavier when he was mad, which forced air through the mask's voice box, causing the internal gears to grind. If that wasn't enough of an indication of his mood, the fiery look in his eyes got the point across.

Regret filled her. She hadn't wanted him to see her drunk ever again.

Costin seemed undisturbed by Alistair's reaction. "I'm helping her to get home safely." He climbed off the horse and reached out to her. She slid into his arms.

"I'll take it from here," Alistair said, stepping forward.

"As you wish," Costin said.

Somewhere behind her sloshy thoughts, Westie knew she should protest being passed around like a sack of grain, but she was too far into the bottle to care.

Alistair stumbled backward, nearly falling, when Costin released her.

"Jesus, she's heavy," Alistair said.

"Hey," Westie mumbled.

Costin laughed and caught Alistair before he toppled over with Westie in his arms.

"Let me go—I can walk on my own," Westie said, pushing at Alistair's chest, not liking the way he was suddenly taking charge of her after he'd ignored her for so long.

When he released her, she canted a bit but managed to stay on her feet.

She said good-bye to Costin and leaned forward to politely kiss his cheek—and if it pissed Alistair off, so be it—but when Costin turned his head abruptly, their lips met instead.

Westie was too stunned to pull away at first, even when she felt his mouth part and the tip of his tongue brush against her lips. It wasn't until Alistair made an ugly grating sound with his mask that she finally reeled back, looking between Costin's lazy smile and Alistair's wide-eyed mortification.

She thought about slapping Costin because that was what she *should* do, but hitting a vampire with her left hand would be ineffective, and using her machine could knock out his fangs, which seemed far too rash for the situation.

She touched her lips, willing herself to curse Costin or say something, anything, to stop Alistair from looking at her like that, but no words would come. If she had been being honest with herself, the kiss wasn't entirely unpleasant except for Alistair being there to witness it.

The front door to the house opened and Nigel walked out, wrapped in his dressing gown.

"Alley," Westie said as Alistair pushed past Nigel and went into the house. There was a slight thrill seeing his anger, but there was guilt too. She didn't like seeing him upset.

"What's the meaning of all this noise?" Nigel demanded. His eyes locked onto Westie's, lips pressed together. "Oh, I see." Westie looked at the ground, shame heating her cheeks. She tried to focus on a single rock in front of her to keep from tipping over. "Get to bed," he said with a disappointed sag in his voice. "We'll deal with this in the morning."

She was more than happy to oblige.

# Nine

Despite a vicious hangover, Westie woke early the next morning. She wanted to be out of the house before Nigel woke up so she wouldn't have to talk about the Fairfields.

She couldn't blame him for not believing they were cannibals. Her memories were not always reliable. Once, when she'd first gone out looking for the killers of her family, there'd been a woman slain and eaten by cannibals in the valley where Westie had gone hunting. She had seen a man lingering in the town nearby who'd had the same beard, build, and deep-set menacing eyes as the man who'd cut off her arm. Taking him off his guard by playing the part of damsel in distress, she'd managed to knock him out and string him up by his feet.

Though no other authorities believed there were cannibals in the valley, Westie had managed to convince Nigel and the sheriff both that there were, and that the man in her possession was one of them.

But just as the man was about to be hanged for his crime, his brother came to town with proof that the accused man had just flown in from New York on an airship days before and couldn't have been the one who'd killed and eaten the young woman the week before.

It had been a great scandal and embarrassment. The only thing that kept her from sitting in the sheriff's cells for her wrongful accusation was Nigel's good word that she'd never pull a stunt like that again—and yet she would have yesterday if Costin hadn't been there to stop her.

Because of past follies, there was no way anyone would believe her based on her word. To get the sheriff on board, she needed Nigel's backing, and for that, she needed proof. Only way she knew to get it was to go back to the scene of her nightmares.

She left the note she'd written for Nigel on the desk in his study and went out to the barn, stumbling when she saw Alistair waiting for her.

Bena was beside him, brushing her horse. She gave Westie a questioning look that Westie replied to with a shrug.

"What are you doing out here?" Westie asked Alistair.

There was a long pause as they watched each other. Alistair was an athlete at the staring game. "Curious why you're sneaking around." He didn't look angry like he had the night before.

"You're spying on me?"

There were dark circles beneath his eyes as if he hadn't slept. "Do you really think that after what happened at the docks I would let you out of my sight?"

He left out the part about her time at the saloon, but she wasn't going to remind him.

Westie slung her saddlebag over Henry's rump. She didn't know what to do. Alistair was a hitch in her plans.

"You haven't cared about anything concerning me for the last three years—why start now?"

"I've always cared about you." His mask whirred and his face reddened.

Westie fought the smile rising up. It was the first time he'd ever admitted anything of the sort, but it was difficult to believe after all the time he'd spent avoiding her.

Alistair cleared his throat—though it sounded more like the clank of metal bits pinging off one another—and continued, "You've always been independent and competent for the most part, but after showing up at the house in the middle of the night, drunk and kissing vampires, no less, I'm not so sure anymore. Clearly you need some assistance with your decision making."

There it was.

"If I didn't know better, I'd say you were jealous," she said, mimicking his statement from the docks.

He gave it right back. "It's a good thing you know better."

Westie ground her teeth. He was only copying the words that she'd said earlier, but they stung all the same.

"Does Nigel know you're leaving?" Alistair asked.

"I left him a note saying I was going to Sacramento with Isabelle for a few days."

"Where are you really going?"

"The cabin."

Alistair moved so close he couldn't be ignored. "The cabin . . . where your family died?"

She didn't answer, just went on about her business, checking her saddle, Henry's bit, and the length of her stirrups. When Alistair took her flesh hand in his, Westie looked down at their tangled fingers as if he'd grown tentacles. How unlike him it was to even stand near her. She could've easily slipped out of his hold, but his warmth and the firmness of his grip kept her grounded as her strength withered away.

He had big, strong hands that were rough to the touch. They were hands that had never shied away from hard work, but were still agile enough to dress wounds and assist Nigel in the surgical rooms.

Seeing their fingers laced together, she was reminded of the day they'd met, the day she and Nigel had found him. The men who'd attacked him and his family took off into the woods, and Nigel, with his cane and horse, went after them. Westie stayed back with Alistair.

The cannibal men had bitten his cheeks, but the worst damage was done to his throat, leaving scarlet craters. Blood gurgled from his open wounds. Air whispered from his lips. His voice was gone, but she understood well enough. His lips moved and he mouthed the words "Kill me."

Though only fourteen at the time and small for his age, he gripped her flesh hand with the strength of a man twice his size, holding on as if she were his last tether to this earth. Westie was in agony as he crushed her fingers together, but she refused to pull away.

Heavy tears fell from her eyes into his wounds. She'd thought about strangling him with her new powerful arm, but looking into his glittering eyes, she couldn't bring herself to end his suffering. After losing her family to cannibals, Westie knew losing someone else— even a stranger—in the same violent way would be too much for her heart to bear. And so she begged him to live. She kissed his forehead and begged and begged.

Nigel came back covered in the blood of the cannibal men and looked like a creature out of her worst dreams. She turned her begging on him and asked him to save the boy's life.

He slid from his saddle and crouched over the boy, examining the wounds.

"You have to save him," Westie demanded, tears blurring her vision.

Nigel smoothed the boy's hair and whispered. "Westie, I don't know if—"

"No! You have to," she cried, her voice echoing off the trees.

He let out a long sigh and nodded. "I'll try."

Alistair sat on the edge of death for weeks after infection ravaged his body, but Nigel managed to save him. Westie stayed with Alistair through his recovery, through his nightmares and sorrow. She never once left his side. Like a silly girl, she believed he lived for her, so he was hers and she was his.

"Don't go," Alistair said, interrupting her memories. "Creatures and bandits are all that travel the wagon trail now that the trains and airships have come back from the war."

Westie closed her eyes, memorized how his touch felt against her skin before shaking him off.

"I have to."

"I am going with her," Bena said. "She will be safe."

Alistair wouldn't give up that easily. "Why are you going back there?"

It wasn't the first time Westie had tried to get into that cabin to learn more about her family's killers. Once, two years ago, she and Bena had ridden out to the cabin in search of clues. An old man had made the place his home and refused to let them in. This time Westie wouldn't take no for an answer.

"Proof," Westie said. "Solid evidence is the only way I'll convince Nigel that the Fairfields are cannibals, and Nigel's word is the only way the sheriff will believe it."

"It's been seven years since your family died in that cabin. What do you expect to find?"

"A photo, a piece of paper with their names—I'll know it when I see it." From what Westie had seen of the old man living in the cabin, he didn't throw anything away.

"What about Emma? Nigel needs the Fairfields' money to finish it."

Westie glanced at Bena, who checked her paint's hooves and acted like she wasn't paying attention, though Westie knew better.

"I won't say anything till they hand the money to Nigel. That'll give me enough time to gather the evidence I need to build a case against the Fairfields, one as solid as a steel wall that neither Nigel nor the sheriff can deny." She mounted Henry and pulled the reins to face Alistair. "We need to get on before Nigel wakes up."

Alistair took a deep breath that made his mask hiss. "I'm going with you."

It had been so long since they'd spent any length of time together that she wasn't sure how to act around him. She tried to breathe around the lump in her throat.

"Suit yourself." She clicked her tongue, urging Henry out of the barn.

# Ten

They left as soon as Alistair's bags were packed. The shock of him wanting to travel to the cabin with her had yet to wear off. She'd been making bad decisions all her life and he'd never been concerned before. She wondered what the real reason was for him wanting to go, and refused to let herself believe it was because he'd missed her.

Bena rode ahead, leaving Westie and Alistair alone. Westie started to think about the red huntress. She thought about James too, wondering what part he played in the family, and if he was one of them. Shaking her head, she rid herself of the thoughts before they consumed her.

She needed a distraction, a way to pull herself out of her head and away from the Fairfields and James for a time. She looked at Alistair. Despite the oppressive heat, he wore a bowler hat atop his thicket of dark tangles, a black wool duster buttoned up to his neck, black leather riding gloves, black trousers, and his mask. He looked like a henchman. Sweat spilled down the sides of his pale face into his mask.

"You're looking a little green, Alley," she said in a goading tone.

There was nothing that chafed him more than Westie pestering him to take his mask off. And there was nothing that gave her more pleasure than chafing Alistair. Picking on him was the distraction she needed.

"You should take a drink of that cool water I packed in your canteen. This trip's going to be a long one—don't want to dry up without Nigel's medicines around," she said.

Alistair's head bobbed lazily with his horse's stride as if he were agreeing with her, which he was not, at least not openly.

"Take that damn thing off," she said. "Don't be such a stubborn ass."

She wanted so badly to see her old friend.

"I'm quite all right, thank you," he said in a metallic voice that reminded her of the idling purr of a steam engine. "Speaking of drying up, perhaps you should be more worried about yourself. You're looking a little sober. Shouldn't your face be planted in Henry's mane by now? I mean, since you're drinking again."

She snarled, wanting to spit an insult back at him, but he had a point. If she was to face the nearly three-day round-trip journey to the cabin where her family died and the memories that went along with it, she'd need more courage than she had.

Reaching into her bags, she shoved her clothes and food aside, but found only leather at the bottom.

"Alley, where's my flask?" It had to be a mistake. She'd packed it the night before, she was sure of it. "Alley?" She looked into his eyes for answers, for guilt. There was no guilt, but there were secrets. Her next words came out like a coiled snake ready to strike. "What did you do?"

"What I should've done years ago," he said.

Suddenly she felt every step Henry took, every hobble, every bounce. Her head was thick with desperation. Like Alistair's presence, sobriety had not been part of her plan. She strangled her reins and dug her heels into the gelding's sides to catch up with Bena.

When she reached her, Westie's neck was hot, but not from the sun. Bena rode with a swayed back, her eyes scanning the forest around her, stoic like the braves of her tribe.

"Alley shouldn't have come," Westie said, wondering what she had done all those years ago to push him away. She remembered the day it had happened, but not the event, or the words she'd said that had led to the demise of their friendship.

It was on her fourteenth birthday. Alistair was a month from turning seventeen. Nigel had insisted on inviting all the teenagers from town to her party, saying she and Alistair spent far too much time alone together and hadn't been properly socialized. Westie knew most of the kids from her short time in school, but Alistair had been homeschooled and never met any of them.

They all went down to the swimming hole. Westie was splashing around with Isabelle when she noticed Alistair sitting on the bank alone, wearing his mask to hide his scars from the others.

"Alley? What are you doing over there alone? Come swim with us," Westie said. She splashed at him, but the water didn't reach.

He stood up and headed toward her, but before he made it, a boy came up behind her, grabbed her waist, and dunked her. By the time she rose from the water, Alistair was gone.

She left the others to go look for him and eventually found him in his room, alone, staring out the window. Standing in the doorway, she knocked. When he turned to look at her, his eyes were impossible to read.

"What's wrong?" she asked. His mask hissed. "Did someone say something about your mask? 'Cause if they did, I swear I'll knock all their teeth out."

She smiled at him, hoping to see his eyes squint, but they remained emotionless. He took several steps toward her. Thinking he was going to go with her back to the party, she took a step back, but instead, he closed the door without saying a word.

Months went by before he spoke to her. Eventually, he started talking to her again, but it was never the same. He stopped taking his mask off, and they no longer swam at the hole, or lay in the field at night counting stars. Every time she'd try to touch him, he'd shrug away from her.

He'd been her rock, her only source of comfort, and then he was gone. They lived in a big house like strangers. Each day of silence caused her heart to break a little more until the pain of her loss turned into an old friend. In Alistair's absence, the night-mares of her dead family returned, and Westie got into the habit of hiding from them behind a bottle. It was also when she became determined to leave Nigel's mansion and seek the cannibals who had killed her kin.

Westie felt a deep ache from the memory and looked down so Bena wouldn't see it reflected on her face.

"Alley's a distraction," Westie said. "If we come across creatures and I die, it'll be because of him."

Bena didn't even pretend interest. She was Westie's oldest friend, but when it came to matters of the heart, Bena was as deaf as Alistair was mute.

"Many travelers have taken this road recently," Bena said, ignoring Westie's outburst.

"Is that bad?"

"Could be if they're bandits. We should avoid the road. I know a path."

"I don't know which is worse, bandits or rattlesnakes."

Bena gave her a cool look. She was being as stuffy as Alistair.

"A rattlesnake will not rape you, take your gold, and leave you for the creatures."

"Fine." Westie rolled her head back, letting the sun kiss her face. "Rattlesnakes it is. They can't possibly be worse company than the two of you."

A cold finger walked up Westie's spine as they passed the blue-painted trees that stood as a warning, letting human travelers know they were leaving the safety of Wintu protection. She looked up at the dome, saw the smooth curve of it like a bell jar over the town, where it had stood for eight years. When settlers had first come to the area, the Wintu—as a peace offering—conjured the dome to protect the settlers from creatures, with the agreement that the Wintu's sacred sites were off-limits. Every time Westie left that protection, she felt like she was running naked through a rose garden. It was only a matter of time before things got dangerous.

They traveled north along a game trail next to the Sacramento River. By the time the sun fell behind the mountain, Westie's stomach was in a riot from nerves.

They cooled their saddles near the river for the night, far enough away from the rushing water so that they could hear anyone approach but close enough to catch the breeze.

Westie was laying out her bedroll when Bena sat down in front of a pile of wood and debris she'd gathered to build a fire. Whispering words to the earth in Wintu, she held her hands over the wood. Westie had seen her do the same thing countless times. Each time a fire would roar to life without a single spark. This time it didn't work. Bena's jaw clenched, and she tried again.

"Shit!" Bena said, and stood up.

Any other time, hearing Bena use a cuss word would've made Westie laugh, but there was nothing funny about seeing her friend so upset.

With a defeated moan, Bena said, "I'm going hunting."

While Bena was away, Westie lit the fire, and Alistair brushed the horses. Westie sat on a fallen tree near the fire, watching him in the saffron glow.

"I'd lend you a hand, but it seems I've grown attached to it." She waved her clockwork arm at him. "Unlike some of those with mechanical parts that are removable." She leaned her head back and grinned even though her face wanted to do just the opposite. "That breeze is something to smile about. Feels nice against my face."

He ignored her digs the same way he always did, but his eyes narrowed and he began to brush faster.

"Maybe you ought to take your mask off?" she said, unlacing her bodice to expose her cleavage to the breeze, pretending she didn't see his cheeks turning red and the front of his trousers getting tight. His sudden fury to hide it made her choke on laughter. She looked away, cheeks hot, heart speeding up. It was the first time she'd ever seen him react physically to her. She felt shy and hopeful, but pushed it down. He would probably react the same way to any woman showing skin.

He mumbled something under his breath—something unpleasant, she was sure—before tossing his brush to the side and disappearing into the woods.

He came back to the camp only when Bena returned with her catch of plump rabbits and blackberries. Alistair left again, walking to the river to eat alone. Westie had a headache and wasn't hungry anymore. She fell asleep and was tossed into the same familiar nightmare of running through the cabin trying to escape from the cannibals, only she was able to force herself to wake before the worst of it.

Her eyes opened to a star-bloated sky and to Alistair sitting beside her, brushing her sweaty hair off her face with a gentle finger.

The light of the dying fire shimmered in his eyes. "It was only a dream," he whispered. "Go back to sleep."

She wondered if she had woken him, or if he'd been sitting with her all along. As he petted her hair, her lids grew heavy, and she was reminded of a time when they were younger, when she was still struggling to use her machine. The mechanical arm had been such a tiresome burden back then. Every time she'd go to scratch an itch on her nose, she'd punch herself in the face, knocking herself out for hours at a time. She was never without a blackened eye or bloody nose in those days.

One day, Alistair came to her while she sat in the barn, cuddling with Henry and crying after breaking Isabelle's hand at school. He'd wiped her tears away, held her metal hand up in front of him, and placed his face in its palm. His blue eyes were bright against the copper as he watched her through the open spaces between her fingers.

*You wouldn't want to crush my skull, would you?* he signed. He didn't use his mask much at all back then.

She sniffed and shook her head.

*Then squeeze my face and try not to kill me.*

He wouldn't budge until she gave it a try. She sat there an hour before even attempting it. Eventually she did and was able to squeeze his face without crushing his skull or pinching his skin between the gears. They practiced every day until she learned how much pressure to apply to each situation. But that was a long time ago, she thought. He didn't even trust her enough now to let her see his face.

"I'm sorry for teasing you, Alley," she said as she started to slip back into the abyss of sleep. She touched his hand with her copper one. And though she didn't hear his reply, she knew when he didn't pull away that she was forgiven.

# Eleven

The next morning they packed and were on their way. To get to the cabin, they had to first get back onto the wagon trail. An hour later Westie started to develop blisters in places blisters had no place being. She put her bedroll beneath her, but it was no relief.

"Are we almost there?" she asked. Though it had been only two years since she'd gone with Bena searching for the cabin in the woods, Westie had no idea where they were. It was before she'd struck her deal with Nigel, so she hadn't been entirely sober during that trip. "I don't think I can sit in this saddle much longer."

"Almost," Bena said.

They veered off the wagon trail again into the woods when Westie finally saw something she recognized. Little figures made of braided twine hung from the branches in the trees ahead.

Those dolls had been there when she'd traveled to the cabin

with Bena, but not when her family had crossed through that part of the forest. Perhaps if they had been, things would've turned out differently. Instead there had been nothing but trees and snow. Fear churned in her stomach, making her insides a cauldron when the hunting cabin came into view. It was smaller than she remembered, barely a shack. The windows boarded up, the wood gray and swollen with fading red symbols painted on the door. The roof, covered in dried moss, was charred and breaking down. It bowed in the middle and had holes all about. It was buried deep on Wintu land, hidden behind giant pines and scrub brush, impossible to see from the wagon trail.

"How did your family even find this place from the wagon trail?" Alistair asked.

He and Westie stayed behind while Bena looked for signs of life.

"By accident," Westie said, her voice thick with trepidation as she scanned the forest. "We'd fallen behind the rest of the caravan we'd been traveling with after my brother Tripp had taken ill. Our wagon had gotten caught in the snow and we were out of food, so my pa took us out into the woods to look for food and shelter."

Westie had been holding Tripp's hand as they'd searched. He was only a year younger than she was, but he was racked with fever and seemed so fragile. She thought about his sweet face and red hair, clutching the doll she'd given him. Its name was Clementine; her favorite, with a burlap dress, brown yarn hair, and button eyes. The memory made her eyes throb with impending tears.

"Why would you try to cross the mountains so close to winter?"

Westie forced air into her lungs, trying to compose herself. Clearing her throat, she said, "We'd heard California was free of the Undying. They'd taken over the prairie. We didn't have much choice."

The Undying's takeover hadn't happened all at once, but it felt like it had. Symptoms of the change were gradual, starting with a fever. No one even knew what had caused it at first. There'd been a drought that had lasted nearly two years, killing off crops and cattle so there wasn't much to eat. Desperate, people began hunting and eating the wolves that roamed prairie. What they didn't know was that those wolves were no ordinary canines but werewolves. What they also didn't know at the time were the dire consequences of consuming creatures of magic.

The Undying had been slow, but there was a church of them and they liked to congregate. They were also hard to kill. Only way to keep them down was to cut off their heads. It took a lot of strength to sever one's neck from its body.

She remembered those days vividly. Her mother hadn't wanted to leave, holding out hope for a cure. But there was no true cure. It was only after Westie moved to Rogue City that she learned from Bena that magic was the only thing that could keep the disease at bay if caught in its early stages. It wouldn't have helped those in the valley though; the settlers had decimated the only tribes on the prairie who could've conjured that magic.

At Westie's father's insistence, they cut their suspenders and braved the wagon trail to get to California.

Westie took a wavering breath. *We should've stayed.*

Westie sat taller in her saddle when she saw Bena come out of the forest. The Wintu hunter's expression was as difficult to translate as her native language.

"What happened? What'd you see?" Westie asked.

Bena shook her head. Despite the unmoving wall of her features, there was tension in her gaze.

"It's abandoned. Looks like the old man who used to live here has been gone for some time, but there have been others."

Westie slid off her saddle and tied Henry to the closest tree. Bena dismounted behind her. She was just as short as Isabelle, but Westie never thought of her that way. Bena was strong and sturdy, which made her seem bigger than she really was.

"I counted six different sets of horse tracks, and manure piles still warm nearby. It could be outlaws," Bena said.

"Let's make it quick then," Westie said as she pushed through the dilapidated door of the cabin, which hung on by a desiccated leather hinge. Birds erupted from nests hidden in the rafters, bouncing around the room until they found escape through the holes in the roof. Westie walked into the middle of the room. Dust glittered in shafts of dingy light.

It was there, in the middle of the room, that the cannibals had invited her family to sup with them.

Westie remembered how delighted she'd been to see the family. The fire shed a yolky glow across their faces, giving their features the soft lines of dreams. There was a female toddler with a tangle of golden curls, a woman her mother's age or maybe a bit younger, and a teenage boy. He had a greasy complexion and a deep voice that cracked when he spoke.

The woman smiled at Westie. She wore a tattered light-blue dress exactly like one a woman from the caravan wore. She had a long hooked nose and a bony face, and she wore her dark hair pulled back so tight that it made her brown eyes slant.

The man's face was covered in hair. He looked strong. He was double her father's weight, and nearly double his height as well. He didn't give their names, nor did her father offer theirs.

"Come share our meal," the woman had said. The sharp angles of her face didn't match her friendly voice. "I've made plenty of stew. You must be famished."

Westie's mouth watered. The food smelled like home, like hugs and laughter and all the good things that came before the voyage west. It had been days since their last meal, which had been horse grain.

"The hunting must be good," her father had said.

The bearded man seemed put off by small talk. Shadows from the firelight danced behind him. "The mountain provides," he grumbled.

They sat on the floor in the middle of the main room, and Westie watched the woman deliver heaping ladles of stew into her wood bowl.

Her first bite was a taste of heaven. The tang of wild onions popped on her tongue, the potatoes were soft and gritty with the skins still attached, and pine nuts gave the stew a sweet crunch. There was plenty of meat. Some of the chunks were tough and stringy and others were mushy like liver or duck. She guessed it to be bear, or horse. It had an odd gamy flavor, fungal like a mushroom past its prime. She ate it anyway. Even Tripp ate some, the pink blush coming back into his cheeks.

Westie pushed the memory away and focused on the present. The cabin no longer held the scent of food. Instead it smelled musty and old. Her gaze shifted. There, in front of the fireplace, was where her family had died. That same familiar fear from her nightmares twisted her stomach.

Tins and jars of moldy food had been left behind by either the old man or those who'd sought shelter in the cabin since his departure. Westie kicked at a heap of rusted tins, looking for anything that might lead her in the right direction. She headed toward the only bedroom. When she stepped across the threshold, her boot fell through a plank of rotting wood.

Pain shot through her calf. She cried out as the jagged edges of broken boards ripped through her pant leg, dragging down her flesh. Bena and Alistair rushed to her side.

"Are you hurt?" Alistair asked. He took her by the arm, his lids peeled back around wide, frightened eyes.

Westie clung to the floorboards to hold her weight. She moved her foot around, feeling cold, empty space beneath. "I don't think so. Just stuck."

Bena grabbed her other arm and they pulled. Westie closed her eyes and crushed her teeth together as exposed pegs cut into her skin. Blood trickled from several spots on her leg, but they were just flesh wounds, not even deep enough for stitching.

She looked back at the hole where she'd fallen and saw a small speck of white through the gloom and spiderwebs. "There's something in there," she said.

Reaching into the dark hole, she moved her hand around. The earth below the floorboards was damp, and she tried not to think about spiders and other things with fangs whose homes she might've been destroying. Her fingers swept across something coarse, and she had to fight the urge to pull away. She grabbed the thing and pulled it from its hiding spot.

It was a scarf.

# Twelve

All three of them stared down at the wisp of fabric in Westie's trembling hand.

"This was my momma's."

"Are you sure?" Bena said. "We found many clothes in this cabin."

Bena and some of the Wintu scouts had gone back to the cabin to hunt for the cannibals after Westie was found. The family had fled by then but left the evidence of their carnage behind. The scouts had taken the bones and clothing of the dead and buried them after the ground thawed in a private ceremony nearby, knowing if they took them to the church for a Christian burial, the natives might've been blamed for their deaths.

They'd tried to burn the cabin after, but the wood was too wet and the fire had fizzled out. Instead they left woven dolls hanging from trees and painted symbols on the door warning travelers of the haunted cabin. Judging by the trash scattered across the floor, not many had heeded that warning.

Westie nodded. She was sure. The cannibals had used the scarf to tie her mother's hands together.

"She was wearing it that night. She always wore this scarf. It was a gift from my pa on their anniversary."

Westie ran her fingers across the intricate pattern. She imagined she could still smell her mother: lilac and honey. The only thing she really remembered was the smell of blood and the faces of those who killed her family.

Tears glittered in the corners of her eyes when she remembered waking up to her mother's screams. She'd blinked several times, eyes blurry with sleep, and found her mother and father sitting on the floor beside her, their hands and feet bound with items of clothing. She looked around for Tripp but didn't see him.

"Run!" her mother had cried.

Westie had imagined an attack: vampires, the Undying, werewolves, or ghouls, but saw nothing.

"What? Why?" She looked around. The nice family she'd shared her meal with earlier stood in the room watching her.

"Go!" her mother shouted again.

The other family surged toward her like a machine, different parts of a single structure working together for a single purpose, to tie her up too. She was drunk on fear and confusion. She did what her mother demanded of her and ran. The boy, much bigger than her, moved in front of the door leading to the woods, so she turned and ran toward the only bedroom. The woman moved to block her way. Westie turned again, slipped on a grimy rug, and nearly went down before recovering and rushing toward the kitchen. She heard the heavy boots of the bearded man as he chased after her.

When Westie reached the small kitchenette, she saw bare cupboards, a stove, a pump for water, and a butcher block in the middle of the room, with a bloody stump of a human leg on it. The skin on the leg was smooth and soft, and the foot was small. A child's leg.

*Tripp . . .*

Beside the leg was a fresh pot of stew.

A scream stuck to the sides of her throat and burned like medicine. She felt herself start to retch when the fetid smell of decay reached her nose. Despite the cold winter month, flies buzzed around a lake of congealed blood pooled on the floor below the block. Westie bent at the waist, and when she did, she saw a pile of clothes and bones behind the butcher block. She recognized the clothes. They belonged to members of the caravan.

Her family had been warned of cannibals on the wagon trail before they left Kansas. Stories were told of folks who had been ill-prepared for the mountainous terrain and would turn on one another for nourishment when the food ran out. It wasn't prairie sickness, the illness that turned one into the Undying, but to eat one's own kind seemed far worse. Westie's father had said it was a bunch of lies shopkeepers told to prevent money from leaving town. He was wrong.

When Westie heard the floor creak behind her, she spun around to face the bearded man. In his hand was a knife that winked in the candlelight. As he swung down on her, she raised an arm to ward off the blow. The knife sliced clean through her bone at her elbow, leaving her arm attached by skin and tendon.

There was hardly any pain, only pressure and a dull ache. It took her a moment to get her breath. When the man lifted his knife once more, she slipped past him. The wife and son of the bearded man seemed confused when they saw Westie come into the room, as if they hadn't expected her to make it out alive. She was able to get past them too.

Westie's mother was screaming. Her father struggled with his ties. "Leave her be," he growled in a voice that frightened her. "Run," he said to her. "Run and don't look back."

So Westie did. She ran out into the dark woods, through the snow without coat or shoes. She could hear the man's heavy footfalls behind her. Her breath was a death shroud around her face. Petals of blood floated behind her as if she were a flower girl at a wedding until her body became so cold it stanched the flow. The man's footsteps had been close at first. She ran and ran without looking back, until the steps slowed and finally stopped. Even then she ran. Soon her battered arm was in so much pain that she could no longer move. She slumped to her knees in the snow. The pain was razor sharp, but she dared not scream. There were moments she wanted to look at the damage but was too afraid of what she might find.

Several times she leaned over and retched, because of the pain, and because she knew she had eaten the flesh of travel companions whose children she had played with. And because she had left her entire family to be slaughtered.

Something moved in the snow. Her breath halted as she listened. She prayed the cold would take her before a hungry mouth.

Her vision had begun to gray. *Good*, she thought, *I'm dying*. She thought the same thing again when she saw the rider atop his painted pony in front of her. It was a beautiful horse, red with white shapes on its hide. Upon its rump were blue handprints, and in its mane feathers and beads. Westie wished she had a pony like that to ride. Its gallop would be so fast they could outrun the pain.

The rider dismounted. The person was too small to be the bearded man, or his wife—the boy, maybe. As the figure got closer and the face became clear, Westie saw the skin was too brown and the hair too long and dark to be anyone from the cannibal family. An Indian, she realized, a woman. Westie tried to speak, but then her gray vision turned black.

# Thirteen

Westie dropped the scarf, not wanting to touch it any longer. It was hardly proof. She was the only one who knew it had belonged to her mother.

They left the cabin after Westie had turned the floors to kindling and pulled down entire walls in search of evidence. But if there were ever pictures or papers bearing the Fairfield name, they were long gone.

When they were outside the cabin, Bena said, "We need to hurry."

But it was too late, for a train of outlaws appeared from behind the trees.

The first to show himself was a man. The only thing she was certain of was the malice she saw in the way he watched her troupe.

The next to show himself was not a man but a leprechaun. Fear kneaded at Westie's stomach when she saw it was the old buzzard she'd played cards with in the saloon. He had a tobacco-pregnant lower lip and boasted cuts and bruises from a previous quarrel. Each outlaw who showed himself afterward had a unique look about him, except his intentions. Those were all the same.

There were six of them all together. Westie's head was no place for a lady when the last outlaw was in view, for all that came to mind were curse words. It was the young leprechaun from the saloon. He wore a sling on his arm and a harder look upon his face than when she had seen him last.

She pulled the parasol from its leather holster across her back and pointed it toward the gang. Alistair stood at her side with his hands resting on the revolvers at his hips.

The young leprechaun slid off his horse and the others followed. He wore an amused look on his face and raised his hands in a parody of surrender.

"You plan to beat me to death with your parasol, tart?"

Westie assessed each outlaw, taking inventory of their weapons. Each had a revolver on his hip and a rifle on his saddle. "I reckon I might have me a try," she said, happy to be sober.

When the young leprechaun moved, there was a shimmer beneath his vest.

"Ace in the hole," she whispered to Alistair, knowing he would be counting guns as well. He nodded without taking his eyes off the gang.

Westie had one bullet secured in the chamber of her hidden gun.

All she had to do was pull the trigger and hope the young lep caught a case of slow. Once she did, it was up to Alistair and Bena to finish the others before they fired their weapons. She prayed it wouldn't come to that. Last thing she wanted was to find herself in a hailstorm of gunfire. If she could just get off one shot and frighten the outlaws' horses, they could make a getaway, though she doubted the horses of outlaws would be gun-shy.

She had to make a choice. It was a corpse-and-carriage event no matter which way she looked at it. She just hoped she and her friends weren't the ones taking the long ride home in boxes.

She took a deep breath and aimed between the young leprechaun's eyes. She pulled the trigger.

Nothing happened, not even a click. Her heart sputtered. She tried again and again. The gun was jammed.

The outlaws were restless, and the young leprechaun was no longer amused by her display of bravery. Their stallions, each one as dark and fearsome as the riders, had also grown impatient. They pawed at the earth and nipped at one another.

Alistair fidgeted with the pistols at his hips. The young leprechaun turned to Alley.

"You half vampire under there?" the young leprechaun said with hooded eyes and a dry smile. "Take off your mask, boy. Let's see your pretty face."

Alistair showed no hint of fear.

"You don't want to see what's under this mask," he said.

The outlaws' horses were startled by Alistair's metal voice.

They whinnied and stepped back.

"You're a metal freak just like she is," the young leprechaun cried in a high keen.

The leprechaun fumbled with the six-shooter beneath his vest but dropped it on the ground. He turned to the holster keeping his rifle strapped to his saddle.

Before he could reach it, Alistair put a window in his skull, and two more bullets in the men on either side of him.

Gunpowder filled Westie's nose and stung her eyes, the screams of the old leprechaun pulsed in her ears. Alistair put a bullet in his chest, shutting him up for good.

One of the outlaws turned his gun on Bena. She darted around to confuse his aim, then reached for her pony's mane and swung onto his saddleless back to get above the man. She leaped from her horse with a battle cry, her knife in her grip, two graceful ladies dancing through the air. A violent pink mist dappled her skin as she hacked through the man's neck before he could get his shot off.

Another of the outlaws took aim at Alistair and fired.

The bullet hit Alistair in the face and threw him back against a tree, where he crumpled to the ground like a discarded jacket.

"Alley!" Westie cried as she unsheathed the blade in her parasol.

She lunged at the outlaw who'd shot Alistair, her sword high over her head, gripped in both her hands. She brought it down upon his head where he was bent on one knee, reloading. He didn't look up until she was right in front of him. The blade cut through the air with the full force of her machine and sliced the man clean through from skull to groin. His twin halves fell apart with a sticky sound.

Westie's breath was erratic as she looked around at the six dead bandits lying in pools of blood and loosed bowels. She turned her desperate gaze to Alistair.

Bena was by his side. Westie was afraid to go to him, afraid of what she would see. Bena dabbled in gore and could stomach such things, but Westie wasn't sure if she had it in her.

"Is he . . . ," Westie started to say, but her voice shut off before she could get the words out.

"No," Bena said.

"No?" Westie went to him then. She thought there would be blood or worse, but all she saw was Alistair's dented mask. His eyes were closed, chest moving with each breath. It simply looked as though he were sleeping.

"It was his head hitting the tree that knocked him out, not the gunshot," Bena said. She poked at his skull with the tips of her fingers, then reached behind his head to unsnap his mask.

"Wait," Westie said, and turned her back to Bena. "Alistair wouldn't want me to see his face."

She waited, wanting so badly to see what Bena was doing, but she knew how angry Alistair would be if she watched.

"You can look now," Bena said. When Westie turned around, Alistair's mask was back on. "A shot like that should have knocked all his teeth out and crushed the bones in his face. There is no damage from what I can see, just a bump on the head."

Westie wiped a tear from her cheek. "Nigel makes durable

machines," she said in a strangled voice.

"Help me get him on his horse," Bena said. "We need to get him back to town to make sure there is no other damage."

When Alistair was draped over his saddle and Bena was back on her paint, Westie took a moment to secure his body with rope and make sure he didn't fall off. She touched his hair and the skin on his neck. He looked so peaceful. She kissed each of his closed eyes and quietly thanked the maker for saving his life.

# Fourteen

Alistair had stirred along the way but had yet to wake by the time they stopped to camp. He still hadn't woken the next day when they got back to Rogue City. Bena and Westie took him straight to Doc Flannigan's.

Westie held her head in her hands as they sat in the doctor's office, waiting. "Thank you for coming with me. I couldn't have gone through that without you," she said.

Bena's copper-colored eyes looked straight forward, but she reached over and put a hand on Westie's back. The gentleness of Bena's touch made Westie want to weep, but she knew how uncomfortable her friend was with tears, so she held them in.

When the doc confirmed Alistair would be fine, Westie let out a sound of relief and left for the mansion to change her clothes.

Nigel waited for her on the stoop with a crushed piece of metal in his hand that had once been a telegraph bird. Westie looked at the broken bird. She should never have believed Doc Flannigan when he said he would wait an hour to tell Nigel about Alistair.

Westie dismounted and climbed the steps. Jezebel pushed her bucket head into Westie's hand, forcing her affection. She scratched the beast dutifully in the spot behind the ear where she liked. Nigel watched her expectantly.

"Would you like to tell me why you weren't in Sacramento with Isabelle as your note said, and how Alistair was shot in the face?" He asked the question as if he were asking about the weather, but Westie could see the emotion of that news lingering in the tremble of his lips.

It was an honest question, so she gave him an honest answer. "No."

His eyes examined the dried blood covering her riding clothes. "Very well."

She opened her mouth to counter his objections, but tilted her head when there was no resistance and closed her mouth again, happy not to disappoint him further.

He said, "I was hoping we could talk a bit."

Talk. Nigel always wanted to talk. He knew a lot of words and he liked to use them: big ones, fancy ones, and some she was sure he made up.

"Later," she said. When she saw the dubious look on his face, she added, "Promise."

He nodded with a resigned smile and led her into the house, where she pulled the parasol from its leather scabbard and placed it in the stand by the door that held the other umbrellas.

Westie hesitated, eyes scanning the foyer, when she noticed that a black suede coat lined in purple silk, smaller and more expensive than Nigel would ever buy himself, hung on the rack next to the umbrella holder.

"Who's here?" she asked.

Nigel's jaw tensed. He tried to smile through it, though it looked more like the grimace of a man constipated with secrets. "James stopped by for a visit today. He wanted to look at some of my inventions."

Westie wondered if James had been eavesdropping, for he walked into the room as soon as he heard his name.

"So good to see you again, Westie," he said. Westie said nothing in return, only fussed with Jezebel, who had been particularly invasive in seeking her attention, nearly knocking her over. She tried to shoo the beast but failed. "How was your trip to the city?"

She thought about the wide, unseeing eyes of the dead leprechauns and the outlaw whose body she'd sliced in two like an anatomy lesson. Her body gave an involuntary shudder.

"Fine," she said. "Where's your family?"

Nigel gave her a stealthy shake of the head. She ignored him.

James shrugged. "Off spending money, I'm sure. I don't really know and I don't really care." The piqued tone he used to speak of his family intrigued her, but not enough to ask why.

Jezebel's behavior had gotten to where it could no longer be ignored. The chupacabra had nearly lifted Westie off the floor with her enormous head. When Jezebel started to tear the fabric of her shirt, Westie had had enough and pushed the beast away.

James leaned in as if he were going to whisper into her ear, then stepped away with a frown. "Is that blood on your clothes?"

"What?"

The entire hem of Westie's shirt was crusted brown with old blood and swatches of dried skin.

"I reckon it is." She tried, unsuccessfully, to hide some of the bigger patches of blood with her hands. "We, um, went hunting, caught us some rabbits . . . could you excuse me? I need to get some air."

Once outside, she sat on the stoop, head tucked between her legs until the sickly feeling passed. When she lifted her head, James was sitting beside her. She held back the sigh waiting in her lungs.

"Are you feeling all right?" he asked.

"Fine. It's a little stuffy in there, is all."

"Maybe this will help." He pulled a silver flask from his trouser pocket, offering it to her. "Scotch, single malt. Not that it matters. Still tastes like hot piss, but it gets the job done."

Westie hesitated. Before drinking at the saloon, she'd gone two years without even a sip, and she'd managed without alcohol on the trip to the cabin. But that was before she'd killed a person, before Alistair was shot. Her resolve couldn't take much more.

*Just one drink to take the edge off,* she told herself when she reached out and took the flask. Closing her eyes and taking a deep breath, she tipped her head back, shivering as she felt the familiar burn.

James picked up a dried leaf on the porch. "I think I'm going to like it here in Rogue City," he said.

"Why?" she asked, wiping her mouth with the back of her sleeve.

He discarded the leaf in exchange for a passing ladybug. It crawled across his fingers. "The company, of course," he said with a wink. Westie rolled her eyes, dismissing his comment as flattery. "There are other reasons too, though. In the city I'm always on guard. Here I don't have to worry about creature attacks or the Undying wandering in."

"The Undying?" An image of the Undying snapped in her mind, blood weeping from their eyes, noses in the air as they sniffed out their prey. She took another long drink and handed the flask back to him. "As far as I know, there were never any in California to begin with, and from what I hear, there's no such thing anymore. President Pierce wiped them out and gave that land to the creatures as part of the treaty to end the war."

James smiled. "I suppose my sheltered city upbringing is really shining through. I didn't know anything about that." The ladybug spread its wings. With a gentle flick of James's hand, it flew away. "Still, it's a strange and wonderful place."

"I've grown up here and even I find it strange sometimes," Westie admitted, looking up at the dome. Again she thought she saw it flicker, but couldn't tell for sure. It might've been the alcohol playing tricks on her eyes. "You don't see all the different species of creatures much on the road, but here in Rogue City, where there's some semblance of law, you'll find every creature you once thought was legend sipping on a tumbler of whiskey at some point or another."

James's smile revealed the little white scar on his lip. "I shared a pint with a vampire last night, and he even offered to pay. It's almost like they're human at times—but don't let Lavina know I said that. She'd probably disown me."

With the mention of Lavina, the scotch in Westie's stomach went sour. Her nausea returned, and so did the tears pushing at the backs of her eyes. The entire trip to the cabin was a waste, and Alistair had nearly been killed because of it. She was no closer to finding any evidence against Lavina and her family. Maybe a ball wouldn't be so bad. Perhaps she could learn something about the Fairfields in a social setting.

"It's been a long ride," Westie said. "I'm bushed."

James bowed his head to her. "It was good to see you again," he said.

She nodded and went inside, bounding for the stairs.

# Fifteen

The next morning Nigel and Westie left for town to pick up Alistair from Doc Flannigan's office. Westie breathed slowly through her mouth. It was hot as a kiln out, but she shivered as her nausea crept up again. After James had left the evening before, Westie had snuck into Nigel's office, where he kept a stash of absinthe on hand for entertaining guests. She'd only meant to have one drink, but somehow one became four.

"Stop the wagon," she said, hopping down before he had the chance. She bent over, hands on her knees on the side of the road, and stayed that way until the feeling passed.

Nigel frowned. "Is this something I should be concerned about?"

Westie spit in the dirt. "Must have eaten something that didn't agree with me."

He mumbled under his breath, then went to his medical bag and pulled out a cup. He filled it with water and dropped what looked like a sugar cube inside. When it started to fizz, he handed it to her.

"Drink this. It will make you feel better."

She wrinkled her face in disgust upon tasting the chalky drink, but once she got it down, her stomach began to settle. They climbed back into the wagon without another word spoken between them.

Their next stop was in front of the doc's office, where an old man sat in a chair, whittling away at a piece of basswood. Westie jumped out of the wagon, her clothes clinging uncomfortably to her skin. A few horses waited in the shade of an awning, but the streets were mostly abandoned.

She reached for one of the boxes Nigel had brought to give to the doc in exchange for Alistair's care.

"What the hell did you pack in this thing?" she asked, lifting the box with her machine and steadying it with her flesh arm. It was big enough that she couldn't see a thing in front of her. She balanced the box on her knee before trying to brave the steps. "Are you and the doc cutting up dead bodies again?"

Westie had been only eleven years old when she'd walked in on Nigel, the doctor, and the old sheriff performing an autopsy. What took less than a minute to witness took years to finally get out of her head.

"Just a few inventions I came up with. Thermometers and alarms, mostly," Nigel said.

As Westie reached the top step, a scream punctured the doldrums of the lazy day, the kind of shattering sound that turned blood to ice and muscles to stone. She dropped the heavy box and heard the tinkle of something delicate breaking within as it tumbled down the steps.

"What in the heavens was that?" Nigel said.

The sheriff barreled out of the jail next door. His shirt was untucked, drool crusted on his chin, and he had the puffy eyes of someone woken suddenly from a nap.

Westie's heart jittered as she looked around, waiting for something to happen.

A woman erupted from the dark space between the general store and the tailor, tripping over the wagon ruts in the road and landing on the ground before pushing herself back up and running again.

"Help me," she cried, her eyes wild, blond hair unraveling from its bun, dress torn and bloodied.

She was just a streak of color and noise as she passed Westie, who pulled the sword from her parasol.

The sheriff reached for his gun, but he wasn't wearing his belt. "Dammit, my gun's still in the jail. Wait right there," he said to Westie, but it was too late. She was already running in the opposite direction, toward the alley where the woman had come from.

Westie's mind scrambled for the different scenarios she might encounter. The hard soles of her boots made it difficult to maneuver over the ruts, and several times she nearly went down when her ankles buckled. She was vaguely aware of the sheriff's shouts from behind her and of the slower steps following behind her. By the time she reached the darkness, whoever had been there with the woman was gone.

Westie panted as she buried her blade in its sheath, the heat of the day making her feel light-headed. Behind her, Nigel leaned heavily on his cane, trying to catch his breath. "Anything?" he said with the toothy grimace of a man in pain.

"Nothing."

The woman had collapsed in the sheriff's arms in front of Doc Flannigan's office, her body quivering from her racking sobs.

Others spilled out of shops, cluttering the porches to see what all the commotion was about. Isabelle stood in front of her parents' apothecary, eyes alight with intrigue. Westie took Nigel by the elbow and helped him make his way back to the sheriff.

"Westie, I told you to wait," the sheriff said in his Texas drawl, and spit a thick stream of tobacco juice on the ground beside her.

Westie wasn't sure why all the women in town thought he was the handsomest man in Rogue City. Sure, he was tall and lean and packed with muscle. But he was also hairy and slightly horseshoe legged. But mostly it was his personality that made him ugly to Westie. If he were a horse with a disposition like that, he would've been put down by now.

"I didn't realize you were talking to me," Westie lied.

"Do you see any other dumb shits around here with a death wish?" The sheriff rarely cussed, but when he did it was usually at her. He still hadn't gotten over the embarrassment she'd caused him when he'd nearly hanged an innocent man for cannibalism.

"Like the kind of dumb shits who forget their gun belts in jails?" she said.

The sheriff's mustache covered his mouth, but the gathering of skin on his forehead suggested a frown. He tilted his tan Stetson, pointed a finger at her, said, "Watch yourself," and focused on the woman once more.

"She was right behind me," the woman said. "Please, you have to do something!" She clawed at the sheriff's shirt, nearly climbing up the front of him in her frenzy.

*"She?"* Westie said.

"Whoever it was is gone now," Nigel assured her. He leaned over, massaging his bad leg.

Westie persisted. "What do you mean, *she*?"

"A woman," she said through weeping hiccups. "She paid for my services and then she . . . she bit me."

Westie noticed for the first time the woman's rouged cheeks and red lips. Black paint melted from her lashes down her cheeks. She was older than most of the prostitutes Westie had seen at the blood brothel. Her scant clothing showed off a plump body, round in all the places men liked.

When most of the gawkers saw she was a prostitute, they lost interest and went back indoors. Only a curious few remained.

"Go on, then, you vultures," Isabelle said to them as they muttered their insults about the woman's profession.

"What's your name?" Westie asked the woman.

The sheriff glared at Westie. "I'm conducting this interview." His voice was so deep it sounded like he was growling when he talked.

"What's your name?" the sheriff said.

Westie bit her words back and pressed her lips shut, afraid if she pushed him too far he'd make her leave.

"Nadia."

"Did you say a woman bit you?" the sheriff said, as if women couldn't possibly be capable of such derangement.

Nadia pushed the loose hair from her shoulder, revealing a deep oval wound gouged out of the curve of her neck. The sheriff paled and brought his handkerchief to his mouth. Nigel used his pocket square to dab away the blood, but as soon as he stopped, the deep crater filled up again.

"You're sure it was just a woman and not an entire family?" Westie said.

Nigel shot her a look full of daggers.

The sheriff seemed too ill to reprimand her.

No sooner had the words left her mouth than Hubbard, Cain, James, and the mayor stepped out of the apothecary, each with a stack of pamphlets in his hands.

"No, just a woman."

So it wasn't the Fairfield men, but what of Lavina? She was nowhere around.

"What did the woman look like?" Westie asked, desperate for any detail that might link Lavina to the attack.

She could tell by the distant look in Nadia's eyes that she was going into shock. "I don't know. I didn't see her. She whispered to me in the shadows, handed me a bag of coins, and told me to—"

"I don't think we need all the sordid details with ladies around," the sheriff said, cutting her off. He glanced at Westie. "And I use that word loosely." He put his handkerchief back in his pocket. The color had seeped back into his lips and he stood straighter. "Let's get you to the doctor for patching. I'll take your statement when you're through."

Westie kicked at the dirt, knowing justice was unlikely, given Nadia's employment.

When the sheriff was gone, Westie said to Nigel, "This is a cannibal's doing." There was no need to say names. Nigel knew exactly who she was talking about.

"Cannibals?" With the excitement of the event, Westie had failed to notice Isabelle behind her. "You really think so? There hasn't been a cannibal attack in these parts for years."

Isabelle was right; there hadn't been cannibals near Rogue City for some time. Cannibals used to be a problem back when Westie's parents and others like them were still traveling the wagon trail, but by the next year, after the creature war officially ended and air travel became more affordable, there had been very few attacks. The only ones Westie heard of were in the valley where she'd been hunting them.

"Rubbish," Nigel said. "It wasn't a cannibal. The woman was working. You see, sometimes when two people are in the throes of passion—when they are . . . let's see, how do I put this?"

Isabelle giggled into her hand. Westie made a gagging sound.

"Copulating," Westie said. "Yes, I know what two people do when they're alone."

The column of Nigel's throat moved when he swallowed. He put a hand on his shoulder, massaging a knot. "Right, anyway, sometimes when two people are intimate, they can get carried away."

"I'm telling you, Nigel, that wasn't a love bite," Westie said.

Nigel ran a hand down the front of his face, stretching his skin. "I need to go see if the doctor needs help with the stitching," he said, hurrying to escape the conversation.

As soon as he was gone, Westie asked Isabelle, "What were the mayor and the Fairfield men doing in the apothecary?"

"Well, the mayor came in to complain about the Wintu, creatures, and pretty much everything else in Rogue City. I think that ridiculous little man just likes to hear himself talk. As for the Fairfields, they talked mostly about Emma. Cain told me they're spending a fortune on Nigel's invention, so they want to spread the word about its capabilities."

The hairs stood on Westie's arm. "You've been talking to Cain Fairfield?"

Isabelle smiled the devilish smile she wore when talking about boys. "A little. Though I have to say, it's difficult to focus on Cain when James is around, wouldn't you agree?"

Westie looked at James, who was about four feet away, still in front of the apothecary. Their eyes met and his lit up. She scratched the back of her neck and brought her attention back to Isabelle. She wanted to tell her to avoid the Fairfields at all costs, but wasn't sure how to do it without revealing her secret about them being murderers. Isabelle loved secrets. She had a trumpet for a mouth, and gossip was her favorite tune.

"He's all right, I suppose," Westie said.

"Well, I'd best get back to the apothecary. I'm sure the doctor will need alcohol and medicines to patch the woman up," Isabelle said, though Westie was sure Isabelle was less concerned about the doctor's needs than she was about being present in case any of those sordid details the sheriff seemed so concerned about just happened to slip from Nadia's groggy lips.

After Isabelle left, Westie realized she'd forgotten to grab the extra set of clothes she'd brought for Alistair. On her way back to the wagon, she noticed someone strolling down the center of the road and froze.

Lavina wore a bright-yellow gown with lace trim and held a parasol shading her from the sun. Her hips swayed ever so slightly. So casual compared to Nadia's screaming and fumbling as she ran down the same path.

As Westie watched Lavina join the Fairfield men, she remembered briefly wondering, while she'd been drinking in the Tight Ship, if the Fairfields were still cannibals. Most who had turned to cannibalism on the wagon trail did it only to survive and stopped once they were rescued. But for some, it became a craving, or maybe it was just madness. Either way, they couldn't—or wouldn't—stop.

It took animal savagery to tear at someone's skin with their teeth, gnawing through fat and muscle, to hear someone's agonized screams and feel nothing. Westie saw no compassion, no regret, as Lavina tilted her head back, laughing at something James was saying.

Perhaps the rest of the family hadn't been involved. Maybe they had moved on from hunting helpless families in cabins, but there was one thing Westie felt certain of: Lavina was still a threat.

The Fairfields headed toward her. She was reminded again of being back in the cabin, woken up by the screams of her mother.

"Westie, so good to see you again," Lavina said when they were facing each other. Her dress was exquisitely made. There were no bumps or wrinkles at all in the fabric. Not something Westie imagined a cannibal would wear when on the hunt, but maybe that was the look Lavina was going for.

"Good to see you too," Westie said with some semblance of grace. She held her ground, not wanting them to see her squirm. She kept her parasol close and twisted a gear at the wrist of her machine that made her middle finger twitch. It reminded her she was no longer that helpless little girl in the cabin, even if she still felt like it. "What brings you out today?"

"Actually," the mayor said, "I was hoping to speak with the little savage girl I've seen you running around with."

Westie bit the inside of her cheek, wanting to tell him that Bena was a woman, not a girl, and she was far from savage. But that would've meant sticking around to give a lecture. Without Alistair and Bena by her side, she wanted to be away from her present company as soon as possible.

"I'm sure I can get a message to her," Westie said.

"Good. Some folks around here are concerned about what's happening with the dome."

When Hubbard took a step toward her, Westie flinched, nearly raising her arm to ward off an attack, but she stopped herself, remaining calm outwardly even when her insides rattled.

"If I'm going to invest my money in this machine, I need to know them savages will pull their weight," Hubbard said. He had a bovine look to him and talked like a man slow in the head. Perhaps that was what eating humans did to the brain over time. If that was the case, it wasn't working on Lavina. She seemed as sharp as ever.

"I'm sure whatever is happening with the dome, the Wintu have their reasons, and it will have no effect on Emma whatsoever," Westie said. "I'll see if I can set up a meeting with the Wintu's chief as soon as possible."

"Excellent," Lavina said, wiping the sweat from her brow. "Now maybe we can finally get off the topic of money."

When Lavina lifted her arm, Westie saw a brown smear on her sleeve and blurted, "Is that blood on your dress?" before she could stop herself.

James leaned over Lavina's shoulder for a better look. "You two must bathe in the stuff. Westie was covered in it too just yesterday. Is this some beauty regimen we should be concerned about?" he said with a smirk.

Westie forced herself to smile at James's quip, but her gaze remained on Lavina, who scratched at the dried brown swatch. She'd been in Rogue City less than a week and was already causing trouble. It was hardly enough blood to suggest she'd attacked someone, but it was there all the same.

"I must have pricked myself with the needle when I was sewing Olivia's doll's head back on," Lavina said. She smiled as if to say there was nothing Westie could do to shake her. "Speaking of Olivia, I'd best go check on her. If she wakes and sees I'm gone, she'll destroy the place."

"I think I'll slip over to the Tight Ship. I'd like to avoid that little terror when she wakes." James looked at Westie in a way that might've sent a flutter through her had they been alone. But as it was, all she felt was sick. "It's always nice to see you, Westie. Good day."

Westie watched the Fairfields leave. As soon as it was safe to turn her back on them, she rushed into the doctor's office, locking the door behind her.

# Sixteen

They arrived back at the mansion just before supper. Alistair was awake and, other than complaints of a headache, seemed no different than before he was shot. They sat down to eat. He wore a red hand-kerchief over his nose and mouth like a bandit after Nigel had taken his mask for repairs.

Alistair lifted his kerchief with one hand and shuttled a broccoli floret into his mouth with the other, careful not to let Westie see the face hidden beneath. She wished she had peeked at him when she'd had the chance.

He raised his hands. *Stop watching me,* he signed.

"Sorry, Alley, I don't remember what those signs mean," she lied. "You wear that blasted machine so often I've forgotten the hand lan-guage."

He glared at her until she broke into a smile. His eyes softened.

"Enough," Nigel said from the head of the table. He'd been so quiet Westie had nearly forgotten he was there. "I want to talk about what happened at the airdocks before the two of you went off seeking adventure."

Westie looked down at the plate of food she hadn't touched. "I was hoping to avoid it," she said.

"You have been, but no longer. Now"—he tossed his napkin onto his full plate—"I want you to stop all this nonsense about the Fairfields being cannibals."

"Nonsense?" She crushed her fork into a silver ball with her machine. "You don't believe me?"

Neither Nigel nor Alistair would look at her. She wished Bena were there. Bena would at least give it some thought before dismissing her completely.

"I believe that you believe they are who you say they are, but *please*, Westie, look at this from all sides. You spent months searching for these people in the valley, always one step behind them, you say. You dug tirelessly into the cases, trying to dispute the reports of skilled pathologists on their findings—"

"They were calling them creature attacks. I've helped you in the surgical rooms enough to recognize a creature attack. There weren't any fang punctures on those bodies. I know a human bite mark when I see it."

Nigel's mustache moved like a living thing as he chewed his lip.

"I realize you saw . . . what you saw as a child, but you are no expert on human bite marks. Vampire and elf bites can look very much human."

Each word that came from his mouth stoked the fire that grew within her. No one believed her. She heard it in Nigel's voice and saw it in Alistair's eyes.

He went on, "And don't you think it is a miraculous turn of events that the cannibal family who killed your own seven years ago just happens to show up on our doorstep—quite literally—the day after you get back into town?"

"You think I'm lying?" she asked with narrowed eyes.

Westie had told some tall tales as a child, and she'd told a few whales to get out of trouble, but she had never lied to Nigel about the important things. It pained her that he didn't believe her now.

"Not lying—I believe you are mistaken. I think you want to find your family's killers so desperately that you see them in every new face you encounter. I mean you no offense, but with the way you've been drinking lately, and some of the mistakes you've made in the past, I have to just come out and say it: you are not the most reliable witness."

Nigel's words tore through her chest and ripped out her heart. She was quite aware of her past mistakes and regretted them, but it hurt no less hearing Nigel throw them back in her face. She felt ganged up on. Ashamed of the mess she had become. She needed Nigel and Alistair more than ever, and they wouldn't stand by her. And worst of all, she had no one to blame but herself.

She left the table without being excused, ignoring Nigel's pleas for her to return.

\* \* \*

That night after everyone had retired to their rooms, Westie slipped out her bedroom window and went down to the barn.

She saddled Henry and made her way to the Wintu village. Once she was outside the city limits and into the pitch darkness of Wintu land, she slowed her horse. To keep from getting an arrow between her shoulder blades, she spoke the Wintu word for *friendship*—that, or the word for being flatulent. The Wintu children used to find it comical to teach her the wrong words for everything, and with *friendship* and *flatulent* being so close in sound, she couldn't remember which word was which. When she heard the quiet laughter of Wintu scouts coming from the trees, bushes, and crags, she knew.

They let her pass anyway. Everyone in Bena's tribe recognized Westie, and she was welcome.

In a clearing was a circle of huts and a large campfire in the middle, with most of the tribe gathered around. Grah sat by the fire, scraping an animal hide with a sharpened bone. He was the closest to Westie's age, and they'd played together when Bena would take her to the village as a child. She'd developed quite the infatuation with him back then, following him around, braiding his long hair when he wasn't able to avoid her. He would tease her about her pale skin blinding him in the sunlight. She hadn't thought about him much since Alistair had come into her life, but seeing him, his long black hair and shirtless broad chest, made her sweat a little. He smiled and winked when he saw her. She had to fight the urge to hide her face in her hands like she'd done when she was young and still shy.

Sitting near Grah was Rek. He looked much older than she remembered, his black braids now woven with stands of gray. His wife had been raped and killed by a white man around the same time Bena had saved Westie, but that hadn't stopped him from gently changing Westie's bandages and treating her wound.

Roasting what looked like a squirrel over the open flame was Chaoha, who'd told her grand stories of a giant eagle that flew around the sun with the earth on its back, and Tecumseh—also known as Tall Buck—who'd sung her songs when she'd woken up from nightmares.

Seeing them brought a burning sense of longing. For Westie, the Wintu village was a place of healing, a place for her tortured soul to be nourished. She'd come to the Wintu with her heart in pieces, and they'd done their best to put it back together with what little they had left to work with.

As she rode by, she was met with words of welcome and smiles as warm as the orange glow of firelight against their skin.

Westie tied Henry up with the Wintu horses and made her way to Bena's hut, which looked somewhat like a beaver nest. It was a round structure, dug deep into the earth. The roof was made of branches and was almost flush with the ground.

"Come in," Bena said without even looking up. She sat on a woven blanket, the blunt end of a spear wedged between her bare feet while she sharpened the tip. "It's been two seasons since you were last here."

Westie looked around at all the weapons on the walls, bows and arrows, hatchets, spears, and guns. The evidence of the warrior Bena was.

Breathing in the familiar smell of wood smoke, she smiled and sighed. "Every time I step on Wintu land it gets harder to leave. I fear one day I'll come for a visit and never leave."

"Believe me, we fear it too."

Bena grinned when Westie glared at her. Bena was always more generous with her smiles when she was with her own people. It made Westie feel a little better after the crushing blow dealt by Nigel's words.

"So." The smile slipped away from Bena's lips as she concentrated on the tip of her spear. "What brings you out at night?"

"I was hoping to speak to Big Fish if she'll have me."

Big Fish was the Wintu chief. The name was much prettier in their native language, but Westie's tongue could never move the way it needed to to pronounce it.

"I am sure she will be happy to see you." The smile was back. "She loves a challenge."

"Well, aren't you just a riot tonight?" Westie said.

Bena chuckled. "She's up on the hill, talking to the spirits."

Westie turned to leave, then stopped at the opening of the hut and faced Bena again. "Is magic really as scarce as Nigel would have me believe?"

Though Westie had seen it with her own eyes when Bena had failed to heal the houseplant and start a fire, she didn't want to believe it was true.

Bena looked up from her work. "I'm afraid so."

Westie had hoped Nigel was exaggerating so that she would behave around his guests, and that the change in the dome was some sort of natural phenomenon that could easily be explained away.

"But how? Why now?"

Bena put the spear to the side, picked up a blunt-edged stick, and began to whittle away at the tip. "More and more settlers are calling this continent their home. As the population grows, so does industry. Entire forests are being destroyed to build cities, waterways polluted. Magic *is* the land. It is in the trees, the mountains, the water, the air. As all those things are destroyed, magic will recede into the earth, deeper and deeper, until those of us on the surface can no longer reach it."

That was why Nigel used gold for his invention, Westie realized. She'd seen Big Fish use nuggets of it during spells. She wore a chunk of it on a string around her neck. Magic had sunk into the earth and soaked into the gold.

"I'm sorry," Westie said.

"As am I."

Westie ducked her head and left Bena's hut. There was nothing she could do about the settlers, and she didn't need another burden right then to wallow in. She'd come to the Wintu village with a purpose, and that was to ask a favor of Big Fish.

Westie hiked up the nearly vertical hill. It was too dark to see her footing. She worked solely on memory to get her there, and it seemed her memory wasn't all that reliable from when she'd been sober either.

She didn't remember trees and rocks in the path the last time she'd walked to Spirit Hill. She fell and scraped her knees. The pain of it nearly pushed her to a breaking point. She cussed the entire way up.

She could see the glow of firelight up ahead and smelled the tangy scent of kinnikinnick burning in the air. The smell brought back a long-forgotten memory of when she had stayed with the Wintu. Big Fish had spent every night on Spirit Hill with her pipe, talking to her creator, asking the spirits for protection over her tribe. Westie had decided she wanted to talk to them too, ask why they'd allowed the cannibals to take her family. She knew only a chosen few were able to talk to spirits, but that wasn't about to stop her from trying. One night after everyone in the village was asleep, she snuck into Big Fish's dwelling, took the pipe, and climbed the hill.

Though not a spirit talker, after smoking enough wild tobacco for three grown men, Westie finally saw them—as well as a pink buffalo and dogs dressed in human clothes dancing through the air. Somehow, through it all, she'd forgotten to ask the creator anything and woke up with a brain-splitting headache the next morning. Since then she'd decided to leave the spirit talking to the chief. It was a hard lesson learned, like most. Still, it was a memory that made her smile when so many others hurt.

By the time Westie reached the top of the hill, she was bathed in sweat and breathing so hard she thought one of her lungs might have collapsed. She crumpled to the ground in front of the fire opposite the chief and grabbed the water skin from her belt, taking deep gulps.

Big Fish wore coyote hides and a colorful woven hat that fit tight to her skull. She looked up at the sky in a trance, unaware Westie was there. Her eyes darted from side to side like a cat following a bird in the trees. Westie followed her gaze but saw only lazy stars. Big Fish was seeing the creator, she knew. Westie sat back on the blankets by the fire, waiting it out. Finally the chief fell out of her stupor.

"Westie. It has been too long," the woman said, offering the pipe to her.

Big Fish was the oldest person Westie had ever seen, with deep wrinkles creasing her face and skin like parchment. Some in the Wintu village claimed she was over three hundred years old, though Westie reckoned it was closer to ninety. She was old and frail, and smaller than some of the mountain dwarves Westie had seen, but there was nothing frail about the woman's mind.

Westie shook her head and waved the pipe away. "My days of spirit talking are done."

Big Fish smiled and nodded.

"The creator tells me you seek something. I'm told you have a darkness growing inside your heart," Big Fish said in Wintu.

Westie picked up a clump of dirt, smashed it between her fingers, nervous.

She replied in her own tongue, self-conscious about saying the Wintu words properly. "I have a whole lot of dark things growing in my heart these days, but I'm here to tackle just the one."

"You want to ask the creator for help?"

What she planned to ask Big Fish was no small favor, and she felt guilty for even asking since it had been months since her last visit.

"Nah," she said, "spirits don't like me much. I was hoping *you* would help me out."

"Oh?" Big Fish raised her brows—only the loose skin around her eyes kept her from looking surprised.

Westie buried her chin in her chest, avoiding Big Fish's clear, wise eyes. "I was hoping you could give me an elixir, something to stop me from . . . from . . ."

"The poison you crave," Big Fish finished for her.

Westie looked up then, meeting her gaze. "Yes."

The chief nodded and frowned. "I am sorry, young one, but there is no herb or spell for sobriety. It takes time and perseverance to overcome such a craving. There is no instant cure."

Westie picked up a rock and crushed it with her machine. "That's not true." She sat straight, suddenly remembering a rumor she'd heard long ago. "There is a cure."

Big Fish leaned over the dying fire and gave Westie a hard glare. "What you speak of is illegal, and immoral. The creator looks down on such perversions."

Westie stood up, feeling angry. Mostly at her own self for even asking. "I reckon if the spirits don't care for me, I don't care for them much neither."

The old woman looked ready to throw Westie over a knee and give her a good paddling for talking bad about her beloved spirits, but her anger was soon replaced with a look of concern.

"Westie, I pray you reconsider. There is no cure. What you speak of may stop the body's cravings for a time, but it is your mind that is diseased. You must rid yourself of the darkness in your heart. Only then will you be free."

Westie took another swig of her water. "Don't you worry about that. I plan to."

# Seventeen

Being denied a cure by Big Fish was a blow Westie hadn't been expecting. She wasn't angry, though. Nigel had told Westie the Wintu's healing spells weren't working, and she was sure their elixirs needed magic. Or maybe Big Fish just wanted Westie to figure it out on her own, only she didn't have time for that. If she wanted to get sober and regain Nigel's and the sheriff's trust, she'd need to figure out a faster way.

A year ago, while in the Tight Ship, she'd heard a drunkard talking about his wife leaving him and how he planned to stop drinking in order to win her back. Everyone just brushed him off and went back to their spirits and gambling. No one thought he could do it until he showed up at the saloon one day, bathed, shaved, and dressed to the nines. Without ordering a drink, he paid his tab and wished everyone well, hardly recognizable except for the shiner he'd gotten in a fight only two nights before. When asked how he'd cleaned up so quickly, he told everyone, "Sheer willpower, my friends," but rumors spread that Doc Flannigan had given him vampire blood on the sly.

The man had since left Rogue City with his wife, and Doc Flannigan was far too skilled at keeping secrets to tell her anything, but she needed to know if the blood really worked. The next morning, without waking Nigel or Alistair, Westie crept into the kitchen to brew some of Isabelle's favorite coffee. She was crazy about the stuff—mostly because it was expensive and rare. Westie refused to even try it. Isabelle would've too had she known those particular beans had traveled through the colon of a monkey in order to earn that price tag. Some things were better left unsaid.

Westie rode into town. The streets were filled with miners and gold panners on their way to work. The musty smell of a summer storm warred with the fresh scent of baked bread that hung in the air. Westie stopped when she saw a brownie pushing a cart full of steaming cross buns. She bought two and headed for the apothecary.

Isabelle worked alone most mornings before school. She was busy crushing herbs in a mortar with a pestle, humming a beautiful tune, when Westie walked in.

As soon as she smelled the coffee, Isabelle looked up, mouth falling open. "Is that what I think it is?" she said, leaving her medicines to examine the canteen in Westie's hand.

"It is," Westie said, pouring some into a tin cup, "and cross buns to go with it."

Isabelle started to reach for the cup, then paused, eyeing Westie suspiciously. "What do you want?"

Westie leaned against a barrel full of medicines wrapped in paper and tied with twine. "Can't a girl just do a nice thing for her friend?"

"Yes, if that girl was anyone other than you."

"Hey." Westie's brow furrowed. "I do nice things."

Isabelle took the coffee and the sack of buns from Westie's hands. "No, you don't."

"Okay, fine. I need a favor."

Isabelle sat down with her gifts. She took a drink, eyes rolling around in her head as she savored the taste. Westie cringed.

"What kind of favor?"

"A tiny one." Westie picked up one of the packets of medicine in the barrel labeled *Pants on Fire*.

Seeing the perplexed look on Westie's face, Isabelle laughed, spitting crumbs from the bite of cross bun she'd just taken. "Father let me name it," Isabelle said. "It's a powder for burning, itching sensations—it's very popular in brothels around the valley."

Westie crinkled her face and tossed it back into the barrel. "Speaking of brothels," she said, trying to ease her way into the subject. "What do you know about the medicinal qualities of vampire blood?"

Isabelle shrugged. "It cures anything from mosquito bites to old age. Why do you ask?"

Not wanting Isabelle to know she'd been drinking again, Westie said, "I'm concerned about Alistair's head injury. I thought it might help."

Isabelle coughed, then hit her chest with her fist. "Have you gone mad? You'll go to jail if you're caught with even a drop of vampire blood. Besides, we don't keep it here in fear of bandits trying to break in and steal it."

"I know, and I would never ask you for it if you did. I just need to look at your father's medicine journal to see the dosage it would take to heal him. I don't want to accidentally turn Alistair into the Undying."

Isabelle took a bite of her bun, covering her mouth as she talked with her mouth full. "My father doesn't let anyone read his medicine journal. You'll need a lot more than a cup of coffee and a bun for me to go against my father's wishes."

"I know." Westie reached into the leather satchel at her hip and pulled out a burlap pouch full of the rare coffee beans, handing it to Isabelle. If Nigel found out it was missing, he'd be livid, but luckily, he didn't drink it too often.

Isabelle's eyes gaped when she looked at the tag. "Is this the price?"

Westie grinned, knowing she had Isabelle by the look on her face. "Sure is."

"I don't know whether to make coffee with these beans or wear them as jewelry."

"It would be better than some of the jewelry I've seen you wear."

Isabelle scowled at her. "You're supposed to be buttering me up, not insulting me."

"Sorry."

Sighing, Isabelle said, "You have five minutes." She reached behind the counter and pulled out a leather-bound journal.

While Westie flipped through the pages, Isabelle kept an eye out the window for her father. Westie barely listened as her friend went on and on about the ball.

"It's coming up soon and I have yet to find a dress. Can you believe it?"

"Uh-huh," Westie mumbled. She felt a surge of elation upon finding the page on vampire blood.

She moved her finger down the page until she found the diagnosis of alcoholism. Beside it was the dosage: five drops.

Five drops. That wasn't so bad. It shouldn't be too hard to get. Her stomach clenched with anticipation, and she had to fight the excitement she felt spreading across her face.

"Thank you for this," Westie said, handing the journal to Isabelle to put back. "Maybe we'll go out later and shop for dresses together."

Hope turned Isabelle's voice shrill. "Really?"

Westie smirked. "No," she said, and walked out the door.

# Eighteen

After everyone had gone to their rooms for the night, Westie grabbed a lamp and went to the main sitting room, where the walls were lined with shelves of books. Next to the fireplace was a light sconce. She pushed it toward the ground. The oil lamp in her hand shed watery light on a panel of books that slid without sound on rails and disappeared behind the fireplace. The hidden room was no bigger than a closet and was stacked to the ceiling with shelves of poisons in dainty glass bottles. Oil of oleander, doll's eyes, and angel's trumpet. Such pretty names. There was also strychnine and other exotic poisons Nigel brought home from his travels. And of course the local specialty, cyanide, which came from mining the iron hills. Nigel preferred the classics: castor plant, mushrooms, nightshade, belladonna, hemlock, wolfsbane, and the rosary pea. The bottom shelf belonged to the tricky poisons that came from the venom of reptiles such as the copperhead, rattlesnake, and cobra. So many poisons, each with their own different way of killing, though killing was what they did all the same.

Nigel used to tell her poisons were like women, placed in beautiful packages but deadly within. Westie had rolled her eyes when he told her women also preferred poisons when dealing in death. Less messy. He knew nothing about women.

"I hope you're not doing what I think you're planning on doing."

Westie started but made no sound when she heard the woman's voice behind her. At first she thought it was Lavina, and that somehow she'd snuck into the house without rousing Jezebel. But when Westie turned, she saw it was Alistair. He stood in the doorway wearing a temporary mask while his was being repaired. The replacement was delicate, made with bits of nickel and lined with lace, and it had a female sound box.

Westie shrugged her lips in a fleeting smile, and then it was gone. "Not today," she said. "And not like this. I want justice. I want to watch the Fairfields hang on a branch like cottonwood blossoms."

"Then why are you eyeing a wall of poisons?"

The lamplight filtered through the colorful glass bottles and cast rainbows across the room. All of Nigel's poisons were the killing kind, but he didn't keep them for that reason. Used in the proper dosages, they had healing qualities. She ran her finger across the labels and stopped on a green bottle the color of a tropical sea. Vampire blood.

When she pulled the bottle of blood from the shelf, Alistair's eyes shone, for he guessed her intentions and approved. It made her smile and gave her more confidence to see his support of her decision. She opened the bottle. It was empty.

The sky was a black sheet over their heads with millions of holes cut out to show the light of heaven behind it. At least that was what Westie's mother used to tell her about the stars.

A full moon lit the road ahead, and the howls of werewolves completing their cycles filled the night. Alistair shoved a piece of paper toward her. He had taken off the temporary mask after she'd teased him about its female voice, and refused to put it back on, trading it for a handkerchief. There wasn't much light to read by, so she had to hold the piece of paper right up to her nose to see it.

*This is a terrible idea,* the note read.

Westie balled it up and tossed it at him. He caught it in the air.

"You thought this was a good idea when I pulled the glass bottle from the shelf," she said.

Alistair uncrumpled the ball of paper and scribbled. He pushed it her way again. Westie rolled her eyes, missing his mask.

She looked down at the piece of paper: *That was before you planned to take it from the source,* it read.

The next time she balled the paper, she tossed it over her shoulder. Alistair looked behind him at the crumpled paper on the road and pulled a tablet from his saddlebag. He waved it in her face like a spoiled child. She laughed and dug her heels into Henry's sides to pick up the pace.

Westie heard the music and raucous laughter before they

reached town. They followed the glow of street gasoliers down the main strip. Alistair steered his horse closer to Westie and tossed a piece of crumpled paper at her face to snag her attention, hitting her nose. She looked at him with a terse glare. He held his tablet in the air, the words written large and dark enough to see in the vague light.

*Let's go back. We shouldn't be here.*

She turned away from him, toward the source of all the sound. The blood brothel was grander and more garish than the other buildings in town, painted a deep, obvious red.

"Vampire blood's the only true cure for addiction. The sheriff won't consider any evidence I find against the Fairfields without Nigel's approval, and Nigel won't take me serious if I don't get sober, not after what happened last time I accused a man of being a cannibal." They tethered their horses at the watering post in front of the saloon and crossed the street to the brothel. "Since Big Fish won't help me, I have no other choice than to go through with this. Besides, I don't think I can face Lavina and Hubbard again without a drink. I need them at the ball. Only way to get evidence of their crimes is to get as close to them as possible."

Human women, naked from the waist up, with pale anemic skin and gaunt features, slumped against the balcony on the second floor, their heads hanging like dying tulips. Alistair pulled his hat over his face to shield his view, but Westie looked anyway. There was no life left in their eyes, and yet they lived. Vampires knew how to drain just enough blood to keep from killing. The women's faces were slack, their lips parted, too wasted away to call to folks who walked by.

Westie shook her head, wondering why anyone would subject themselves to being drained of their blood until they were nothing more than shriveled slugs. Rumor had it that the venom vampires injected from their fangs before opening a vein was intoxicating, but so was whiskey, and she preferred the latter.

Two vampire guards stood at the front doors of the brothel, blocking their way.

"We'd like admittance. We have money." Westie pulled out a sack of coins from the pocket of her duster and let them jingle.

"All our girls are busy now," a big vamp with a lazy eye said.

"I just saw them." Westie looked up, but the girls she'd seen before were gone.

"We don't cater to friends of the mayor." The smaller, stocky vamp whistled through missing teeth. Without them his fangs looked far too long for his mouth.

Westie made a sour face. "We're not friends with the mayor, and we're not here for any of your half-dead skinny girls either. I'm here to see Costin."

"Every bloody human girl is here to see Costin. He's busy, now go away."

Alistair reached for Westie's hand. She pushed him away and grabbed the big vamp by the throat with her machine, sending him to his knees. Alistair's six-shooters were in the smaller vamp's face before Westie had time to blink.

"Now that I have your attention, I'd like to see Costin, if you please," she said, trying to mimic Isabelle's society politeness.

Costin's voice drifted out the brothel doors to find his guards. "Let her in," he said. "The boy stays out."

"That wasn't so hard, was it?" she said.

Westie released the big vamp and watched him cough and shrink into a ball on the ground. Alistair put his guns back in their holsters and grabbed her shoulders, forcing her to look at him. He shook his head at her, his brows drawn, eyes pleading.

"I'll be fine," she said.

She stepped over the big vamp. He looked up at her and hissed. Alistair tried to enter the building with her, but a group of guards emerged from the building and formed a wall to block his way.

"Wait for me by the horses." Westie was pulled into the building, and the doors shut behind her before she could get out another word.

She was pushed into the center of the room by the guards. The overwhelming scent of perfume went straight to her head and made the spot just above her left eye throb.

Heavy black tapestries embellished with gold tassels hung at the windows. The walls were covered with black-and-white floral-patterned wallpaper, and the floors were blanketed in lush red carpet. To her right was the bar. It was well stocked with bottles of both whiskey and blood.

It looked much like any other high-end gentlemen's club except for the soiled doves—as wives liked to call the human women working for the vamps—sitting around tables waiting for either their next customer or their next fix. And then, of course, there was the rumpus of fornication coming from the curtained partitions upstairs and the swings hanging from the ceiling.

"Come," she heard Costin say.

She followed his voice to a dark corner of the enormous room, blinking to adapt her vision to her hazy surroundings. Costin was slumped in an oversize chair like a heartbroken king, hair pooling around his shoulders. He had beautifully long limbs and perfect symmetry. She thought about him helping her home from the Tight Ship, his hands on her stomach, his cool lips on hers when they kissed, and started to feel giddy with nervousness.

"Off you go," Costin said to the others. The girls grabbed their drinks and rushed off without prodding, up the stairs and into their individual partitions. The guards were more hesitant. They knew Westie's reputation for losing her head whenever she was angry. It was hard to kill a vampire, but Westie's mechanics made a fair foe. "The rest of you too," Costin said to the guards in the room.

They looked ready to protest but eventually left Westie and Costin alone.

Costin stood, grabbed a chair from a stack against the wall, and placed it next to his. He lit the candles in their sconces for her benefit and motioned her to sit. She did.

"It's quite an honor having you here. There is only one reason a human girl comes to a blood brothel," Costin said with a mischievous grin.

Westie screwed up her face. If he thought she was going to let him drink her blood, he had another think coming.

"I need vampire blood," she said.

Even with blown pupils black as pots of coal dust, she could see the disappointment in his eyes.

"All right, two reasons, but what you're asking is against the law, as is barging into my establishment and threatening my guards. You could be hanged for your offenses if I were to go to the sheriff."

Westie knew the sheriff didn't like her, but his hatred for creatures went deeper than any petty dislike. A fact she didn't mention.

"If I were the guest of honor at a string party every time I offended, I would've died as a child," she said.

The sultriness crept back into his voice. "Yes, you're quite contrary, aren't you?"

She smiled sweetly, then let her lips fall back into a serious line. "Now about that blood."

"For your long-standing illness?" he asked.

She remembered her kicking and flailing at the airdocks, and Nigel's quick lie about seizures. "Yes."

He lifted his head so that he could gaze incredulously down at her. "You come in here wanting vampire blood, which could get us both killed were anyone to know I gave it to you, and yet you lie to me."

Their eyes dueled for a long moment before Costin turned his gaze away from her. "I know a seizure when I see one, and that display at the airdocks was no seizure. That, my love, was a fit of rage, though I have yet to figure out why." Westie opened her mouth to speak, but Costin stopped her. "No. Don't tell me. I like a good puzzle."

"I wasn't going to. I need that blood, and I need it before Nigel wakes up and sees I'm gone."

Costin peeked at her through the corners of his eyes. "What will I get in return?"

"I have money."

"I have more money than you can imagine. Why would I want your little bag of coins?"

"I don't have time for games, Costin. What do you want?"

"I want you to drink from my vein."

She nearly choked when she heard those words. Drinking from a vampire's vein was erotic for creatures, like sex was for humans.

"No," she said. "No way, nope."

He smiled, looking smug. "Then no blood. Do have a good evening, Westie, and be careful on your way home. The werewolves are out tonight; wouldn't want to get fleas."

Westie stood from her chair and fought the urge to break it to splinters. "I need that blood, Costin—you don't understand." Her hand shook. "I need to cure my addiction. If I don't get sober for good, Nigel won't believe a word I say, and he won't let the—" She started to mention the Fairfields but stopped herself. The fewer people who knew about her vendetta, the better. "I just . . . I need it."

"What is it you need Nigel to believe?" he said.

She bit her lip to keep from screaming at him. "I can't tell you."

"Then no blood for you." He stood up to walk away.

"Wait!" She put her hands on top of her head, cringing at the stupid choice she knew she was about to make. Costin stopped in midstride and turned to face her. "All right," she said. "I'll drink blood from your vein, but I can't tell you why I need Nigel to believe me."

He put his hand to his chin in thought, though Westie could tell by his smirk that his mind had already been made up.

"Very well. We will go to my room, where it will be more private. This could get messy," he said with a wink.

# Nineteen

Costin's room was nothing like Westie had imagined. There was no coffin, no dirt floor, no blood on the walls, no horrible smells. Instead the walls were covered in white gauzy fabric and the room smelled like citrus. There was a circular bed in the center of the room, with mounds of feather pillows covered in silk. Everything was neat and in its place. Costin was a tidy creature.

Westie's neck arched as she took it all in. She was growing even more nervous, she realized when her stomach began to flutter.

Costin fussed with pillows to carve out a space for her on the bed.

She took off her duster and shoes, tossing them onto a chair across the room so she wouldn't get blood on them. He watched her with brows raised and a curious smile. "Eager, are we?" he said.

She plopped down on the bed, wriggling to get comfortable. "I want to get this over with. How do we start?"

"Lie down," he said.

Leaning against a stack of pillows, she watched Costin pull a box from a dresser drawer beside the bed. Inside was a red glass dagger.

Westie sat up, her muscles tensed for a brawl.

"Relax," he said. "It's for me. Lie back down."

*Alley was right,* she thought. *This is a terrible idea.*

But she didn't leave. She needed Costin's help. Vampire blood was the only way to achieve sobriety, even if it upset the Wintu spirits. She took a deep breath and melted back onto the pillows.

Westie felt something stir deep within her belly when Costin removed his shirt, revealing a smooth white chest. He was lean and solid-looking, with cords of muscle beneath his skin.

The mattress dipped when he climbed onto the bed and settled beside her, propped on an elbow. Her heart pulsed in her ears, and the stirring in her belly became more insistent.

*He's a creature,* she had to remind herself. But what she told herself and what her body was feeling were two very different things.

Costin held the blade in his hand. When he moved, she noticed three perfectly spaced scars on his upper arm that looked almost like brands.

"What are those from?" she asked. Vampires healed so quickly, she didn't think they were capable of having scars.

"General marks from the war."

She felt him shiver as she traced her finger over the bumps. "You were a general in the creature war? For how long?"

"Five years."

"I was just a child back then," she said. The war had ended while she was staying with the Wintu.

Costin put a finger to her lips. "No more talk of the war. Shall we get on with this?"

Westie gathered her wits and nodded.

He smiled, slicing the skin of his wrist open. She'd never seen anyone so happy to bleed. Red satin beads bubbled slowly out of the wound. His blood didn't have a metallic, tangy scent like the human blood she'd smelled while assisting in Nigel's surgical rooms. Vampire blood was different. It smelled sweet and buttery.

Westie pulled long, slow breaths into her lungs. "I'm going to do this," she said, "but I don't want any funny business. You keep your hands to yourself." If things got carried away, she wasn't sure if she'd be able—or willing—to stop.

"I promise. Now drink." His voice was like a soft kiss.

Costin held his wrist out to her. Cold, velvet orbs dripped onto the bare skin of her collarbone.

All it took was five drops for a cure. *One drink,* she told herself.

She took one last breath, held it, and braced herself as she put her lips around his wound.

A cold drop trickled down her throat. His blood was thick and sweet like honey, just the way it smelled. As soon as it hit her stomach she felt serene. Not exactly like the tranquil daze that overcame her when drinking whiskey, but something deeper. It was the same kind of lovely ache one felt in one's soul when hearing a beautiful song.

Soon Westie's tentative licks became greedy slurps. She knew she'd consumed more than the five drops necessary for a cure, but it was difficult to care about that when feeling the rush it gave her. She wrapped her legs around Costin's waist to keep him from pulling away.

Costin let out a moan as she sucked at his vein. The taste was pleasant enough, but it was the feelings being dealt to her body that kept her mouth clamped to Costin's skin like a deer tick. It was like waking up, like seeing everything beautiful in the world for the first time, and all at once. The blood was cold going down her throat, but it warmed every part of her until she was a puddle in his arms.

She felt her bodice give and his cool lips touch her chest. When Costin started to kiss her neck, she reluctantly pulled away from his wrist and grabbed him by the throat with her machine. The amount of pressure she used would've killed a human but only made Costin wince.

"I said no funny business." While her mechanical hand squeezed his neck, her flesh hand caressed his cheek. Though she still had some of her wits, it was a losing battle. There was no telling how long she could keep resisting him. If she were to take a guess, she was at the end of the countdown.

He choked out a laugh, barely able to get words through her stranglehold. "You said to keep my hands to myself. You didn't say anything about my lips."

Her body quivered, knees shaking. When he offered his wrist to her once more, her breaths became urgent. "Just . . . behave."

By the sound of his laughter, he knew the effect he was having on her. She let go of his neck and grabbed his wrist again, latching on.

She was enveloped, too submerged in bliss to notice his dark eyes drinking in her curves, her ripe, warm skin. His mouth parted, and a carnal growl escaped from deep in his chest.

He pulled his wrist away and she was finally able to fill her lungs. She sat up just in time to watch his mouth open and his fangs bury themselves deep into her inner thigh. She gasped in surprise at first, and then in pleasure.

The luxury of his bite was more than she could have imagined. Somewhere, deep within, she knew she should stop him. Not that she had the greatest reputation to begin with, but if anyone found out a vampire had drunk from her, she'd be ruined. In that same deep pit of thought, she knew she would regret giving herself to Costin, but right then none of that mattered.

Bursts of color popped in front of her eyes. Greed was royal blue with sparks of gold. Her machine clawed at the bed, shredding the sheets. She saw her desire in shades of rich, dark purple.

Forget whiskey, forget everything. She wanted to live beneath Costin's teeth forever. She finally understood why the living dead girls gave their lives to the blood brothels.

The blood swirling in Westie's stomach turned from cold to warm to blazing hot. Her pleasure was diluted with tendrils of pain. That was new. She'd liked it at first, before her pleasure thinned and only the pain showed through. Splashes of black smothered all other colors.

Westie's stomach cramped. Pain raced through her, hooked its claws onto every nerve as it passed, and pulled her from her pleasure stupor. She wrapped her machine around her waist and groaned as the cramps dug deeper.

Costin sat up. Her blood dripped from his fangs onto his chin. "What is it?" he asked. His face showed more concern than she'd thought a vampire was capable of. "What's wrong?"

She didn't know. She couldn't speak. It felt like a serrated blade had sliced through her abdomen. When she opened her mouth to speak, a scream came out instead. Her body slammed against the pillows, back arched off the bed as a new barb of pain cut through her consciousness, causing her muscles to stiffen. She could hear Costin's voice and other voices around her, but the pain was too agonizing to care about her modesty.

"I don't know what's happening," she heard Costin's desperate voice say. "Find Alistair, tell him to fetch Nigel—and tell him it's urgent."

When everyone was gone, Costin appeared above her. His face went in and out of view, the lights flashing as she blinked.

His hands clutched the sides of her face. "Westie, my love, stay with me," he begged her. His voice was a high tremor.

He was frightened. *A frightened vampire—now there's a first,* she thought just before she blacked out.

Westie woke up in her own bed. Her cramps became straight razors cutting into her intestines. Each stab of pain was worse than the last, like fingers had reached inside to braid her guts. Her tongue felt stretched and heavy in her mouth. She went back and forth between blanket and cold rag as fever and chill battled for supremacy. If she'd known the pain vampire blood would inflict, she might have thought about the idea more thoroughly before seeking Costin's help.

Her insides felt like they had liquefied and were coming out at all ends. Any hangover she'd ever had paled in comparison. Embarrassed by her lack of control over her body, she begged Alistair to leave her. He wouldn't. Luckily, Bena insisted Alistair leave when it came time to change Westie's bedpan and clean her. Still, the humiliation was complete.

Nigel gave her sugar-grass milk—which was anything but sweet—to help her body absorb the healing qualities of the vampire blood and flush out any toxins. She got devil's claw root to ease her pain and fluids to keep her from dehydrating.

When the sun was high in the sky, her fever finally broke and the pain had turned from a savage flogging to a mere stab in the belly. Every muscle in her body was wound tighter than a banjo string, but she no longer wished for death, and the thought of whiskey sat worse than a bad smell. By nightfall she felt better than she had in years, and she was famished. Bena sent up a bloody steak the way she liked it and a fire-cooked potato with fresh-churned butter.

There was a knock on the door, and Alistair and Nigel walked in. Nigel sat on the chair beside her bed while Alistair, still wearing a red kerchief, stood by the door.

"What happened?" Westie asked. She knew vampire blood was a

cure for alcoholism, but she'd never heard of it causing the pain she'd felt.

"Your immune system was compromised because of your alcohol abuse over the years. When you drank Costin's blood, it became toxic in your system."

"It worked, though, didn't it?" Westie said. "I'm cured."

"One more drink and you would've turned into the Undying, but yes, it worked. You are as healthy as a girl your age should be, and with magic in your veins, will probably outlive us all by a hundred years," Nigel said.

Alistair's eyes burned with anger. He paced around the room, his hands moving in a flurry. *I should've been there in the room with them to make sure she was all right. I can't believe I left her with the vamps,* he signed.

Westie felt her cheeks warm when she remembered the lusty sounds she'd made, and Costin's hands and teeth all over her. She felt guilty, which made her cross. She had nothing to feel guilty about. It wasn't like Alistair loved her. Loyalty was not something she owed him. She could tell herself those things until her tongue fell out, but it wouldn't matter. The guilt had set up camp and was there to stay.

"Neither of you should've been there," Nigel replied. With a sigh he turned to Westie. "You should eat hot oats, something that will be gentle on your stomach."

She put a protective arm around her plate so Nigel wouldn't take it from her. "I want steak. Don't you see I have my appetite back? I feel good, Nigel. Better than I have in a long time."

She ate her food and drank her glass of apple juice.

"Normally you would ask for a glass of wine with your steak," Nigel said.

Even the mention of wine made her stomach clench. "I'd rather drink hot piss."

"Lovely." Nigel shook his head and dropped his shoulders in resignation. "You're definitely back to normal." He looked at Alistair, who continued to pace the room. "Alley, would you be so kind as to fetch more devil's claw root from my office? And bring clean sleeping clothes for Westie from the washroom."

Once Westie and Nigel were alone, he turned to her, a serious look in his eyes. Westie knew she was about to get an earful of something.

"I can't believe you would break the law and go to the vampires for help when you know how I feel about Costin. Not only did you put your own life in danger, but you put Alley's life on the line as well." He folded his arms over his chest. Westie grumbled and sat back, waiting for the rest of the tongue-lashing to go by so she could finish her meal. Nigel was no slouch when it came to sermons against brothel vampires. Only what she thought would be a lengthy speech fell short, and his chin began to quiver.

"After Alistair being shot and now you nearly being poisoned to death, I don't know how much more I can take. The two of you are all I have left in this world."

Westie's throat balled up with emotion. It wasn't what she'd expected him to say. She struggled to swallow her mouthful of food.

As often as she'd disappointed him over the years, it was hard for her to believe he truly cared for her. She'd often wondered if he wished he'd never brought her back from the Wintu village.

"You are my child," Nigel said. "Parents should never outlive their children. Don't frighten me like that again."

Westie shook her head. "I won't. I promise."

# Twenty

Three days passed before the effects of vampire blood poisoning finally wore off. Westie crawled out of bed and stretched, spine popping, making a sound like dragging a stick across a picket fence. It was the first time she'd been out of bed since being home.

After a bath, she stepped out of her room and was met by the dim chatter of conversation. When she got to the bottom of the stairs, she nearly ran into a rotund man in a white baker's cap wheeling out a cart of flour and sugar.

"Whoa," she said, dancing away just in time to avoid the collision. "What's that stuff for?"

He had streaks of flour across his face and dots of sugar absorbing his sweat. When he noticed her mechanical arm, his eyes widened and he took a step back. "Ingredients for a cake, miss," he said with a wobble of fear in his voice.

"Where are you going with them?"

"I'm taking them back to the bakery, since the party has been canceled."

Canceled? *No.* The panic of missing out on a perfect opportunity made her heart speed up. How else was she to learn more about the Fairfields without it being obvious she was snooping? The party had to happen, even if she had to drag people by the scruff of the neck and lock them inside.

"Take the cart back to the kitchen. The party isn't canceled," she said.

"But—"

Westie balled her copper hand into a fist. "Put. It. Back."

His eyes opened wider. "Yes, miss."

Others were leaving the house as well. She sent them back inside, including a pretty female elf who'd made clever clockwork invitations that opened with a push of a button.

"Make two more, please," Westie said. "Address them to James Lovett and the Fairfields, and send them to the inn by telegraph bird at once—Nigel will pay extra."

The house was swarming with workers packing their things and preparing to leave. She found Nigel and Alistair in the dining room, overseeing the exodus.

Alistair pointed wordlessly at the hired staff. Westie watched the serving girls as they stole glances Alistair's way and whispered. Some giggled. It was obvious that without his mask, he intrigued more than frightened the fairer sex. She found herself staring at him too and had to admit that the handkerchief made him look myste-rious. How anyone could find Alistair frightening was confusing to her. His beautiful eyes gave him away. They were trustworthy eyes.

"Why are you canceling my party?" Westie demanded.

Nigel tugged at his shirt and smiled. "Good to see you up and around. How are you feeling?"

"Fine. Why are you canceling my party?" she repeated.

Nigel adjusted his top hat. He wore loose trousers and a gussied-up smoking jacket even though the heat of hell had risen to the earth's surface that day. "I wasn't sure you'd feel up to a party, and since you don't like them to begin with, or people for that matter, I didn't think you'd mind the cancelation. You weren't supposed to know about it anyway, but Alley told me Isabelle had informed you. I should've known the Johanssons couldn't keep it under their hats."

"Well, I do mind. I already told everyone I know about it."

"You know five people and three of them are in this house."

Westie frowned. "Isabelle told everyone she knew. I'll look like a fool if I have to tell folks there won't be a party."

"You've never cared about looking like a fool before." He tucked his hands into his pockets and lifted his chin, looking down at her. "You're up to something."

"Am not."

"Yes, you are." His voice rose. "No doubt it has something to do with the Fairfields."

Westie shook her head, focusing on the cleft in his chin to keep her eyes from shifting so he wouldn't see through her deceit.

"Do I look stupid to you?" he asked.

"Do you really want me to answer that?"

He growled at her.

"All right," she said. "I just want to observe the Fairfields, is all."

His back straightened. "Absolutely not. Besides, they wouldn't have shown anyway; they were never invited."

"Well, they are now. The invitations have already been sent."

"What?" Nigel's voice echoed in the room. Workers stopped what they were doing to stare.

She shrugged.

He twisted the tips of his mustache. "Dammit, Westie."

"I'll be on my best behavior, promise."

His shoulders wilted. "I've heard that before."

"I mean it this time."

Alistair cut in, hands moving to sign, *Everything has already been paid for. Might as well.* Westie held back a smile when he glanced at her. *And we'll all be there to make sure things don't get out of hand.*

"Oh, fine," Nigel said. "We'll have the party, but you must promise that you won't drink. Not even a single sip of wine."

Westie cupped her hand over her mouth. The mention of alcohol stirred her stomach. "You have my word."

He started to walk away, then paused. He was as tall as he was brilliant and had to bend so their eyes were level. "You stay out of trouble."

Alistair watched Nigel leave, then turned his curious gaze on her. His hands started to move in familiar motions.

*I vouched for you. If you're planning on doing something stupid, it's my ass too,* he signed.

Westie's signing was rusty, but she understood well enough.

"Relax," she said. "I just want to watch them."

*So you do remember hand language after all.*

She signed back, *No, I don't,* and walked away.


Westie went to her room for a nap. When she got there, she found her oak wardrobe open and her dress for the ball hanging inside. Nigel must have put it in there while she was talking to Alistair.

She lifted the dress carefully, peeled back the protective shroud it was encased in. It was white silk with black velvet trimming and pearl buttons, and was covered in lace wherever it had a chance to be plain. She imagined the smile on Nigel's face—no, the smirk—when he'd had the dress made and hung in her closet.

"Ick," she said when she hung it back up. It was a dress for a Southern belle. Her cannibal friends might mistake her for a sweet cake and eat her alive, wearing a dress like that.

# Twenty-One

After her nap, Westie went to the barn to saddle Henry. A horse snorted behind her just as she noticed Alistair's mare wasn't in her stall. Westie closed her eyes and shook her head. Alistair seemed to know every move she made before she even thought to make it.

She adjusted the stirrups on her saddle without looking at him and said, "I thought you were planning the party."

There was no reply. She'd forgotten Alistair was still without his mask. She didn't bother to face him so they could try and communicate. She knew well enough that he meant to babysit her.

He followed several feet behind as she made her way into town. When they neared the assay office, a horseless coach stumbled into view. It was made of black metal with gold accents and had smoke pouring from its stacks. Red velvet curtains covered its windows. It looked exactly like a traditional stagecoach, only with four pointed metal legs on each side.

Pulling Henry closer to the assay building, out of harm's way, Westie watched as the coach tilted and swayed like a drunken spider. It crushed watering troughs and anything else in its way until finally coming to a stop after hitting a beam outside the post office. The beam snapped in half, causing the awning to sag.

Westie's mouth fell open as Isabelle stepped out of the coach, adjusting her skirts. She looked at Westie with a frown. "When did they put that beam in front of the post office?"

Westie swallowed back laughter. "When they built the town."

Isabelle giggled. "Oops."

"When did you get that?" Westie asked as she moved closer to get a better look at the coach.

There were brass levers and buttons all over the driver's cabin. *Children and small animals beware,* Westie thought as she imagined Isabelle trying to figure out what they were all used for.

"My parents bought it for me when I told them your coming-out ball would be more extravagant than mine was."

Westie had stayed at Isabelle's coming-out party only long enough to prove she was there before disappearing into the servants' quarters for a game of poker, but she did remember fireworks and the gaudy white coach drawn by a team of pure-white draft horses that brought Isabelle to the house. If Westie's party was more extravagant than that, she'd have a bone to pick with Nigel.

"I was surprised to get your telegraph bird," Isabelle said. She gazed at Alistair in the distance as though he were in her crosshairs.

"You know that thing crashed right through my window, nearly frightened me half to death."

Westie imagined Isabelle flailing her arms, her hair in curlers, and smiled.

"Sorry for the short notice."

"Honestly, the bird wasn't what shocked me the most. It was you being serious about wanting to go shopping for a dress. I don't think I've ever known you to buy a single thing that didn't have a blade. Does this mean Nigel finally told you about your party?"

"He told me."

Westie mopped the sweat from her forehead, squinting against the light that filtered through the trees. Heat made opaque waves in the distance.

"Well, I'm glad you called on me. Shopping for a dress with the debutante will be so much fun!"

Westie sighed inwardly. "I reckon I ought to find a dress I like rather than that thing Nigel hung in my closet."

"Don't you think you're cutting it a little close to the party?"

Westie shrugged.

"Why did you have to bring him?" Isabelle hooked a thumb in Alistair's direction.

"I didn't. He followed me." Both girls watched Alistair. A loose smile formed on Westie's lips as he fidgeted in his saddle from the attention. Even at a distance she could see his forehead blush. His Irish skin always gave him away.

"His head seems better," Isabelle said. "I take it the vampire blood worked."

"Better than I could've imagined."

Westie's smile quickly faded when she saw Cain Fairfield strolling along the sidewalk across the street, browsing through store windows. Alistair tied his horse to a post and stepped up next to her.

"There's Cain Fairfield," Isabelle said.

"Sure is an ugly cuss, don't you think?" Westie said, hoping that someone else's low opinion of Cain might change Isabelle's.

Isabelle shrugged. "Yes, but look how well he wears that jacket."

Cain looked at them and tipped his hat. Westie stiffened. Isabelle smiled bashfully and waved a gloved hand at him.

Taking Isabelle by the elbow, Westie ushered her away from Cain before they were forced to talk to him. "Come on, we've got a dress to find."

"I think I like this new you, talking boys and shopping. Does this mean I can stop pretending to care when you tell me about your new weapons?" Isabelle said with a teasing smile and a hop in her step.

"You've been acting this whole time?" Westie said, feigning shock. "Well, since we're faking it, let's pretend I want to be here shopping with you."

Isabelle laughed, knocking her shoulder against Westie until they both nearly fell in the street.

For Westie, shopping with Isabelle Johansson proved more taxing than it was worth. The girl had introduced Westie to every clothing vendor new to Rogue City, including a succubus who offered to make Westie a beautiful gown made of human skin. With a polite "No, thank you," the girls took off running.

Alistair caught up with Westie and Isabelle at the general store after lagging behind. He wore a black handkerchief, which made him look like a proper bandit.

When Isabelle went into the general store, Westie pulled Alistair to the side. "Why are you so eager to go shopping with us?" she said. "You fancy Isabelle?" She wished she could see his mouth, for his eyes gave nothing away.

A poster was glued to one of the gasolier posts outside the general store. Westie pulled it off and started nervously picking at its edges. The poster had a picture of President Pierce, with a reminder that harming creatures was illegal. Someone had drawn a profane sketch of a creature next to the president's face and had written *Creature lover* beside it.

She turned her back on him. "Never mind." If he cared for Isabelle, she didn't want to know.

He took Westie by the shoulders, forcing her to face him, and signed, *I fancy Isabelle the way a snail fancies a block of salt. I promised Nigel I wouldn't let you out of my sight, but I'm bored. Can we go home?*

It was difficult reading his hands with his mouth covered up. A lot of signing had to do with facial expressions, but she understood him for the most part.

"Does he think I'll end up with my face planted in a pool of vomit at the Tight Ship?"

Alistair shook his head. *If I had to take a guess, I'd say his distrust has something to do with the Fairfields. He finds your eagerness for this party worrisome. And I have to admit, so do I.*

He and Nigel had every right to be concerned. If she was in a room with the family who killed her own, there was no telling what her emotions might force her to do, but she was willing to take the chance if it meant learning their secrets.

Isabelle called Westie into the store, dragging her over to the fabrics in the back. Westie was eyeing a swatch of white silk when bells chimed over the door.

"Oh look," Isabelle said, "it's Lavina and Olive Fairfield."

Westie whipped around, nearly knocking over a shelf of flour. She held her body against the wooden case to steady it, but when it continued to wobble, she realized it was she who trembled. She watched Lavina and her sour whelp walk up to the front counter, where the clerk smiled with his moon-shaped face. Westie sought out Alistair and met his gaze with a silent plea.

Alistair rushed toward her, grabbed her by the machine, and tugged her to a crouch behind the bolts of fabric stacked near the wall. If one didn't know better, one might think the two were lovers looking to be alone.

Isabelle squatted beside them. "What in blazes are you doing?"

Westie's thoughts buzzed in her ears. She didn't know how to explain her actions to Isabelle. She wished for Alistair's quick lies, but without a voice, he was of no assistance to her.

"Have you ever had a conversation with Lavina Fairfield?" Westie asked.

Isabelle thought about it. "No, I can't say that I have."

"Pray you never do. That woman's got more lip than a muley

cow. She'll talk your ear clean off, and she will . . . she will . . ." Westie couldn't think of a single thing to follow.

Isabelle smiled, all gums and tiny square teeth. She wasn't so much beautiful as she was cute, which gave her an innocent quality that boys and men alike adored.

"Don't be silly," Isabelle said. "Lavina has wonderful taste in fashion. She could be most helpful—"

Westie yanked Isabelle down when she tried to stand. Isabelle's smile was gone, replaced with an unbecoming scowl. "What has gotten into you? I swear the two of you become odder as the years pass. Before you know it, you'll be holed up in Nigel's strange mansion and people will whisper rumors about you like Mrs. Shelley's monster."

"I'm dressed in rags." Westie waved a hand, bringing Isabelle's attention to her outfit, the same clothes she'd worn that morning to feed and brush the horses. "I'm not fit for an audience with someone like Lavina Fairfield." Not that she actually cared what Lavina thought of her attire. It was just her attempt at avoiding the woman. After her last encounter with Lavina, Westie had sat in the doc's office, gnawing on a piece of devil's claw root to get rid of her headache. It had taken hours for her knees to stop shaking.

"Please. You are Nigel Butler's adopted daughter. She will not mistake you for common."

When Isabelle tried to stand again, Westie grabbed the girl's fingers with her machine and squeezed. She knew by the shocked look on Isabelle's face that she had read the threat.

Westie was stormed with guilt about using force against such a fragile thing as Isabelle, but she was given no choice.

"I'm sorry, Isabelle. Please forgive me," Westie said. Isabelle yanked her hand back, rubbing her fingers. "If we can avoid Lavina just this once, I'll give you the white French dress I wore at the airdocks."

Isabelle watched her, the fear in her eyes leaking away. "You ruined that dress during your seizure."

"Not ruined. Nigel sent it in for mending. It's good as new, maybe even better. I'll send for my own personal dressmaker to fit it to your body just right. It's far richer than anything you'll find in Rogue City."

Isabelle looked up in thought, the gears in her head turning like clockwork. "I don't know . . ." It felt like an eternity while Isabelle swished the idea around. Each second she spent thinking, Lavina drew nearer. Westie couldn't remember a time when her friend had been more tiresome. "Everyone has seen you in that dress before."

"Then we'll change it. We'll add embellishments of pink velvet and jewels on the bodice." That perked Isabelle up. Westie continued in hopes of sealing the deal. "And you can wear my gold-and-diamond earrings you love so much."

"I don't know . . . ," Isabelle said again, twisting a strand of her hair. "I think the bronze owls will go better with a dress like that."

Westie seethed. Nigel had made the bronze owl earrings for her thirteenth birthday. They were her favorite.

"Fine. You can borrow the bronze owls."

Isabelle's face lit up. She crawled into their cramped space and somehow managed to keep from touching Alistair. Westie hadn't tried so hard. She could feel his heartbeat tapping her shoulder. His hand touched the skin of her arm, raising gooseflesh despite the heat. She looked into his kind, open eyes. He stared back.

"The little girl is coming our way," Isabelle nearly shrieked.

Westie shook herself out of the trance his gaze held her in.

Olive walked across the room. She had a new doll tucked under her arm and a lollipop in her hand, lips candy red from the dye. Her blond ringlets bounced with each step. She walked past a row of white kid gloves, touching each pair with sugar-sticky hands. Westie thought the girl would skip right by them, but with a sudden turn, Olive bent and poked her head behind the fabric bolts. Westie jerked in surprise. Alistair held her firm against him.

"You thought I wouldn't see you?" Olive said. She was hell with the hide off and had an obnoxious way about her: taunting voice, pinched eyes, and a puckered mouth caught somewhere between smugness and accusation.

Westie struggled to smile. "You're too clever for us."

The girl stuck her rainbow tongue out to lick her lollipop.

"Is this a game you're playing?" the girl asked.

"Sure is," Westie said. She could feel Isabelle stiffen beside her, but not for the same reason Westie was. For Isabelle it was the fear of humiliation in front of a distinguished family. "We're hiding from grown-ups."

The girl's face hatched open with a grin. "Can I play?"

The thought of being in such cramped quarters with the girl

had Westie looking for an alternative way out. But there wasn't one, not without Lavina seeing her.

"Yes, of course," Westie said. Olive began to crawl into their hiding spot. Westie stopped her. "Wait. We need someone to be our lookout. Stand in front of the bolts and give us a signal when a grown-up is coming, and let us know when they pass."

The girl, with her doe eyes and her Cupid's bow mouth, gave her a chilling look, reminding Westie of a demented doll in the scary stories the boys used to pass around when she was in school. Olive knew she was being played for a fool.

*This girl really is clever,* Westie thought.

"All right then, I'll give you a signal," Olive said with an angry jut of her hip that made Westie think she would do just the opposite.

Westie tried to make it right. "Good. You have the most important job of the game."

It was clear by the harsh line of the girl's lips that she didn't believe her.

Olive stood vigil as she was directed. Westie could hear footsteps coming toward them. Through the diamond-shaped spaces between the bolts of fabric, she saw Lavina heading their way and wondered what signal Olive would give them—if any—and if it would be too subtle for her to notice.

"Olivia, what are you doing over here? There's no time to be fooling around," Lavina said. "You should be picking out the fabric for your ball gown."

Westie waited for a signal. She thought she must've missed it until Olive turned and kicked her in the shin. Westie gasped and clutched her leg. Alistair covered her mouth with his hand before she could cry out.

*Well,* Westie thought with her teeth bared, *we don't have to worry about missing the signal. Little pissant.*

Every one of Westie's muscles turned to iron when Lavina stepped toward them. Alistair brushed his thumb soothingly against the skin of Westie's arm as Lavina Fairfield studied the fabric. If Lavina peered through the cracks, she would see them—

Their eyes met, for a brief, horrifying moment. Lavina looked at Westie like she was trying to figure out exactly what she was seeing.

"Westie, is that you?" Lavina said. She walked behind the bolts where the three of them were crouched. "What are you doing back here?"

Westie planted her back firmly against Alistair's chest and let his steady heartbeat help pace her own.

"They're playing a game," Olive answered for her. "They're hiding from grown-ups." She lifted her head proudly. "I'm the lookout."

"Doesn't look like you've done a very good job now, does it?"

The proud angles of Olive's face formed angry curves. The look on her face had potential to become a fit, but it was quickly snuffed out when Hubbard appeared from around the corner and lifted Olive onto his mighty shoulders. Olive's laughter was like a knife being dragged down Westie's skin.

Cain and James rounded the corner next.

*Jesus,* Westie thought, *they're like a pack of wild dogs.*

"What's all this?" Hubbard asked in his dull way when he noticed Westie's group.

Lavina said, "A game, it seems."

Alistair helped Westie to stand.

"And who do we have here?" Lavina asked when Isabelle crawled out from her back corner. Her head was down, cheeks flushed crimson. "I don't think we've met."

"Isabelle Johansson. My parents own the apothecary," she said to the ground.

"Well, aren't you just the cutest thing," Lavina said. Isabelle looked up then, her smile like an exploding sun. "I could eat you up."

Alistair clutched Westie's flesh hand. Lavina looked at Westie as if gauging her reaction. Westie's entire body was frozen; she couldn't look frightened even if she wanted to.

"What are those pamphlets I've seen you carrying around?" Westie asked Cain to take the focus off Isabelle. She didn't like the not-so-subtle looks Cain was exchanging with her friend.

"Information about Nigel's magic amplifier—costs and sales projections, mostly. Things a girl wouldn't understand," he said with a dismissive shrug.

James huffed out laughter. "You see, Westie, a girl homeschooled by the most brilliant man of our time couldn't possibly keep up with Cain's fifth-grade education." His smile faded when he saw Westie and Alistair's interwoven fingers.

With an ugly scowl, Cain pushed James into the bolts of fabric, knocking them off their rollers and onto the floor with a startling clamor. James might have been small compared to Cain, but he was scrappy and got right back on his feet. He tackled Cain to the ground, knocking down a shelf. Bags of flour broke open, filling the room with white dust.

The shopkeeper grunted something from the front of the store. Isabelle hid her open mouth with her hand. It would've been a fine time for them to slip out had Lavina not been blocking the way.

"Boys! Stop that at once." Lavina looked to Hubbard for help. "Please deal with this."

Hubbard grabbed James and Cain by the collars of their jackets, lifting them off the ground as if they were oily rags. "Always nice to see you, Westie," James called out as he was dragged from the store. Olive rode her father's shoulders, clapping and shouting, "Punish them, Daddy. Punish them good."

Lavina appeared genuinely embarrassed when facing Westie again. "I must apologize. I hope you'll still welcome us to the ball. I promise my children will be on their best behavior."

"I wouldn't have it any other way," Westie said, tugging at Alistair's hand once Lavina had moved enough to clear a path.

There was a painful throbbing at the back of Westie's neck from tension, and her teeth hurt from clenching her jaw. She couldn't remember ever being as wound up as she was in Lavina's presence.

# Twenty-Two

For the next two days, Westie watched the Fairfields from the shadows, finding excuses to go into town or bring up their names in conversation to local busybodies who thrived on gossip. In a conversation she had with Huan Zhao, a Chinese woman who sold dumplings at morning market, she learned Lavina was dull and mostly talked about expensive dresses Huan could never afford. From the accounts of the whittler in front of Doc Flannigan's office, she knew the mayor, Hubbard, and Cain were all about politics and Emma, and from everyone else Westie talked to, James cared only about fun and games. In all that time she hadn't learned a single useful thing.

When it was finally time for the ball, Westie felt as if she were about to combust. She'd wring her hands, pace the room, sit, then repeat. Outside her bedroom window, she heard the creaking joints of carriages, the clopping of hooves, and the excited murmur of voices blending together as guests arrived for the ball.

Westie let a slow breath deflate her lungs and shook out her arms. "Are you sure James and the Fairfields have arrived? This entire party will be a waste of time if they don't show up," she said to Bena.

"As sure as I was five minutes ago." Bena stood behind her, pulling curlers from Westie's hair. Each curl was pinned and tucked just so, and adorned with gems to match her eyes. For a wild thing, Bena could pin and curl with the best of them.

Westie let out a bleat of impatience.

She'd spent the afternoon in Bena's care. Her friend had used a homemade concoction of plant oils and springwater to make Westie's auburn hair shine as bright as her polished machine. Her body and nails were scrubbed, and she was in full war paint.

When all was done, Westie stood in front of the mirror wearing the dress Nigel had given her. She'd given up on trying to find one she liked better after running into the Fairfields at the general store.

She laughed at her reflection. "Have you ever seen anyone look as silly as I do right now?"

Bena's smile was a straight, unmoving line. "You do not look half as ridiculous as Nigel."

"He's not wearing his red suede shoes with the brass buckles, is he?"

Bena's smile cracked until it broke, exposing white teeth that sparkled against her dark skin. "I am afraid so. And the purple coat with the gold cuffs."

"You reckon he was raised by circus folk where he comes from?"

Westie said. She looked at her reflection, tugging at a clump of hair wound up in the gears of her machine, and gave a shrug. "At least I won't be the only silly thing there." She turned to Bena, who fussed with a hem. "Do you think this is a bad idea?"

"This dress? Yes."

Westie smiled. "You know I'm talking about the plan."

The plan—the only reason for the ball—was to get ahold of Lavina's key to her rooms at the inn so that Westie could look through their belongings for anything that might prove they weren't polite society folks like everyone thought.

Bena gave her a smile, the kind that made the skin around her eyes crinkle. Westie loved that smile. It reminded her of her mother, even though the two women looked nothing alike.

"I think using this party for your scheme is a terrible idea, but I would do the same if I were you. Just try not to get caught. If Nigel finds out, it will break his heart," Bena said.

Westie nodded. Though there were a lot of parts to her plan, she was sure they could pull it off.

Bena took Westie's hand in hers and gave it a maternal squeeze. "If it looks at all like there could be trouble, walk away."

Westie swallowed hard and nodded.

"We had better get downstairs before Nigel gets suspicious," Bena said.

Nigel waited for her at the entrance of the ballroom, where a black curtain had been draped to hide Westie from the guests.

Westie asked, "Where's Alley?"

"He's parking carriages out front," Nigel said.

She found it harder to breathe with each passing moment and wished Alistair were there.

Bena said good-bye, leaving Nigel and Westie alone.

Nigel gave her the dance card in his hand. It wasn't a card at all, but a paper fan with red satin backing lined with copper. A few names had already been scrolled on the flat part of the folds in gold ink calligraphy.

She took a closer look at the names. There were spots for Nigel, the mayor, and Costin. She noticed only one spot for Alistair—she would have to make that dance count.

Nigel gave her the pen to fill out the rest of the names. Next to Nigel's elegant script, her penmanship looked like someone trying to write with their toes. She wrote James's name in most of the spaces. Even if he was unaware of the Fairfields' dastardly hobbies, he might be able to add the missing pieces she needed without him even knowing he was exposing their secrets.

There were places on her dance card for Cain and Hubbard as well, but only one for each. She would have left them off completely, but that would've looked suspicious.

"Remember," Nigel said when she was finished writing. "Not a single drop to drink."

The mention of alcohol made Westie's stomach twitch with the acidic pang of vomit. Before she'd tried it herself, she'd doubted the healing ability of the vampire blood, for there had been times when she'd craved the drink so fiercely, she'd rather have died than be without it. The revulsion she felt as she remembered the sting of whiskey down her throat had turned her into a believer.

"Not a drop," she promised.

"Good. Now, I've asked James to escort you, since Alistair is busy with the carriages."

She nodded.

Nigel went beyond the curtain to announce her arrival. She barely heard his voice as he spoke the common words of one's coming-out. He told the crowd she was a proper lady now, fit for society and suitors. When Nigel called her name, she took a deep breath and walked into the room, a shaky smile on her lips.

# Twenty-Three

It seemed everyone in town had shown up for the ball. Even the sheriff was in attendance. Westie had never seen the sheriff's family before. He had a pretty young wife and seven daughters. He was younger than Nigel, maybe in his early thirties, but the comfortable way he wore his authority made him seem older. She'd seen him take down men twice his size with his bare hands and had always thought of him as a cowboy, but the tender way he danced with his wife and daughters was enough to melt the stoniest of hearts.

As Westie looked around, her eyes lit up at the sight of several Wintu in the crowd: Grah and Chaoha, and three women whose names she couldn't remember. Nigel had invited the tribe but hadn't expected them to show, since no one but her family wanted them there. They probably came in defiance of the mayor, but a part of Westie hoped they were there for her. Either way, she was happy to see them.

James waited for Westie, his arm crooked for the taking. He looked dashing, with tall, fitted boots over his trousers, a black tailcoat, a high-collared white shirt, and his dark hair oiled as it always was. Other than Nigel, she'd never seen someone wear a suit so easily.

"You're even more beautiful than I remember," James said when she took his arm. He led her onto the floor just as the band began to play a new song.

She blushed. Not because of the flattery, but because he hesitated before taking hold of her machine. It was only a brief pause, but it was there. When he did take her machine without being crushed, he finally loosened up and settled into the dance.

The music was more modern than anything she'd encountered at other coming-out parties. The singer was a young woman with long knotted hair and filigree tattooed on her face. She plucked and thumped at the strings of her stand-up bass, the gears and cogs spinning and steam coming from small stacks on the side as she played. A frantic banjo solo turned ladies' skirts into chiffon turbines as their dance partners spun them across the floor.

"You dance wonderfully. Who taught you?" James asked. There was a hint of a black eye still remaining from his fight with Cain in the general store.

"My pa."

"Nigel?"

They were both looking at Nigel. He was dancing with the widow Myrtle Grey, arms barely able to wrap around her ample waist. At first glance he looked elegant with grace and an exquisite carriage, but south of his waist Nigel was a mess, stampeding all over her feet.

"My real father."

Her father had loved to dance. Mostly dances made for country folk, but he knew the proper ones too. He could waltz with the best of them.

"Do you still miss him?" James asked.

She returned her focus to James. He had the kind of strong jaw girls lost their manners over, and kissable lips. She thought of Alistair's lips too and was saddened to find it hard to remember what they looked like with James standing there.

"Every day." She glanced at her machine, noticed how James's fingers grazed the copper pieces. How she wished she could feel it. "What about you? You must miss your family, with you being here and them being—well, wherever they are."

"My parents also passed away when I was young, and I have very little memory of them. I know my father had the same name as me, and he was the mayor of Sacramento before Ben Chambers, but that's all."

She scolded herself inwardly, remembering the news about the former mayor's passing. She'd just moved in with Nigel when she'd heard about the horrible accident. "I'm sorry to hear that." She hurried to find something else to say, but it didn't feel right going into trivial topics like parties and talk of investments. She decided to take a chance and speak from the heart. If she was going to learn anything about the Fairfields, she needed James's trust. "It gets lonely at times, doesn't it?" she said.

"Yes, though there are times I am thankful not to remember my parents, for seeing their faces and remembering their touch would make me feel all the more guilty."

The faces of her family flashed into her mind, her parents bound by the fire waiting to be slaughtered while she ran to her salvation. Tripp's severed leg...

She swallowed hard. Guilt was a feeling she knew all too well.

"Why would you feel guilty?" she asked.

"My mother and father died in an airship crash over the Sacramento airfields when I was just a boy. I was sick and they were traveling to seek medicines for me. If I wasn't such a weakling, they would never have been on board."

"I'm so sorry, James."

"Don't be sorry for me. Your life is no less full of heartache."

She didn't want to travel down the path of her own heartache with him, so she steered clear, keeping to his story.

"It was very kind of the Fairfields to take you in," she said.

He let out a humorless snort. "Good indeed."

"They haven't been good to you?"

Her eyes met his. She remembered them being a lighter green when she first met him. Under gaslight, with the sparkle of the chandelier overhead, they were the color of emeralds.

"Good enough, but anyone would be with the amount of gold they were given to take care of me. Since they're my only living relatives, my parents left them money with the stipulation that they'd keep me in their charge until I could take over my trust when I turn eighteen."

"It must have been a great deal of money for them to take care of a sick child," she said.

"Eight gold bars."

"Eight gold bars?"

She choked on the words and looked around, afraid she had spoken too loud. No one seemed to notice. Nigel still danced with Myrtle, and the Fairfields sat at a table talking to the mayor.

"One could live two lifetimes on eight gold bars."

"Not the way Lavina and Hubbard spend money. They're likely to blow through the whole thing and dip into my trust when they're done."

"They can't do that," Westie insisted. "There are laws."

"Lucky for them, they know a former lawyer who's excellent at finding loopholes."

Ben Chambers, of course. She remembered Nigel mentioning that he'd been a property lawyer before he became mayor. No doubt he knew his way around tied-up estates.

"Mrs. Fairfield was a good mother to you, wasn't she?" Westie asked, hoping to find some glimmer of light in James's childhood since his parents' passing.

He shrugged. "She made sure I ate well, went to the best schools, and had the best doctors. If I were to get sick and die, they would lose everything. She wouldn't want anything bad to happen to me—at least not until I'm eighteen and sign my will."

"Why do you stay? Why not stay with friends for a time? As bright and charming as you are, I'm sure there's someone."

A smile erupted on his face. "You think I'm bright and charming?"

She looked away from him, feeling her face heat up. "You're all right, I suppose."

James spun her round and round on the dance floor. Despite being overheated and feeling a bit faint, she was surprised how much she was enjoying his company.

"I'm afraid there's no one. Being a sickly child didn't allow me much time to make friends. . . ." His words trailed off. "Are you all right? You've gone pale suddenly."

James stopped spinning her, but Westie felt as though the room were still moving.

Her legs started to wobble. James held her tight as she collapsed in his arms.

"I think Bena may have tied my corset a little too tight." It felt as though her ribs were being crushed..

She put her head against his chest. He smelled of spiced cologne. She'd never liked the false smells of perfume before, but didn't mind it on him. "Will you walk me to my seat, please? I need to rest a bit."

James walked her to her table and helped her to her seat. She liked the attention somewhat. It wasn't often someone treated her like a lady. It wasn't often she acted like one.

She smoothed her skirt around her, feeling better once she sat.

"I'll go get you something to drink."

While James fetched her drink, she looked around at the other guests. There were humans and creatures alike. Nigel invited creatures to all his social events to keep politically neutral. Westie had never minded their presence in the past as long as they didn't hog the booze. Now dry, she still didn't mind. The socialites' discomfort upon seeing the creatures amused her.

Banshees, ghouls, elves, and werewolves had shown up. There were also vampires. She'd almost missed Costin sitting in his dark corner with his posse all around him, long hair nearly covering his face. He looked paler than usual. His cheeks were gaunt, and there were lavender pouches beneath his eyes as he trained them on her, following her every move as though there were an invisible web that linked them together.

Isabelle slipped into the seat beside her. "You look positively green," she said.

*Good,* Westie thought, thankful for the distraction. At least Isabelle couldn't tell she was flushed.

"I feel like all the colors in the world mushed into brown paste," Westie said.

"You can't get sick—you're a debutante," Isabelle said.

"I wasn't aware debutantes were immune to illness."

Isabelle plucked a garlic-stuffed olive from the hors d'oeuvres on the table and delicately put it into her mouth. "Well, they are."

"Why aren't you wearing the dress I had fitted for you?" Westie asked.

Isabelle was wearing an off-the-shoulder red silk dress with a plunging neckline, much like the one Lavina had worn when she landed in Rogue City. The bronze owl earrings were the only thing Isabelle wore of the ensemble Westie had given her.

"That old thing?" Isabelle took a cheese ball from the platter and bit into it with a grimace before she spit it into her napkin. "Lavina says red is all the rage in the city."

*That old thing?* That old thing had been a cherished gift from Nigel. Westie had spent her entire allowance to have it cut up and fitted to Isabelle's smaller frame, ensuring that Westie would never be able to wear it again. Isabelle threw it away to look like Lavina. Westie wanted to rip the bronze owl earrings from Isabelle's ears but contained herself. At least those she could get back after the dance.

Westie sighed. "So Lavina likes red. How . . . appropriate."

Isabelle was about to bite into another garlic-stuffed olive but thought better of it. She cupped her hand to her mouth, breathed into it, and sniffed. The result left her face crushed.

"That's garlic in the middle of that olive. I thought it was a pimiento. Why didn't you warn me? Now I'll have garlic breath when I dance with James."

"Is James on your dance card?"

Westie was surprised by the jealousy she felt. Knowing there was no love lost between the Lovett heir and the Fairfields had changed the game. He was smart, and he hated the Fairfields as much as she did. It was possible he could be an ally in the war against her family's killers.

Isabelle removed her small leather-bound booklet from her cleavage. "Well, no, but there are a few spots open should he want them." She gave Westie a curious look. "Do you mean to keep him all to yourself?"

"What? Of course not."

Isabelle snagged the fan rudely from Westie's copper fingers, nearly ripping it.

"This is your dance card?" Isabelle said. "Why is everything you own more beautiful than everything I own?" she complained while studying the list of names on the fan. She looked up with a mischievous grin. "I was wondering why none of the other girls had James's name on their cards. It looks like someone is squirreling him away for herself."

Westie snatched the fan back.

"It's not like that. I have no interest in James Lovett."

"That's obvious enough." Isabelle studied a glazed carrot round carefully and gave it a sniff before dedicating herself to eating it. "Everyone knows you're waiting for Alistair."

Alistair walked into the room just then. His mask was repaired and gleaming in the gaslight. Isabelle's lip curled in disapproval.

"I don't get what you see in him," she said as she looked around the appetizer tray for more treats. "I just don't get it."

"He's not yours to get," Westie snapped.

Isabelle smiled, raising her hands to pantomime surrender.

When Alistair saw Westie, he waved. He moved through the crowd, politely acknowledging guests he knew, then breathed a sigh of relief when he sat down beside her.

With a roll of her eyes, Isabelle left the table to seek out more popular company.

"What's her problem?" Alistair asked.

"She's a bitch."

He nodded.

"You look beautiful," he said.

The compliment meant nothing. He told her she was beautiful each time she wore a new dress. It was good manners. Nigel used to say her beauty was like a spider's web. *Those poor, poor boys,* he would say. But what good was beauty if it couldn't capture the heart she wanted?

"I look stupid."

He studied her dress without argument.

"Your face is pretty," he said.

She waved off the shallow comment with a swish of the fan she held between copper fingers.

He took hold of it. "When do I get my chance to sweep the floor with that hideous gown of yours?" After reading the names, his face turned ashen. He had obviously found Cain and Hubbard Fairfield on the list. "I suppose it's a good thing Nigel had me hide your parasol."

"So that's where it went to."

"I agree it is good strategy to befriend James Lovett, but your dance card suggests he's courting you."

She thought about her dance with James, his unfortunate story, those deep eyes. "Spending time with James won't be the worst way to get information about the Fairfields."

Alistair gave her an intense look that made her fidget. "Sounds a little like you fancy the heir." He turned away from her. "Wouldn't that be something? Imagine the fortune you'd inherit if the pair of you wed," he said.

"I hate it when you use Nigel's British words. What man uses a word like *fancy*?"

He didn't seem to care if she and James walked out together. The thought hurt her more than she cared to acknowledge. Suddenly she lost her taste for the food being carried out of the kitchen by servers, as well as the taste for music and dance.

James wove his way through the dancers to reach her. "There you are." He held a champagne flute. "I had to calm Mrs. Fairfield. She's a bit cross that she wasn't seated at the debutante table."

Westie took the flute from James, stared into the familiar bubbles, and heard her stomach gurgle. Alistair took it from her before she could get sick.

"It does seem rude," Westie said. "I'll have to make it up to her." She looked around, noticing Nigel had put the Fairfields at the opposite end of the room from Westie's table. Smart man, but she wouldn't learn anything by avoiding them.

"I'm sure Lavina will get over it. She's not one to hold a grudge," James said.

*No, but I am,* Westie thought.

Alistair stood and pushed his chair back. He was a head taller than James and wore a similar tailcoat, with a black shirt beneath instead of white.

"I believe the Lovetts and Fairfields aren't friends of Westie's. They have no claim to her table," Alistair said.

James didn't seem intimidated by Alistair's greater age and height and seemed not to fear the mask as everyone else did. Instead he smiled, washing his face in a brilliant glow.

"Yes, which is why I feel honored to be placed right beside the debutante," James said.

Westie looked down at the place cards, and just as planned, James was seated next to her with Nigel on the other side. Alistair wasn't even at her table.

Alistair's mask began to hum with his heavy breathing. There was no sign of the gentle boy she was used to when his eyes narrowed. In that moment she could see why everyone feared him.

# Twenty-Four

From across the room Westie watched Alistair and Nigel argue. Alistair's face turned red as he maniacally pointed a finger in Nigel's face.

"He looks mad," James observed with a hint of amusement.

"I'll say."

By the curious looks on the faces around her, Westie could tell the guests wished they could hear what was being said. The band had become the runner-up in entertainment. Westie looked toward the kitchen. While everyone was distracted by the argument, Bena slipped out of the kitchen into the great room, prowling like a cat without anyone noticing.

Westie held her breath as Bena slid her hand into Lavina's handbag. There was no going back now.

She glanced back as Alistair put his hands down and stalked

out of the room. When she looked toward Bena again, she was gone. Westie's breath burst from her lungs.

After the meal, the dancing resumed. Ignoring the sneering crowd, Westie danced with the Wintu men. They didn't know any proper dances so they just made it up as they went, and Westie enjoyed trying to keep up with them. She also danced with James twice. Afterward she found the sheriff and was curious about what had happened with Nadia.

He was dancing with his wife when she approached. "May I have this dance?" she asked.

The sheriff muttered a curse. "Must I?"

His wife hit him in the arm. "Don't be rude," she scolded. It was clear who the authority was in the relationship.

The sheriff, with the face of a man caught in the rain, took Westie by the hand. As they danced, Westie said, "Have you found anything concerning Nadia's attacker?"

He looked away from her, toward the crowd. "Not yet."

"I know you won't believe me, but there are still cannibals out there, and I think Nadia was attacked by one."

The sheriff made an exaggerated noise of annoyance. "Not this again."

Westie held a hand up, trying to sound reasonable instead of nettlesome. "I don't blame you for not trusting me. Back when I accused that man of being a cannibal, I wasn't in my right mind. But I'm sober now. You don't have to believe me, but can you please just keep an eye out?"

"I'll tell you what. I'll look further into Nadia's case as long as you stay out of it."

"Deal!" Westie kissed his cheek, hardly able to contain her excitement. Perhaps if he pushed Nadia further, she might remember details that would lead the sheriff to Lavina. It was more than she'd expected to get. With a grumble he went back to his wife.

On her way back to the table, Nigel approached her with a man she didn't recognize.

"Westie," Nigel said, "I'd like to introduce you to my banker from Sacramento, Amos Little."

The man had a white slick of hair on his head, a matching mustache, and a stature befitting his name.

"How do you do?" Westie said, still glowing from her conversation with the sheriff.

"Oh, fine," he said, all smiles until the mayor walked by. The two of them stared each other down like two dogs with their ears pinned back. Westie's curiosity was piqued when she saw the exchange. "I just wanted to meet the debutante before I head back to the inn." Amos's posture eased when the mayor disappeared in the crowd.

"You're leaving already?" Westie said, hoping he'd stay long enough for her to learn what the cold look between Amos and the mayor was all about. "The night is young."

Amos put a hand on his belly. "Afraid I must. This blasted ulcer is acting up again."

"I've given him a treatment and a sedative to help him through the night," Nigel said, patting him on the back with a sympathetic frown.

"Unless you feel like dragging my body around the dance floor with your machine after I've passed out, I best be off," Amos said.

Westie winked at him. "Wouldn't you know, that's how I get all the men to dance with me."

Chuckling, Amos said, "I doubt that very much," and shuffled off toward the exit.

"What was that between the banker and the mayor?" Westie asked Nigel after Amos was gone.

Nigel pursed his lips. "I haven't the faintest idea, but I'm sure two of the most powerful men in the valley are bound to butt heads at some point."

Though curious, Westie let it go for the time being and took Nigel up on his offer to dance. She thought it was a fluke that he'd stomped all over Myrtle Grey's toes, but alas, it was not.

While Nigel spun her around the room, Westie watched Olive Fairfield dance on her father's feet. The love she saw in Hubbard's eyes as he twirled his child around reminded her of her own father. She inwardly reprimanded herself, furious that she'd even let Hubbard near her father, even if it was in her head.

Olive spun and laughed while her cornflower-blue dress floated around her and her golden locks danced about her little round cheeks, pink with merriment. The father and daughter looked so utterly normal, almost sweet.

After her dance with Nigel, a new song began. She was about to check her dance card to see who was next when she looked up and saw Isabelle's face bright with happiness as she danced with Cain across the room. Westie's heart came to a sudden halt, and so did her feet.

Other dancers bumped into her, glaring until they noticed it was the debutante.

Her legs began to move again. She headed toward the couple, ripe with anger but no plan, and was jerked to a stop when someone grabbed her flesh arm. She spun around to find Nigel. He looked at Westie, then back at Isabelle and Cain. She tried to pull away from him, but his grip was tight.

"Do not make a scene," he warned her. "Tell Isabelle that Cain Fairfield has a reputation for whoring, nothing more."

He was close to her ear, breath blistering against her skin, and when he spoke his *s*'s were too crisp. That was all she heard.

When she finally wriggled free of him, Westie smoothed her skirts and gathered her wits before she stepped up to the smiling couple. Cain was like a monument beside Isabelle. He was broad through the shoulders like his father, with the sharp, predatory features of his mother. He wasn't ugly really, but he was no James. There was no hint of family resemblance between the Fairfields and Lovett. Still, youth made everyone appealing to some. Money made everyone appealing to most, which Westie gathered was the reason behind Isabelle's sudden interest in Cain. His evening attire reeked of money. He wore tall boots with brass buckles, and a matching tailcoat with gold-and-diamond buttons on the cuffs.

His hair was oiled and slicked like James's, and it was the same dark color too instead of his usual gold. It made Westie wonder what the true color of James's hair was. Though Cain wore his hair in a similar style as James, it made him look more like a rodent than ever before. If there was one thing that could distract Isabelle from a person's looks, it was money.

"Well, aren't you two a lovely couple," Westie said. Her sugary-sweet words burned on her tongue.

Isabelle looked at Westie and beamed.

Cain bowed to her. "It's wonderful to see you again, Miss Butler." He didn't carry the same bruises as James from their fight, but he held his left arm like he was favoring it. "I look forward to our dance."

Like Westie, he still had the slightest twang of poor folk when he spoke, just as she remembered from their brief time spent in the cabin.

"As do I. I believe our dance is up next, isn't it?" She checked her card to make sure.

That made Isabelle pout.

"Could I borrow my friend a moment?" Westie said. "Girl talk, you know."

Isabelle giggled annoyingly. Her brain turned to pig slop whenever she was interested in a boy.

Cain bowed again. Westie had Isabelle towed to the opposite end of the room before Cain had straightened.

"You're hurting me," Isabelle complained, trying to shake Westie off.

Westie held tight with her flesh hand. She wanted to grab the girl with her machine and shake her, but Isabelle was already nervous around her copper as it was.

Westie said, "I don't want you spending any more time with

Cain Fairfield," more bluntly than she'd meant to.

Isabelle looked thunderstruck. "Just because it's your coming-out party doesn't mean you can tell me who to spend my time with." She took a deep breath to compose herself. When she spoke again, her tone was less hysterical than it was vicious. "Besides, why should you care? You're caught up with James Lovett now because we all know you're in love with Alistair, but he won't have you." Her eyes were at a crouch, a look as mean as her words. "Leave Cain for me."

Westie's hand went to her chest, her heart constricting. Isabelle's words had struck their target, and the pain they caused could be felt all over.

She wanted to say something hurtful in retaliation but calmed herself.

"You're my friend," Westie said. "I'm not trying to hurt you, or take Cain away. I'm just trying to protect you. I hear he's got a reputation with the ladies and a terrible habit of stealing a girl's flower. By the time he's done using her, no other man will have her. He spends most of his time in brothels. Costin just told me he's a frequent customer."

Tears sprang to Isabelle's eyes. "You lie. You're just jealous that he wants me and not you. You want every eligible man at the ball for yourself."

Isabelle pulled away when Westie reached for her, and ran from the room in a gathering of skirts and tears.

It was suddenly too hot, and Westie felt like the room was spinning. At least her words had shadowed Cain in doubt. She only hoped it would be enough to keep Isabelle away from him. She watched

Isabelle slip through the door, nearly knocking over Bena as she walked into the room.

Bena wore a simple white dress and beaded necklace, her hair tied back into a knot. She held a box wrapped in pretty white paper with a blue bow, drawing stares and whispers from the tables around her. Seeing Bena again was the only saving grace in an otherwise dreadful night.

"For the debutante," Bena said, bowing and handing the gift to her. "Are you ready for this?"

Westie was still shaken from her fight with Isabelle, but she was ready. "Ready as I can be. Wish me luck."

"Be careful." Bena smiled and headed toward Nigel.

People glanced at her but didn't seem too curious as she tore at the paper. Upon seeing the gift inside, she paused with the lid in her hand. The plan had been for Bena to steal the key, make a clay impression of it, then take whatever she could find in Westie's room and put it into a box to give to her as a present at the party in order to smuggle Lavina's stolen key back into the ball, but what was in the box wasn't anything she owned. It was an actual gift. A dark tunic, supple leather leggings, and a pair of beautiful beaded moccasin boots. They weren't just any Wintu clothing, they were hunting garb. Westie had been asking Bena for a set of Wintu hunting clothes since she was a young girl, and Bena always said, *Not until you're grown.*

Hugging the tunic to her chest, she could smell the undeniable scent of the Wintu: woodsmoke and wild rosemary. It instantly settled her frazzled nerves. She wanted to rip off her ugly dress in exchange for her new clothes. There was a card inside the box. *For a true wild thing.* Beneath the card was a key. She took it and stuffed it into her cleavage. She looked around the room for Bena and smiled when she saw her dancing with Nigel.

Westie was so caught up in the moment that she forgot about her dance with Cain until he found her.

Because of the plan, she'd known she'd have to dance with the Fairfield men, and thought she'd feel more confident when the time came, but she wasn't. It felt as though there was an animal trapped inside her stomach, clawing its way out.

Cain led her to the floor, but instead of holding her metal hand, he put both of his hands around her waist. Normally a blatant move like that would have stung, but not now. She didn't care what Cain thought of her.

"That was quite a scene earlier with you and Miss Johansson," he said. "I do hope everything is all right."

He was head and shoulders taller than Westie. Her neck cramped looking up at him.

"It's nothing. We have spats all the time. I always seem to say the wrong thing."

"I doubt that very much. I believe you knew exactly what you were saying. In fact, I think you picked your words quite strategically."

Westie was taken aback by the knowing grin on his lips. "You heard what I said to her?"

"Every word."

He wasn't mad. The opposite, in fact. He seemed flattered by it.

Perhaps he liked the idea of having the reputation of a wealthy playboy.

"But how?"

He had been nowhere near when she and Isabelle had been talking.

"I have my spies."

Westie's gaze floated around the room until she found Olive looking right at her. The precocious girl smiled, then rudely stuck out her tongue.

She'd have to be more careful around that little beast.

Westie hung her head, wondering how she would get herself out of the mess she was in.

He surprised her again by saying, "I know your game." She braced herself to look at him. "You thought you would try to get close to James, but you know the fortune will soon be in my hands after we invest in Nigel's machine. That's why you turned on your own friend, to seek my notice."

He didn't know the game after all. She felt more confident when she met his eyes.

"I won't deny that I have bigger goals in mind than James." She smiled sweetly.

His smile was less sweet. "I like a girl with ambition."

She gave him a flirty poke to the chest. "Then you will *love* me."

# Twenty-Five

After getting through her dance with Cain, Westie was confident she could handle his father. She fished the key from her bodice and clutched it in her hand as she made her way to the Fairfields' table, where Hubbard and Lavina sipped glasses of wine.

"Lavina, I'm so grateful you could make it to my party," she said with a practiced smile. Lavina stiffened when Westie bent to hug her. Westie took the opportunity to slip the key back into Lavina's handbag.

Once released from their embrace, Lavina relaxed and looked genuinely happy about the interaction. She wore a gorgeous blue gown with a floral bustle so large it practically required its own chair.

"It's we who should be grateful. I'm surprised you would even want us here after the way the boys behaved in the general store," Lavina said.

Westie shrugged. "Boys will be boys."

Lavina chuckled at that and seemed to relax.

"I believe it's time for me to steal your husband away for our dance."

Lavina looked at Hubbard, then back at Westie, shedding some of the cheerfulness she'd been putting on, replacing it with confusion. "You want to dance with Hubbard?"

"Of course. Why wouldn't I?"

Westie was sure Lavina knew exactly who she was, but if Lavina thought Westie didn't remember them, she might let her guard down over time. What better way to feign cluelessness than to dance with the man who'd cut off her arm?

Trying not to quiver, Westie took Hubbard by the hand and led him to the dance floor. He was not as copper-shy as his son and was a fair dancer. What she first thought were pockmarks on his face looked to be scars upon closer inspection, like something—or someone—had gouged at his skin with their nails.

"So," Westie said. She was getting much better at her forced smiles. "You're a lovely dancer. What a relief. After dancing with Nigel, I'm lucky to still have use of my feet."

Grunting in reply and leaning back, Hubbard seemed to want to dance with her as much as she wanted to with him.

He had a permanent scowl that dug lines into the corners of his mouth. Thick brows grew together in the middle, making it difficult to see the deep-set hazel eyes lurking beneath. Seeing his eyes up close again was like looking through a filthy window into her past. They reminded her of being in the cabin, her breath in her ears, his heavy footsteps behind her as she ran. Candles shed just enough light for her to see the clothes, blood, and bones of her traveling companions behind the butcher block when she ran into the kitchen. And then she turned, seeing those eyes, the look of absolute indifference, as if killing her would be no different from shooting a wild rabbit for their supper. Then she remembered the screaming.

"Westie!"

Someone shouting her name pulled her from her memories. She looked down, confused at first as she saw Hubbard on the ground, his hand crushed between her metal fingers.

"Westie, let him go!" Nigel shouted.

The music had stopped. Everyone watched her.

Dropping his hand, she jumped back. "Oh God," she breathed.

Lavina and her children rushed to Hubbard's side, their accusing eyes reaching out to her.

"What have you done?" Nigel said, more to himself than to her.

"I'm sorry," Westie pleaded, afraid she'd blown her plan and any chance she might have had at learning their secrets. "It's this damned machine. I—I—can't always control it."

Hubbard had a voice like a coffee grinder. "I'm all right," he said, letting Nigel haul him to his feet with his good hand. He tested his fingers to make sure they still worked, pain twisting his lips. After some stretching, they seemed to be fine.

Westie was shocked to see his smile, sharp as a scythe. It started at his lips and stretched until reaching his eyes. "If Emma works near as good as that mechanical arm does, then you best believe you have my investment."

He began to laugh, exposing chipped yellow teeth. The sound reached across the room to the dark corner where the antisocial vamps were sipping flutes of blood. Costin looked at her with a raised brow.

Nigel forced a smile, sweat dribbling down his temple. "Wonderful." He turned to Westie and gave her a *we'll talk about this later* look before walking away.

After the party, Westie knocked on Alistair's bedroom door but didn't wait for an invite before barging in.

"Did you get the mold?" she said.

He sat on his bed, his clothes wrinkled, holding up a piece of dried clay with the impression of a key stamped into the middle of it.

"All we need to do is take it to the foundry and have the key made." The metallic screeching that had once accompanied his words was gone now that his mask was repaired, and the hum of his breath was less noticeable too.

"Where's Bena?"

"Here." The voice in Westie's ear caused her to jump.

"Sonofabitch," she said, and grabbed her chest. "Bena, stop scaring me like that!"

Bena replied with a smile.

"Now what?" Alistair said.

"Now we wait for an opportunity to break in. Do you think

Nigel fell for your angry act about me being seated next to James?" Westie said to Alistair.

"He bought it," Bena answered for him as she casually flipped through the pages of a medical book on Alistair's dresser. "If there's one thing that Nigel knows will get under Alley's skin, it's a handsome boy like James Lovett looking after you."

Westie and Alistair blushed equally, as if a blood main that connected them had burst.

Westie cleared her throat. "Thank you for your help, Bena. You're always putting yourself on the line for me."

"I want those people caught as much as you do," Bena said, touching her arm. "I've seen what they're capable of."

Westie woke to an uproar of men's voices and baying hounds. It was early morning, still dark, the air colder now that fall was near. The ruckus hadn't fully penetrated her consciousness until she heard Jezebel pawing at the door, cutting deep valleys into the wood.

"Hold on," she told the worried chupacabra as she slipped into her dressing gown and house shoes.

The moment Westie opened the door, Jezebel shot out of the room and downstairs. Westie walked out onto the catwalk above the grand entrance. A stream of men flowed beneath her, weaving around one another like worms during a rainstorm, holding guns from Nigel's armory.

Alistair slid into the maelstrom from the dining room with his revolvers on his hips.

"Alley," she called to him. He didn't hear her, and there was no way she would reach him before he made it to the door.

Nigel was behind him. He looked up just as she was about to call his name. He pushed through the crowd and took the stairs two steps a time to get to her. It seemed every man in Rogue City was in their house. The place had turned into some kind of headquarters while she slept.

She ran to meet him at the top of the stairs. "What's happening?" she asked.

Concern made a ledge of his brow. "Isabelle is missing."

# Twenty-Six

"Missing?" Westie said. "How could Isabelle be missing? She was just at my party."

"Her mother sent a telegraph bird saying Isabelle never made it home from the ball, and her coach is still here," Nigel told her.

Westie remembered seeing Isabelle's parents leave before the food was brought out, and Isabelle complaining when they'd told her to be home by ten. Westie looked around as if she might find her friend hidden among the men below.

"She was mad the last time I saw her. Maybe she went for air," she said.

Westie shook herself awake. Her brain had clearly slept in after her body got out of bed. For a moment she thought the theory made sense, but she knew Isabelle better than that. She was more likely to gather her hens and cast nasty rumors about Westie to ease her pain than to walk it off. Isabelle wasn't the walking kind.

"Not at all hours of the night," Nigel said.

"I'm getting dressed. I'll help you find her."

If Isabelle's disappearance was some game she was playing for sympathy, Westie meant to give the girl a bite of copper.

Westie checked Isabelle's walking coach first. The metal legs on each side were folded beneath it, making it easier for a woman to get in and out wearing full skirts. Obviously it hadn't moved since the party. There had been a light rain during the night, enough to dampen the ground, but the patch of dirt beneath the coach was still dry.

Westie raced her horse to catch up with Alistair. She found him following a stream near the river. She slowed, checking to see if her parasol was in the saddle holster as Nigel had said it would be. It was. She also found comfort in the rifle slung across her back, even though she was a terrible shot.

She told herself Isabelle would be all right, they would find her. The Fairfields weren't crazy enough to kill a pharmacist's daughter right under their noses. She repeated the thought over and over again until she almost believed it.

"Isabelle is fine. I'm sure there's a perfectly good explanation for where she is, which will most likely involve a boy," Alistair assured her.

They rode a mile downstream. Hounds sang their sorrowful song behind them. Werewolves pitched in. They were still in human form, but their noses were better than any dog's. They looked under every rock, and behind every tree, and still they found nothing. Isabelle could've been anywhere.

"Westie!" she heard someone shout from the woods.

She thought it was Nigel at first until she realized the rider had no accent. And his horse was clumsily splashing over the slick rocky stream—definitely not Nigel.

"James," Westie said when he emerged. She and Alistair shared a glance, for James was a direct link to the Fairfields. "What in damned hell are you doing out here? You don't know these woods—you could get lost."

He was short of breath, as though it were he who had been running instead of his pampered city horse. "I heard people shouting, saying a girl was missing. I had to make sure it wasn't you."

He was coated in sweat, his skin the color of an overcast morning.

"It's Isabelle—she's gone."

"You already knew that, though, didn't you?" Alistair said.

"Alley," Westie warned. If James knew they suspected the Fairfields, it could ruin everything.

James's face was pinched with confusion. "How would I know that? I just told you I didn't know who the missing girl was."

"You look like you're fixing to unload the chuck wagon," Westie cut in. "Are you all right?"

His face had turned a sickly shade of green, and his lips were pale as death.

He leaned over, vomiting down the side of his horse. Westie

lifted her lamp, then quickly turned away when she saw the mess he'd made. The sweet, rancid smell of stomach acid made her head swim. She was afraid she'd be the next link in a chain reaction.

"How much did you drink at the ball, man?" Alistair's eyes were slivers, and he made gagging sounds under his mask.

Westie didn't recall James drinking anything but a flute of champagne at the party, but then again she'd had other distractions.

James wiped his mouth with the sleeve of his sack coat, looking embarrassed.

"Too much."

"Might want to get back inside the bubble if you're not feeling well," Westie said. "Creatures pick off the sick ones first. There's nothing anyone can do if they carry you away."

James looked at her like a frightened child. "I thought creatures couldn't take anyone against their will within the confines of the Indian ward."

"They can't," she said. "But we're not inside the ward. See those blue trees over there?" She lifted her lamp to show him. "Those are the markers of magic. You need to stay inside those lines."

"Oh, I see. That's good to know."

Westie and Alistair led James back to the safety of the Wintu ward. The color had started to come back to his cheeks. Westie was about to inquire further about his health when she heard hooves beating the ground, heading straight for them. A lamp swung in the distance, the light making it look as though the trees were dancing.

Nigel burst from the gloom with Bena close behind him. "The

wolves picked up her scent," he said. His hand shook so violently, Westie was afraid he would drop the lamp and burn down the forest.

"Where?" she said.

"Follow me."

They rode hard. She hoped James and his clumsy horse could keep up or they would have to send out a second party to find him later.

They followed the wolves toward the river, deep into the brush. Ahead, a spot of color on a low-hanging branch caught the light. Westie pulled her horse to the side to avoid a collision with other riders and grabbed the swatch, rubbing the fabric between her fingers. The patch was a red piece of silk chiffon like the dress Isabelle had been wearing. The scrap she'd found was riding height, meaning Isabelle had been on horseback. Westie juggled the scenarios. She wanted to keep an open mind, if only to make herself feel better about the situation. Maybe Isabelle had taken a horse and it had gotten away from her. The girl couldn't ride anything wilder than a wheelchair. Westie didn't want to believe the Fairfields would be so bold as to kill her friend. She couldn't deny the possibility either.

"Here!" someone shouted nearby. "She's over here."

Westie dug her heels into her horse's sides, hoping they would find Isabelle cold and scared but otherwise unharmed. When Westie neared the scene, she knew that was not the case. Her light caught slashes of red like cave paintings all around her, smears of blood against rocks and trees. A howl cut through the silent tension. She thought it had come from a werewolf at first, but it wasn't the sound of any lycanthrope. Westie slid off Henry's back, held the reins in a trembling hand. She could hear the preacher's mumbled prayers under someone's cries. When her tentative steps took her past the crowd that had gathered, she realized the howling sound had come from Isabelle's father. He was hunched down on the ground with the preacher by his side, holding a mangled corpse, unrecognizable as human other than by the red dress it wore.

Westie had stayed home while Alistair and Nigel did the autopsy. As she waited for their return, she jabbed and hacked at a dummy with her wooden practice sword. It was all she could do to battle her pain. Her friend was dead. The last thing she'd said to Isabelle was a lie.

The armory had always been one of Westie's favorite parts of the house. It was more like a museum, really. There were suits of armor and chain mail, polearms, lances, flails, and maces. In the middle of the floor was a pugilist's ring and, beside it, a fencing mat. She stood on the mat, holding the sword with her machine. With a sweeping arc, she slashed down on a dummy with such force that it shattered into a thousand pieces. She was sweating and smelling none too fair when Nigel and Alistair walked in.

Nigel scanned the mess she'd made. She had destroyed all but one of the wooden practice weapons and bent the metal ones into crude sculptures. There were spears broken in two scattered across the floor, and dummies (wood and cloth alike) had been slaughtered. Westie waited for the lecture on tidiness and tranquility. It never came.

"Where's Bena?" Westie asked.

"She went home," Nigel said. "With the confusion about the changes in the dome and now *this*, some people in town think it's the Wintu's doing."

Westie's shoulders slumped. "What did you learn from Isabelle's remains?" She held up the sword as if she could slash through any news she didn't want to hear.

Alistair and Nigel both looked ragged, their hair matted with sweat and filth, their clothes askew. There was horse shit caked on their boots and blood under their nails. Nigel pulled a crumpled handkerchief from his pocket and wiped the dried blood from his face.

"The teeth marks we found on the bones were definitely human," Alistair said.

The wooden hilt crumbled beneath Westie's machine. Tears blurred her vision. It felt as though someone were driving nails into her heart. If that were the case, she hoped it would be nailed shut and never opened again to such pain. She turned her back on her family before they could see her tears.

Her jaw flexed. "I told you it was the Fairfields who killed my family, and now Isabelle's dead too."

It wasn't the time to be laying blame, she knew. If she had a better way to stop the pain and guilt she felt, she would've chosen it.

Nigel hung his head. "I believe you now, Westie, and I'm sorry for ever doubting you. But we don't have proof that it was the Fairfields themselves who killed Isabelle. You said there were cannibals on your travels in the valley. It's possible they made their way to Rogue City and found easy prey with Isabelle," Nigel said.

*Oh,* now *he believes me about the cannibals in the valley,* she thought.

"Again with the damn proof," she mumbled just out of his hearing. "Who else knows about the human teeth marks on the body?"

"Only Alistair and I. I ordered Isabelle's body sent to my surgical rooms for examination. The sheriff was with us, but I didn't tell him my findings so he wouldn't immediately suspect the Wintu."

The Wintu were always blamed for everything. While she knew there were native tribes that consumed the flesh of their enemies in war rituals, it wasn't the case with the Wintu. They were a peaceful tribe living on the river. As long as foreigners kept to themselves, they had no quarrels.

"What happens to the Wintu?" she asked.

"I told the sheriff the attack was most likely a bear," Nigel said. "That takes the suspicion off the Wintu."

"That's good." She pretended to scratch her face while she wiped away a tear. "That also leaves the townspeople vulnerable to another attack by the Fairfields."

"There is a mandatory curfew in place until the bear is caught. Women and children are to be escorted at all times."

Westie threw the bits of shattered hilt across the room so hard, the splinters pierced the wooden dummy carcass as though they were arrows shot from a bow.

"Everyone in Rogue City is a hostage now, and the no-good

zealous hicks of this town will be crawling all over the woods killing innocent bears because the Fairfields are a bunch of flesh-hungry gluttons." She wanted to scream but knew if she tried she might melt into tears instead. "We should just out them and be done with it. Let the town and Isabelle's folks do what they will with them."

Alistair picked up a sword, inspecting the damage. He said, "There's no evidence to prove the Fairfields killed Isabelle, and even if there was, no one would believe it. They are the wealthy kin of the Lovetts, not savages."

No one mentioned Emma or the need for the Fairfields' money. It would've been in bad taste. But the worry of losing investors was not far from Nigel's and Alistair's minds; she could tell by the guilty way they lowered their gazes.

"Nigel, you better get that money soon. I plan to take the Fairfields down before they get the chance to kill another one of my friends."

"It's not that easy," Nigel said. "Investors don't toss their money around willy-nilly. It's a process."

Westie's lips tightened against her teeth. There was no time to sit around and wait for money. She needed to expedite the process.

# Twenty-Seven

The next day Westie sat on her bed and filed the sharp metal edges of the key they had made. She tried to think about anything but Isabelle. It was impossible.

*Isabelle.*

It was hard for Westie to wrap her head around the fact that she was gone. Westie had already lost so many people she loved that somehow she thought she'd be used to the pain, but it hurt no less than before.

Alistair knocked once and walked in. He sat beside her on the bed. "Are you sure you want to do this?" he asked.

Westie finished rounding the last edge and inspected her work. "Yes."

It was a lie. She wasn't sure. There were so many things that could go wrong. But if she didn't at least try, more lives would be lost at the hands of the Fairfields. She'd weighed the consequences, and decided it was worth the risk. If all went according to plan, the Fairfields would lose everything, and Nigel would get the money for his machine.

The men's riding trousers she wore gathered in places meant to accommodate parts she didn't possess. She picked and pulled at them.

"Leave them alone," Alistair said, his eyes smiling. "No one will believe you're a man if you're always pulling at yourself."

She slid him an easy grin. "That's exactly why they'll believe I'm a man."

His laughter wrinkled the skin around his eyes, making the eyes themselves more beautiful. It was the only thing that brought her any comfort.

She continued to fuss with herself. She wore full cowboy dress, with a long duster, angora chaps, and supple leather gloves to hide her machine. Her hair was pinned up, hidden beneath a flat-brimmed Stetson, and she wore a red kerchief to hide her long, slender neck and the Adam's apple missing from her throat. Alistair wore a black kerchief over his mask and a blond, shaggy wig that made his skin look paler than usual.

They housed their borrowed Wintu horses at the livery yard and asked for a room at the Roaming Inn. When the Fairfields had first arrived in Rogue City, Nigel had set up a demonstration of Emma for today in the old mining caves at the edge of the dome. It would've stirred up too many questions if he were to cancel last minute. Because of the demonstration, they didn't have to worry about running into the family at the inn. Westie and Alistair told Nigel they were going to check on the Wintu and would be gone for the day, knowing he would never approve if they told him what they were really up to. After everything that had happened the day before, Nigel was too flustered to be suspicious.

The Roaming Inn might have had the nicest rooms in Rogue City, but they were hardly *nice*. One could pick up a stubborn case of pant-rats without the coin to pay for the better rooms. Westie assumed the Fairfields had taken the best rooms, so she asked for the second best. In her deepest voice, she told the innkeeper she and Alistair were brothers just passing through.

Alistair settled the bill while Westie waited in the lobby. The Roaming Inn was run by a family of werewolves. There were paintings of wolves on the walls. Clumps of shed fur covered the wood floors and were tangled in the rugs. The whole place smelled of wet dog.

A young werewolf boy, naked as the day he was born, stood in the middle of the room aiming at a rose design on the rug before unleashing his bladder.

Westie frowned. "Maybe you ought to housetrain your pup," she said to the woman behind the counter. The woman snapped her jaws in reply.

Westie jumped back. Alistair grabbed her arm and pulled her up the stairs toward their room.

"It would be best not to draw attention," Alistair said.

Westie pulled out of his grip. "Fine."

The room was spacious, with a large bed and a mattress that stank of piss. If their room was second best, she would hate to see the worst. She tossed her satchel onto the quilt and was attacked by a cloud of dust and the lingering scent of mold.

Alistair flushed crimson. "One bed?"

Westie shrugged off her duster and continued to peel away the layers until she was rid of the heat.

"Relax, Alley. We're not sharing the bed. We'll be out of here before you know it."

"Do you have the key to the Fairfields' rooms?" Alistair had the red gingham curtains pulled to the side and was staring down at the main strip.

Westie dug through her satchel until she found it. "Right here." She lifted the key to show him.

They had a plan. They were all set to go, and yet she had a horrible feeling all tangled up in her guts.

"Don't lose that. If anyone finds that key, it will lead them straight to the foundry. I had to pay for it on Nigel's account," Alistair said.

She took a breath, shook it out, then gazed at Alistair. He looked sinister. There was a thrill in that dangerousness, but she knew better of the man beneath the mask, willing to risk his own life for the good of everyone. If Nigel lost everything because they were caught, Alistair would be completely on his own. He was no longer a young boy. No one would foster him without an allowance. No one would be there to fix his machine were it to break. And once he was out of jail, no one would hire a mute except outlaws and desperate ranchers.

"Maybe we shouldn't do this," she said. "There's too much at risk."

He dropped the curtain and stepped toward her until they were face-to-face. He took the hat from her head and pins from her hair so that it was an auburn waterfall around her shoulders. He used to love touching her hair when she was a child. He said it looked like copper wires. It was innocent the way he had touched her hair then, but now, in that rented room, it felt like more.

She drank in his touch, lingered in it, remembering back when they were young and still close. She'd spent every waking hour with him after his wounds had healed, teaching him to read and developing a language of their own with their hands. She'd loved living in that blissfully silent world with him. Even after Nigel made the mask, Alistair hadn't used it much at first. Westie had preferred it that way and liked how he'd always touch her to get her attention.

She was so lost in the memory that she reached up and caressed his hand without even thinking. Alistair reeled back as if she had struck him.

"I'm sorry!" she said, desperate to make it right. "I didn't mean—"

"We should get this done," he said, flustered.

*We all know you're in love with Alistair, but he won't have you.* Isabelle's words stayed with Westie like a greasy meal in her belly.

"Yeah, I suppose so."

She cleared her throat and chewed up her pride, then gathered her satchel and the key before they slipped into the empty hall.

Alistair put the key in the door of the Fairfields' rooms. With a click, they were in.

"Let's make this fast," Westie said.

The Fairfields' rooms were the best she'd seen at any inn, even compared to the ones she'd stayed in during her travels in the valley. There was the one big room for the family to spend time in together and three attached sleeping rooms. The linens were soft green satin. On top of each bed was a fluffy quilt.

While Alistair busied himself in the main room, Westie wandered into the sleeping rooms. One of the rooms was for the married couple. It looked like Cain and James shared another, judging by the different-sized starched and pressed clothes draped over wood hangers in the wardrobe. The last room belonged to Olive; clothes were strewn across the floor along with an army of dolls.

"Found them," Alistair called from the main room.

Westie left Olive's room to join Alistair. He stood in front of an open cabinet. Westie saw the glow of the gold bars on Alistair's mask before she saw the gold itself. It was there for the taking, almost too easy.

"How'd you know it would be here and not in the bank?" Alistair asked.

Westie was certain the Fairfields hadn't always been the city dwellers they claimed to be.

"Country folk don't trust banks."

She knew from her time in Kansas with her parents that people like that preferred to keep their treasures close.

She stared at the gold awhile before reaching out and touching a smooth, gleaming bar.

"Looks heavy," she said. "You think we ought to grab another satchel from one of the rooms?"

She looked up when Alistair didn't answer and found his head cocked, ear to the wind.

"Did you hear that?" he said.

"Hear what?"

They stood together in silence.

Westie heard it then. Voices.

"Shit," she said.

Alistair shut the cabinet door. Westie's heart felt like a stampede in her chest.

The voices grew louder.

"We need to run," Alistair said.

They piled beside the door, listening. The voices sounded as though they were still downstairs. If the two of them were swift, they might be able to make a good go of an escape. Westie cracked the door just enough to peek out. She saw the top of a hat by the stairs, a green suede hat with peacock feathers and beads, an expensive hat. A hat so hideous it could only be fashionable in the big city. A hat only Lavina Fairfield would wear.

Westie shut the door, her mind racing.

"They're too close. If we run, she might see us. We have to hide," Westie said.

Alistair wasn't one to dawdle when it came to tricky situations.

He grabbed her by the machine and yanked her toward Olive's room. It made the most sense. If the Fairfields came home and they were caught, they could snatch the little girl up and use her for leverage. Of course, their lives would be ruined for it, but there was no time to think about that.

"Wait!" she said. "The key."

Alistair stayed in Olive's room while Westie went back for the key. When she opened the door to grab it, she heard Olive's voice. She chanced a look and was relieved to see it was only mother and child coming up the stairs, too busy conversing to see Westie at the door. *They must have forgotten something,* she thought. She grabbed the key, went back inside, and closed and locked the door behind her. All she could see when she got to Olive's room were the whites of Alistair's eyes in the shadows beneath the bed.

"Hurry," he said. She bent to see him better but stopped when she heard a crunch. She slowly moved her boot to find the crushed head of a porcelain doll beneath it. "Leave it. There's a small country of dolls lying around. She won't notice one."

Westie saw a red cape slung across one of the bedposts, grabbed it, and tossed it on the floor to hide the evidence before shimmying under the bed. She was thankful to be wearing men's clothes, for she never would've fit in the cramped space had she been wearing full skirts. She tried to move farther back, but there was a box blocking her way.

"It's on my bedpost, Mommy," Olive shouted to her mother from the doorway of her room. "I'll only be a moment."

Under her breath, Olive mumbled curses too grown-up for a girl her age, just quiet enough so her mother couldn't hear.

The only thing Westie had seen on Olive's bedpost was the cape....

She was struck with a sinking, hollow feeling. They had come back for the cape, and it wouldn't be on Olive's bed where she'd left it.

Olive bent to pick it up off the floor. Her hand froze, hovering just over the material. Westie wondered if the girl had heard the whir of Alistair's machine as he breathed. He too seemed to share her thoughts, for he held his breath as soon as the girl bent.

Though Olive's face was blocked by the mattress, Westie knew by her pause that Olive was curious about the fallen garment. The girl lifted it up, exposing the broken doll beneath.

Westie was sure Olive would look under the bed and they would be caught. She gripped handfuls of hair from the bearskins that covered the floor and held on.

Olive didn't look under the bed. Instead, she put her little boot to the head of a doll beside its broken mate and stomped down until it shattered. She did it to another doll and another after that until she was laughing and dancing.

*Demented little thing,* Westie thought.

"Stop wasting time, Olivia. We're late as it is," Lavina called.

Olive cursed again and skipped from the room with her red cape fluttering behind her like a red gloved hand waving good-bye.

Only then did Alistair breathe again. "That was too close," he said.

Westie agreed. She went to crawl out from under the bed, but her shirt caught on a nail. When she tried to reach behind and unhook herself, the box she was wedged against blocked her way. She kicked it to the side, then untangled her shirt. Curious as to what the little girl had been hiding under her bed, Westie pulled the box out with her.

Alistair was already out, brushing the dust from his clothes. "Let's go. We don't have time for that." His mechanical voice made it impossible for him to sound nervous, but she saw it in the way he tapped his leg with one hand and raked his fingers through his hair with the other.

"It'll only take a second."

There was a blanket folded on top of the box. Beneath it were stacks of dolls. Only one caught her eye. Westie made a horrible, painfully sad sound as she reached into the box with her flesh hand. The doll was mangier than she remembered, but still had its brown yarn hair, burlap dress, and button eyes. Anger built a slow-burning fire in the center of her chest. It spread into rage the longer she sat there. The sad, humming sound she made became louder.

Alistair moved closer to her, his eyes fearful as he watched her grief turn to rage. Westie grabbed the doll, smelled its dusty smell, and clutched it to her chest. Her throat tightened, eyes throbbed with impending tears. She pinched her leg with her metal fingers, the agonizing pain meant to keep her fire from burning out of control, but when she looked back into the box and saw the pair of bronze owl earrings, it was too late. Alistair grabbed her before she could get to her feet and gain the full strength of her machine. He wrapped her in his arms, pinning her machine the way Nigel had at the airdocks, and held her face to his chest to muffle her screams.

# Twenty-Eight

Westie sat in Alistair's room, in his closet where they used to build forts. It had once been their sanctuary, a place to escape a world not ready—or not willing, as it often seemed—to accept metal children with missing parts. The men's clothes and boots that now filled the space killed some of the childhood magic, but it still comforted her to be there.

Alistair sat cross-legged in front of her with a water basin in his lap. The glow of the lamp beside him gleamed off his mask. She briefly wondered what he looked like under there. Did he wear a beard? Did he look like a man, or the boy she remembered? Was he still as beautiful as he was then?

Westie closed her eyes as he washed her face and neck with a damp rag, feeling the edges of her headache begin to dull.

"Will you be all right?" he asked. "We don't have to go to Nigel just yet."

It had been several hours since they'd left the inn, and it had taken two of those hours for Alistair to get her to speak. Her lips still trembled, but she was able to form words.

"I need to do this," she said. "I finally have the proof I need. I don't want to sit on it longer than I have to."

Alistair set the basin aside and took her by the flesh hand, giving it a reassuring squeeze before helping her to her feet.

Westie had sent Bena a telegraph bird, telling her she had news. Once she arrived, Westie gathered Nigel, Alistair, and Bena in the dining room. When they were all seated, Westie tossed her evidence on the table.

"You wanted proof," she said with a shaky voice. "There it is."

Nigel and Bena stared at the cache. "There it is," Nigel said. Astonishment opened his mouth as he lifted the owl earrings he'd made for Westie's thirteenth birthday. He let them dangle from his fingertips, studied the dried blood still caked in the folds.

Bena picked up the doll. "How does *this* prove anything?"

"Lift up the doll's skirt," Westie said.

Bena did, and read the name aloud. "Clementine. Who is Clementine?"

Westie stared at the doll in Bena's hand and chewed her bottom lip. "Clementine was me. My momma sewed my name on the dress so I wouldn't lose my doll. I gave it to my brother when he was sick. I thought if he was going to die on the wagon trail, he could take it to heaven with him and always have me by his side."

"Your name is Clementine?" Alistair said, his confusion almost registering in the sound of his mechanical voice.

Only Nigel knew her real name. After Bena had rescued her in the woods as a girl, she was too traumatized and confused to remember her name when Bena had asked for it. All Westie could mutter was *We were going west.* So the Wintu called her Westie, and it stuck. It wasn't until a year later that Westie's memories rushed back to her in a dream. She decided to keep the name the Wintu had given her. It was a new start.

"It was. It's not anymore. But that was my doll, and that proves the Fairfields were there the day my family died. And those earrings prove they killed Isabelle."

"It does prove they are who you say they are," said Nigel, putting the earrings back down next to the rest of the stolen items. He scratched at the stubble growing on his chin, eyes shifting to the pile of gold on the table. "But why would you take their gold? You're a lot of things, Westie, but you're not a thief."

"Alley said no one would believe the kin of a wealthy heir could be cannibals. Without James's gold, the Fairfields are nothing, the kin of no one important."

Nigel put his elbows on the table and held his head in his hands.

Westie's eyes were wide and desperate as she continued. "I had to do something, Nigel. They've killed Isabelle. Things have changed. How long do you suppose a little bitty meal like her will last an entire family? We need to stop them now before it's too late."

Nigel raised his head and steepled his fingers in front of his mouth. "I agree that something needs to be done about the Fairfields.

One can't argue with the evidence laid out before me," he said with a string of nods, "but I do wish you had come to me first. Delicate matters such as these take time and planning. I can't mention that the two of you found the earrings in the Fairfields' belongings without implicating you in a crime. And I can't use the stolen gold to purchase machine parts until after the Fairfields are convicted and hanged."

Westie felt a grin coming on. "You don't need to worry about that. We'll tell the sheriff that Alistair—not me, for obvious reasons—saw Olive wearing the earrings and followed her into the woods to wherever she goes off to play. We'll say he took them from her. The sheriff trusts Alistair—he'll believe him over the girl. The sheriff will have the Fairfields strung up in no time. He likes himself a hanging as much as the rest of the ghouls in this town. Then after, when the machine is finished and you've made your fortune, you can pay back James's inheritance with interest."

Nigel sat back and wiped his weary eyes. "That's it? That's the best the two of you could come up with?"

Westie folded her arms over her chest. "Not all of us can be geniuses, but it sounds pretty good to me—doesn't it to you?" she said to Alistair.

Alistair looked at Westie, his eyes showing nothing of his emotion, then back at Nigel. He shrugged.

Nigel groaned. He placed the stolen contents back in Westie's satchel. "We need to deal with this, but let's take a little time to come up with a better plan."

Westie and Alistair glanced at each other, concern sculpting identical lines around their eyes.

"What?" Nigel said, glancing between them. "What is that look about?"

Westie filled her lungs and winced. "Thing is, Alley already sent a telegraph bird to the sheriff saying we were on our way with evidence against the Fairfields concerning Isabelle's death."

Nigel rolled his head back between his shoulders. "Bloody hell."

He looked ready to launch. Westie wanted to slink out of the room, for if Nigel were to explode, she knew the devastation would land on her.

Nigel stood with much effort, his knees popping. He collected himself and smoothed the wrinkles from his shirt. "Give me an hour, then meet me at the jail. Perhaps I can salvage this dreadful plan of yours. Lucky for us the sheriff likes to shoot first and ask questions later."

Westie and Alistair left the mansion an hour later as directed. When they reached the jail, Nigel and the sheriff were waiting for them under the eaves.

The sheriff watched Westie approach like a horse eyeing a snake in the road.

"I reckon you had something to do with all this cannibal business," he said to her in his gruff way. "I thought I told you to stay out of it."

Westie put her hand to her chest as if to say, *Me?*

"This wasn't Westie's doing," Alistair said.

The sheriff shook his head. "Well," he said, cocking his hip and hooking his thumbs in his belt loops, "we best get on if we're to do this before the sun goes down."

Westie's heart gave a happy leap. "You're arresting the Fairfields now?" she said with more enthusiasm than she'd meant to convey.

"No, ma'am, we're off to see the mayor."

"The mayor . . . but why?"

The sheriff spit into the lake of chaw juice gathered around the silver tips of his pointed boots. "The mayor's the law in these parts. He outranks me."

Westie felt her bodice dig into her ribs, crushing her lungs. "He's friends with the Fairfields. He'll defend them. It's not fair."

He pinched one eye closed, glaring against the sun behind her. "Darlin', if you wanted fair, you come to the wrong town."

Westie and Alistair rode with Nigel in his carriage. Nigel's lips were sealed together, knuckles white.

"Convincing the mayor will not be easy. He won't be pleased to learn his guests have been deceiving him right under his nose, in *his* county," he said.

Westie hung her head. "If I'd known the mayor would have the last say, I'd never have done what I did."

Nigel slumped forward. "Nothing we can do about that now. Let's just hope for the best. Things may work out in our favor."

They reached the little office space tucked between clusters of shops. The mayor wasn't in Rogue City often, but when he was, he liked a place of his own to exert his authority.

They stepped inside the room. There were antlers and stuffed animal heads on the wall, trophies of his kills. The place smelled like food and body odor. It was no wonder he was a lifelong bachelor, Westie thought. It would've taken a special kind of desperate woman to marry a man like Ben Chambers.

The curtains were drawn, and there was just enough candlelight to see the mayor leaning back in his chair, arms folded over the tub of his belly.

"Nigel, good to see you again." The mayor's arms unwound to fiddle with the broken telegraph bird on his desk, with the sheriff's official star on the stationery tucked in its beak. He snuck a glance at Westie before turning his attention back to the men of the group. "Please, have a seat."

Westie looked in the corner of the room for an extra chair and felt a jolt when she saw Hubbard and Lavina in the shadows. Lavina was putting something into a safe. She closed the door before Westie could see inside.

Though startled by their presence, she wrestled those fears to the ground and forced her expression into a mask she hoped was as unmovable as Alistair's.

"What are they doing here?" Westie demanded.

The mayor's smile was an ugly slash of pink across his face.

"You're branding my guests as heathens. They have the right to face their accusers."

Westie looked at the sheriff, who only nodded, then at Nigel, who seemed confused.

"I have to admit I was quite surprised when the mayor said you believe us to be cannibals," Lavina said, taking a seat beside her husband. Her eyes burrowed into Westie. A drop of sweat crept down the front of Westie's chest into her bodice. "And there we were, about to hand over our fortune after Nigel's explanation of Emma's capabilities this morning. What a shame."

Westie glanced at Nigel. He was a heap against the mayor's desk. The crestfallen look in his eyes crushed her heart, but it wasn't the time or the place to be worrying about Nigel's mood. She had to focus on taking down the Fairfields.

She wondered if they had discovered their gold was missing yet. She doubted it. No one could hold a smirk such as the one on Lavina's lips if that were the case.

"All right, then," the mayor said. "Let's hear these ridiculous claims you've made."

Nigel cleared his throat, looking as if he were about to be sick. "Yes, well, about the Fairfields . . ."

It took some muscling through, but Nigel, with the sheriff's help, delicately explained the story they'd concocted. Nigel elaborated a bit, told the mayor that he'd examined the bones of Isabelle Johansson for a second time after Alistair expressed doubts about his conclusion, and upon doing so, discovered that not only had Isabelle not been attacked by a bear, but she wasn't attacked by an animal at all. The teeth marks he'd found upon reexamination were human. He even had a signed affidavit by Doc Flannigan, who agreed with the findings—which was a forgery, but Nigel had insisted the doctor owed him a favor and wouldn't mind.

Once Nigel was done speaking, he presented the mayor with the owl earrings as evidence and the story of Alistair finding Olive wearing them while she played in the woods.

Westie wasn't sure, but she thought she saw a panicked twitch in Lavina's eyes before she blinked it away.

From his stack of papers, Nigel pulled statements from witnesses testifying they had seen Isabelle wearing those exact earrings at the ball.

Near the end of Nigel's report, the sheriff pulled the cuffs from his belt. All the while the mayor sat at his desk listening, his blank expression never changing.

When Nigel was done speaking, the room was quiet except for Alistair's breathing. He fussed with his machine as if he might find a kill switch.

The mayor finally spoke, voice booming, shaking Westie in her chair. "Earrings, you say." He studied the earrings up close, picked at the dried blood with the tip of his long fingernail. "And you say young Olive was wearing them?" He looked at Alistair, whose dark hair clung to the sweat dotting his forehead.

Alistair nodded.

"Did you ask where she got the earrings?" the mayor asked.

Westie looked at Nigel. His Adam's apple bobbed in his throat.

"That's unimportant. The fact is she had them," Alistair said.

The question of where Olive had gotten the earrings hadn't come up in their planning. Most little girls got their jewelry from their mother, so Westie thought people would assume Lavina had killed Isabelle and had given the earrings to Olive. Westie wanted to mention it, but then thought better of it in case the mayor turned that logic back on her, since it was Westie who'd given Isabelle the earrings in the first place.

Westie cursed inwardly.

"Just answer the question, please," the mayor said.

Alistair's mask hummed. "No, sir."

"So it's possible the girl found the earrings in the forest where she'd been playing, the same forest where Isabelle Johansson met her unfortunate demise."

"Yes," Nigel interjected, "but—"

The mayor slammed his hands against his desk so hard Westie could feel it in her feet, cutting off whatever details Nigel might've added to the wispy remains of their story.

Westie fought the emotion that had started to make her chin quiver. She looked away from the mayor so he wouldn't see, and focused on the safe in the corner instead. It had three locks. Now that the Fairfields didn't have their gold, she wondered what Lavina possessed that was so important she needed to hide it in a safe.

"Unless the Fairfields have blood on their hands and skin in their teeth," the mayor went on, "I will have no more of these accusations. If there are cannibals running amok, it has nothing to do with my guests." The mayor pointed a bloated finger at the sheriff. "What you have is circumstantial evidence," he said, peppering his speech with words from back in his lawyer days, "nothing more. If you want to keep your job, you'll have to do better detective work than that."

Westie felt as though the floor had dropped out beneath her. Her vision blurred as tears flooded her eyes. She mopped them up with her sleeve.

The mayor dismissed them. Westie rushed from the room. Outside, the sheriff leaned into Nigel. "This ain't over. We'll get them." Westie reckoned his determination had more to do with the mayor's threat than it did with seeking justice. He seemed like a man who didn't take kindly to threats. She knew all too well that passion and determination weren't enough to catch killers. They needed a solid plan, and because she'd stolen the Fairfields' gold without one, she feared she'd ruined everything.

Westie plopped down in the carriage seat beside Alistair. She folded her hands in her lap and fought her panic. "It really is over. The Fairfields will leave because of this."

Alistair's hand twitched, inching toward hers as if he might take it. But with a flinching move, he placed it at his side. "Don't give up just yet," he said. "They're broke. They won't leave before trying to get their money back. It's too much to just walk away from. James doesn't strike me as the type who'd be content on government handouts. I imagine the Fairfields will keep a low profile till then. At least they won't kill anyone for a while."

Westie sighed. "Until they run out of food and realize killing and eating a man won't cost them anything."

The conversation came to an abrupt end when Nigel sat behind the reins. His mustache had been twisted to thin points—a habit when he was angry.

No one spoke on the ride to the jail. Once Westie and Alistair retrieved their horses and made it back to the mansion, Westie waited for a good verbal beating. Instead, Nigel went straight to the great room for the rest of the night, which to Westie was far worse than being yelled at.

# Twenty-Nine

The next morning Westie heard the brass sounds of tinkering coming from the floor below and got out of bed. She got dressed and followed the racket downstairs to the double doors of the great room. Opening one of the doors, she hit a wall of stagnant air. The room was barely lit except for a candle here and there. Daylight followed her in and smeared the gloom.

Nigel shied away from the light like a vampire. When he raised his hands to fend off the light, Westie noticed a bottle of whiskey gripped in one of them. He sat atop the great magic-amplifying beast, his face oily with sweat. His eyes looked hollow, his cheeks dug out. Alistair stood below, holding an assortment of tools for the assist.

Westie shut the door and crowded them with shadow again. She put her hand to her nose. That sour, swampy smell was all too famil-iar. It was the smell of old booze seeping from wasted pores, the smell of forgotten nights and drunken mornings after she'd woken up in a pile of her own puke.

"What are you doing?" she asked.

Nigel, mouth opened like a panting dog, tucked the bottle between his legs and reached for a towel to wipe the grime off his face. "Trying to build this machine with the parts I already have. What does it look like I'm doing?" he said in a tone with jagged edges.

"It looks like you're giving up. We should be getting together with the sheriff to come up with a new plan."

His humorless laughter rang out in the copper maze as if he were sitting in a bell. "That's funny, because it's your *plan* that got us into this mess in the first place."

Westie tried to tell herself it was the booze talking and not sweet, patient Nigel.

He continued, "No, we don't need a plan. We need a miracle." He looked down at the machine, rubbed a finger down its spine. It was tall, nearly reaching the ceiling, with gears the size of her head, chain belts, bearings, coils, and so on. It looked like nothing, really, just a confusing ball of metal parts.

*"Plan,"* Nigel said again, and repeated it over and over as if it had lost its meaning. He shook his head and belched—something he'd typically be embarrassed about but made no apologies for now. "No," he said, "no more plans for you. You've done quite enough. Whatever plans are made going forth regarding the Fairfields and this machine will no longer involve you."

He looked at her with the hollow, glassy stare of the inebriated.

She wanted to think it was the drink looking at her and that Nigel didn't detest her as much as his gaze would suggest, but she wasn't so sure.

Alistair spoke up. "You can't put all of this on Westie. I agreed to go with her to the inn and steal the gold."

Nigel looked down at Alistair and took a long pull from the bottle he kept at the ready. "Yes, you did, just as you always have." *Hiccup. Burp.* "Even as children she would scheme and you would follow blindly. And every time, without fail, she'd lead you right into a wall."

Westie's head jerked and her nostrils flared. Not once had she ever heard Nigel talk about her that way. She'd never seen him drunk either. With so many pieces out of place, it felt like her world was falling apart.

She looked at Alistair. He stared at the ground. He didn't confirm or deny what Nigel had to say.

"Now," Nigel said, sweeping a hand at her, "go on with your destructive ways. You've successfully made a mess of things . . . unless you'd like to take your machine to my invention while you're at it."

Westie's anger boiled over. "At least I did something! Maybe if you'd believed me in the first place, Isabelle would still be alive."

She backed out of the room, not waiting for a response, and closed the door behind her. She stared at the doorknob, wondering if she'd just imagined the whole thing and was about to walk in for the first time.

She took a breath, but as she let it out, a furious sob escaped instead. She brought her copper fist down on a side table holding a

Japanese vase and watched the vase shatter to small pieces, then ran from the house.

Henry ran faster than ever before, as if he sensed Westie's need for escape. She touched his long neck. *You've always been the most faithful male in my life,* she thought with bitter self-pity. When she reached the general store, it was locked up because of church services.

Punching through the door with her machine, she took an expensive bottle of aged Brave Maker brand whiskey, her favorite, from the top shelf. She didn't crave the drink like she had before drinking Costin's blood, but she missed how it made her feel. She just wanted to feel different than she did in that moment.

She rode Henry to the forest, not letting up until she reached the stretch of woods where Isabelle's body had been found. If she couldn't have her justice, Westie reckoned she could have a drink with an old friend's ghost.

The blood on the rocks and trees was still there. Westie sat on a rock and opened the bottle. As soon as she smelled the thick, heady scent of the liquor within, she plugged the bottle with the cork and bent over.

An excessive amount of saliva filled her mouth as sickness twisted her stomach. The nauseous feeling kept her in a sick purgatory between keeping it in and giving it up. She wanted so badly to feel nothing once more, but it wasn't going to happen. Her body might have been cured of its longing for alcohol, but her mind definitely wasn't.

Westie had been sitting with her head between her knees,

waiting for the feeling to subside, when she heard a strange yipping sound. She stood, the ill feeling temporarily forgotten as she went to investigate. A fire had swept through that particular part of the woods the summer before, after a lightning storm. It had left the trees bare except for a few stragglers.

Once she was closer, she realized it was a dog. It sounded hurt. Caught in a bear trap, she reckoned. Since Isabelle's death, no one could step into the woods without a close call.

She regretted leaving her parasol back where she'd tied up Henry. What if she needed it to put the mutt out of its misery? She'd have to use her machine, she decided, though the thought of it made the muscles in her stomach quiver once more.

The sound was farther away than she'd thought. She'd gone well beyond the perimeters of the magic ward by the time she came to a clearing. The hot summer days had turned the field into yellow weeds. Grasshoppers bounced around with each step she took, like fleas on a dog.

The wind carried a scent, something rancid and decomposing. It was the smell of her childhood in Kansas with the Undying, a sweet and pungent finger down the throat, tickling the gag reflex. She slowed to a stop, looked around. In the middle of the field was a single tree, a manzanita untouched by the fire, with tiny white blossoms and smooth red bark. Tied to the tree was a dog—a shaggy black-and-white cattle dog, from the looks of it. Next to the dog was Olive Fairfield.

The wind grew stronger, for a moment relieving the odor. She looked around to make sure the other Fairfields weren't lurking nearby, not wanting to seem a convenient meal. She didn't think digestion would be a good look for her.

After a few minutes she moved forward. The girl's back was to her. Olive held a willow switch high in the air above the cowering dog. Her blond ringlets were pulled back into an abalone shell clip. She wore a white knit, high-waisted day dress that was adorable next to her sun-kissed skin.

The smell of death was worse the closer Westie got to the tree. She had thought it was the smell of the Undying, but no, it was the been-dead-awhile. Strips of putrefied flesh were baking in the sun. Dead animals hung all over the lower branches, their smell warring with the floral scent of the manzanita blossoms. There were gray squirrels and baby raccoons without their tails, birds without their wings, frogs without their legs. Macabre ornaments for a gruesome summer Christmas tree. Standing there, in the middle of the stink and the city of flies, was a little tow-headed angel.

When Olive brought the switch down on the dog and Westie heard his painful howl, she cried out, "Stop that!"

Olive jumped nearly a foot in the air, eyes so wide they were like to fall out of her head.

"I wasn't doing anything wrong." Olive's bottom lip shook. She went on to concoct a story about how the dog had attacked her where she played, and how she'd found the tree with the dead animals already hanging there and they just happened to all be within her reach.

Westie went to the dog. He slunk away from her touch. She cooed to him soothingly.

"It'll be all right," she said as she untied the knot around his neck. The dog was just a sack of bones, his fur sticky with blood. From the bite marks on the red bark of the manzanita, and the shit all around, she reckoned he had been tied up for several days. "Shoo now, go on," she prompted. The dog wouldn't leave. He stayed beside Westie, keeping watch over Olive with accusing eyes.

If Westie had thought the dog was capable of retribution, she would've let him have his way with Olive. However, to Westie's dismay, he showed no signs of malice. He just seemed happy to be out from under the switch. Westie stood from her crouch and rushed toward the girl, grabbing her by the collar of her dress.

"Your momma will hear about this," Westie said, though she knew it was an idle threat. Most likely Olive had learned her despicable behavior from her mother and the other members of her family.

Olive melted into tears. "Oh please, you can't tell her."

Westie knew fake tears when she saw them. She'd mastered the technique herself long ago when she broke Nigel's things while learning to use her machine.

"Stop the tears," Westie said. "I'm not buying your bullshit."

Olive watched her, a smile growing on her lips. The tears had been an act, just as Westie suspected.

"Fine." Olive's eyes narrowed dangerously. "If you tell my mommy what I did to those animals, I'll tell her you took our gold."

Westie's thoughts skittered to a neck-breaking stop. "Wha—

what?" she stammered. "I never—"

"Don't try to deny it. I saw you and your friend in my mirror." Olive's lips rolled back from her teeth to form a wicked smile. "One of you crushed my doll and tried hiding it with my cape."

Westie bit her lip. If Alistair went to jail, it would be all her fault. It would ruin him, and possibly Nigel too.

"Your threats don't mean anything," Westie said. "You probably already told them I did it."

"I didn't tell them. I even lied for you. I told them it really was Alistair who found me wearing the earrings and took them from me. I didn't say a word about you finding them under my bed, or being in our rooms."

Westie studied the girl to see if she was being lied to. "Why would you do that?"

Olive held the hem of her skirt, stretching it out and twisting it the way little girls did when showing off a pretty dress.

"Well, partly because my mommy would be cross if she knew I took earrings from a dead girl. I'm not allowed to take things from the people we kill." She smiled. "I do anyway. But mostly I didn't tell because you and I are friends. I don't squeal on my friends." Olive's gaze slid sideways to meet Westie's, a challenge. "We *are* friends, right?"

Westie knew that if she didn't play Olive's game, it could mean Alistair's freedom. She shrugged on her poker face and swallowed the clot in her throat.

"Of course we are," she said. It almost sounded believable.

"Besides," Olive went on, seeming satisfied by her answer, "I hate that gold. It made us ugly. It's all Mommy cares about now. Before we were rich, we used to live off the land. My papa was happy then. Now we have to parade around in these stupid clothes."

Olive pulled at her dress, tearing the skirt.

Westie wasn't sure if she could keep Olive's secret. The girl was clearly deranged. She enjoyed killing things and took too much pleasure in her craft to just walk away from it. And what of the future? Olive seemed content with killing and torturing small animals for the time being, but what if she grew bored with it? Would she graduate to larger animals, creatures, or maybe even children? It was an addiction, a disease, just like Westie's alcoholism.

"Olive, if we're gonna remain friends, you'd best never hurt an animal again."

Olive looked down at the willow switch in her hand. There were no willow trees around. The beating had been premeditated. She'd brought it with her. Olive tossed away the switch with a dismissive shrug. "It was tiresome anyway."

A lie, Westie knew, but it would have to suffice. Noon was drawing near. Folks would be leaving church and . . .

The sudden, horrible clarity of what she'd done stopped her short. She put her hands to her head, panic surging through her veins. Once the owner discovered the robbery and Westie's favorite brand of whiskey to be the only thing missing from his store, he would tell Nigel, and Nigel would certainly put the clues together. As if Nigel needed another check on his list of reasons to be disappointed in her.

She needed to find an alibi and quick.

"We should go. It's getting late. We can take my horse back to town," Westie said.

They took a shortcut. There was an old bridge crossing the river that would take them right to her horse. She wasn't sure if it was still usable. The bridge had been feeble the last time she'd crossed it as a child, but it was worth a try and wouldn't take them any farther out of their way than they already were. The dog followed them at a distance, keeping a steady eye on Olive the entire way.

"Look!" Olive said. She was crouched next to the riverbank, pointing to the ground where a lizard was sunning on a rock. "It's a blue belly. I hear you can pull off their tails and they'll grow back."

"I reckon the lizard wouldn't like that."

Olive reached for the lizard, taking it in her grip and exposing its blue underside. "I don't care. It's just a dumb ol' lizard." She giggled as it squirmed to escape.

Not even a half hour had passed and already Olive had forgotten her promise.

"Don't you pull that lizard's tail, you hear," Westie said. "You made me a promise, and a person's worth is only as strong as their word."

Olive looked over her shoulder at Westie, her eyebrow raised, smirk on her lips, the kind of look made of mischief.

"Words are just sounds a mouth makes. They don't mean anything." She looked down at the lizard, ran a finger along its prickly back, and gripped the tail.

Westie raised her voice. "I swear to the Almighty, I'll blister your hide, Olivia Fairfield. I don't care who you tell about the gold."

Olive's smirk slid into a smile. "We'll see about that."

Westie watched helplessly as Olive gave the lizard's tail a quick yank and tore it off. The lizard writhed in her grip, snapping at her fingers. Olive only laughed when she dropped the lizard and it scurried away with the rest of its life.

It wasn't as if Westie had never seen an animal hurt before; she had, plenty of times. She'd hunted with Bena as a girl, stuck her fair share of hogs, even taken down a buck or two, but she did it to eat, to feed a tribe. It was done with respect and gratitude. Watching Olive beat a dog and pull the tail off a lizard for no other reason than to be cruel took more stomach than God had bestowed upon Westie, and so she turned her back on the girl and walked away, the dog following behind.

"Where are you going?" Olive called after her.

Westie swallowed back the words that would void the truce between her and Olivia. "I'm going home. You'd best do the same." *Before I change my mind about our deal,* she thought.

"I don't know the shortcut across the river."

"Go back the way you came."

Olive tried to keep up, but Westie ran, leaving her behind. She went the long way around to get back to Henry, needing time alone with her thoughts to come up with an alibi in case Nigel or the general store clerk accused her of stealing. If she passed the airdocks on her way, she could make sure one of the dockworkers saw her, and she could say she'd been there all morning watching aeroskiffs take off and land like she used to as a child before Alistair came to live with them. It was as good a plan as any.

Westie reached Henry and climbed into the saddle. Just as she was about to head off, a piercing scream sank its teeth into the back of her neck. The dog cowered, birds scattered from the trees. Westie looked back. If Olive had walked home the way she'd come, the sound would've come from the opposite direction. Unless she'd found the bridge and tried to cross. . . .

"Oh, hell," Westie said.

# Thirty

Westie dug her heels into Henry's sides as they cut through a field, rushing toward the river. When she came to the bridge, she leaped from her saddle and slid down the rough embankment. It was a steady flogging all the way down. She had to dig her machine between the rocks and packed clay to stop her fall before she rolled into the brambles.

As she feared, the ancient bridge was far more unstable than when she'd last crossed it as a child. It was made of rope and driftwood planks for stepping. Between the sun and storms, the ropes were tendrils of hair.

"Olive?" Westie shouted when she saw the hole in the middle of the bridge where the planks were broken.

"Help!" The cry came from downriver.

Her heart a charging bull in her chest, Westie looked all around until she caught a glimpse of what looked like a white sheet caught on a branch in the middle of the river not far from the bridge.

She ran as best she could over the rough terrain, but the slick soles of her boots put her in danger of falling. She cursed as she maneuvered the shore, wishing she had worn her hunting garb and moccasins. She'd have made it to Olive by now had she not been weighed down by her dress.

Olive's screams became shrieks.

"Hold on, Olive, I'm coming!"

Though the girl was a demon with a secret that could destroy Westie, she was a child all the same, and Westie would jump into the river if that was what it took to save her.

When she was close enough, she saw Olive's arm crooked around the branch of a pine caught in the rapids. The river was a giant beast that had taken many lives in the time Westie had been in California, and once it had a victim in its clutches, it wasn't likely to let them go. Olive was but a morsel in its gullet, and she wouldn't have the strength to hold on for long.

Wading out into the anger could be the death of them both, but she couldn't just leave the girl. She had to try.

Sweat ran into her eyes as Westie pushed through the tangle of blackberry vines along the shore. Some of the thorns were as long as fangs and shredded her skin until her flesh hand was drenched in blood.

"Hurry, I'm slipping." Olive coughed as water forced the back of her head forward. Westie knew if the weight of the water didn't kill the girl, the debris—some of it logs the size of grown men—surely would.

Westie finessed her way through the water, wedging her feet between rocks for stability and taking hold of boulders with her machine. When she was beside Olive, she reached out.

"Grab my hand!"

"I can't." Olive swallowed water when she opened her mouth, triggering a coughing fit. "I can't reach."

There were still inches between their fingers as Olive reached out with her free hand, but Westie had nowhere left to go. There were no more boulders between them to grab hold of.

"Olive, you need to listen to me," Westie said, her voice rising over the rush of water. "When I tell you to let go of the branch, I need you to do just that, you hear? The water is shallow where you are. Your feet will touch the bottom. As soon as you let go of the branch, I want you to leap for my hand. I'll catch you. Do you understand?"

Olive was able to focus long enough to nod her head. Westie nodded too. She leaned farther toward the girl. One good jump and Olive would be in her grasp.

"Okay, now, look at my eyes," Westie said. When Olive's gaze met hers, she saw a scared little girl, not the monster she'd seen in the field with all those dead animals. Westie smiled for reassurance, even though she had little faith in her plan. "Are you ready?" Olive's fear seemed to ebb at the sight of Westie's smile. She nodded again.

Just as Westie was about to tell her to jump, Olive cried, "Look out!"

Westie glanced back, heart in her throat, mouth opened into a silent scream, as she saw a fallen tree barreling toward her on the water's surface. There was no time to avoid it; she didn't even have time to try before the trunk hit her with the force of a steam train.

Though shallow in most parts, the river swallowed Westie down into its black frothy maw, chewing her up on the rocks below. The light tumbled in front of her eyes as she was washed in the current. Clawing at the endless wall of water, she was sure she'd met her end until something tugged at her skirts and she felt herself being dragged to less abrasive waters. When she was in the calm, she looked up to find the dog, his wet coat showing off every rib. He released her skirt from his mouth and began to bark. Westie hugged the dog to her chest as she struggled to catch her breath.

And then she remembered Olive.

The spot where the girl had been was now just a wrinkle on the surface.

Westie stumbled along the shore, her dress like a sack of rocks weighing her down. The dog, as if knowing exactly what she was looking for, hopped along the shore in a happy display of barks and tail wags, leading her directly to Olive's body, which had washed to shore and caught in the rocks.

"No, no, no." Westie fell to her knees beside the girl. There was no blood, just a few scratches. Westie tried to pump the water from the girl's lungs like Alistair had once done to her when the weight of her machine had pulled her down to the bottom of a pond they'd been swimming in, but it was no use.

The girl was gone.

Westie's hand shook. She wanted to bolt from the scene and go back to where things made sense. Only she wasn't sure where that place was anymore. She crouched beside the Sacramento River, feeling hot even though the river water was nothing more than melted snow flowing down Shasta Mountain. Thin saliva filled the space under her tongue, and she tasted the salt of sickness. She washed the bloody scratches on her hand and squeezed it into a fist to stop the shaking.

She had to do something, tell someone, but if she went to Alistair or Nigel, they wouldn't believe it had been an accident. She'd have to keep it a secret. But that didn't sit right either. There were plenty of secrets in her closet, but this one was too big to keep inside, for as she'd learned when she was young, guilt had teeth, and it ate folks up if they didn't know how to tame it.

She bundled her knees to her chest and cried a good long time. When the last of her tears were shed, she got up and walked back toward her horse, back toward Rogue City.

Westie had snuck into the house and changed out of her wet clothes without Nigel or Alistair noticing. She stood at the top of the stairs, with the dog she'd rescued nuzzling against her leg. He had to be touching her, as if she were a dream that he feared would flitter away. A search party had been organized, reminding her of the morning after Isabelle disappeared. It had been only four hours since she'd knelt beside Olive at the river. The sun hadn't even set, but after what had happened to Isabelle, people were on edge and not taking any chances.

When Nigel passed below, he stopped and looked up at her. Déjà vu, they called it in France. Her heart began to race. He came to the top of the stairs and looked at the dog, an eyebrow raised with questions.

"I rescued him," she said. He only nodded. The tension between them was unmistakable. They were both quiet for a moment. She couldn't take it any longer, so she asked, "What's happening?" because that was what someone innocent would say.

"Olivia Fairfield is missing."

A proper lady would have said, *That's awful,* or *What can I do to help?* She didn't have it in her. Nigel wouldn't have believed the act anyway.

Her feet fidgeted beneath her skirt as Nigel watched her. She felt as though her face were a scripture of all her sins.

"I'll bring news when I find out more," he said as if she'd asked, then turned on his heels and left.

Westie's knees bobbed. She waited, worrying about the search. Hours later the party was back. She rushed onto the catwalk to see. Dirt-smeared men beat their hats against their legs, raising clouds of dust. They lumbered around, exhausted and possibly saddened by the search. It was obvious by their gloomy expressions that the girl had been found.

Alistair walked in, looked up at her, and nodded, then retreated to the great room. It hurt her that he hadn't come to see her since the fight, but that was the least of her problems. Nigel was the last to come through the door. He marched up the stairs.

Westie's stomach roiled with anticipation.

"What happened?" she asked. "Did you find her?"

He wiped at his stubble. It was the longest she'd ever seen his beard. "Yes, she drowned in the river."

Westie's hand went to her mouth, which she hoped gave a look of shock instead of the lack of it.

"How did it happen?"

"I'll tell you more about it later, but first let's sit. I need to talk to you."

Fear curled in Westie's stomach as she wondered if word had already gotten back to him about the robbery and the missing bottle of Brave Maker.

Nigel led her down the catwalk to the library. It had been her favorite place to play when she was young. She used to run through that room as a child, squealing war cries with her sword in hand while Nigel hobbled after her yelling, "Good God, Westie, no running with blades!"

The memory warmed her for a moment before she remembered why they were there.

They sat down on a bench beneath a shelf of books. It took Nigel a while to speak. He kept starting and stopping. Finally he dedicated himself to words that sounded rehearsed.

"Westie, I'm very sorry for the things I said to you this morning." She didn't care about that. She was more concerned about what had happened during the search, but she let him continue. "I mean, I'm upset that you went behind my back and stole the Fairfields' gold without confiding in me first, but I'm not upset that you took it. You at least *tried* to do something. You were right. I should've done more, and now Isabelle is dead. I won't make the same mistake twice. The Fairfields will get what's coming to them. Whatever it takes, whatever schemes there are to come up with, we'll find a way."

She sat up straight, his words taking some of the edge off her frazzled nerves. "You really mean that?"

"Yes, I really mean that. But we will do it quietly. Don't make any decisions that might draw attention to yourself."

Oh, right, she thought, like breaking into the general store and stealing booze, or a girl dying while in her care.

"There's something else I need to say," he continued, looking down at his boots. "You stood at the table clutching the doll you shared with your late brother, and all I could think about were the creatures and Emma, and how you taking that money had ruined everything. I didn't stop to consider that you have had to face the killers of your family every day since they arrived in town—you even danced with them at the ball. If it were me, I most certainly would have killed them by now. You've been strong and I've been terribly insensitive. Can you ever forgive me?"

Westie's throat tightened. She picked at a loose thread on her skirt. "It's nothing. Let's just forget about it."

"Very well," he said, looking relieved.

After an uncomfortable silence, Westie asked, "When's the funeral?"

"After the investigation."

Westie dropped her hands, and her eyes and mouth opened in astonished O shapes. "What investigation?"

"The mayor seems to think the drowning looks suspicious. The girl was far from where she typically played. It's possible she was lured to the river, though personally I think she was playing on the old bridge and fell in. More children have fallen into that river than I care to count. But the mayor is a stubborn man. Can you believe he looked me right in the eye and said, 'Folks in this town seem to have it out for the Fairfields,' as if I killed the child? It's madness around here. Someone even broke into the general store while people were in church!"

Westie's guts felt full of acid. If the mayor was investigating Olive's death, that meant he'd be out there looking for clues, and it wasn't like she'd taken the time to clean up after herself. There was no telling what messes she could've left behind that would lead the mayor right to her doorstep.

"What's missing from the store?" she said in a tremulous voice.

"I don't know. The shopkeeper is going through his inventory. I'm sure I'll hear more in the morning."

Westie's thoughts spun in circles. She'd left the bottle of Brave Maker somewhere at the scene but couldn't remember where.

She reached over, gave Nigel's hand a squeeze, and stood. "I promise I won't do anything stupid till you figure out how to go over the mayor's head."

He smiled. "Good. Where are you off to?"

"I've got a few things I need to take care of."

* * *

Westie spent most of the night combing the forest for the bottle of whiskey and any other evidence she might have left behind. Retracing her steps, she hoped her new dog would be of some use. As the hours passed, it turned out Lucky—the name she'd given him—was not the retriever she'd hoped for. If the bottle was out there, someone would've found it by then, and in the morning after the shopkeeper finished cataloging his inventory and found only a bottle of Brave Maker missing, she'd wake to someone pounding on the door and the angry voices of a lynch mob.

She shook out her hands, trying to calm herself. If she left town, it would only make her look guilty. She had to stay and face whatever was coming to her. They couldn't convict her on a bottle of stolen whiskey just because it was her favorite brand.

What little sleep she got that night was plagued by nightmares. She dreamed that the mayor and the Fairfields had come to the house and banged at the door in the early hours of the morning, and that when she opened the door, a firing squad waited behind them, ready to send her to her maker.

The next morning she couldn't shake the nausea that the nightmare had left her with. She tried to ignore it by nursing the bloody, matted mess that was her new pup back to health. She fed him chunks of Jezebel's meat mixture. Jezebel came sniffing around when she smelled her food. Westie would've been more concerned about the dog and the chupacabra's first encounter had Nigel not stuffed Jezebel so full of raw meat, she was as plump as Myrtle Grey.

Westie scrubbed the dog in the tub. When she heard someone

pounding on the door downstairs, her back stiffened. Her eyes darted around the room, looking for escape. They'd come for her. She thought about fleeing out the window and shimmying down the lattice on the side of the house. Then she thought again how guilty that would make her look, and so she decided to stay and deny having anything to do with Olive's death.

But what if they saw the manzanita tree, and the evidence of the dog? They'd find her bathing him and know she'd been at the scene.

She heard footsteps making their way upstairs. She closed her eyes and leaned her head against the tub. When the door to the washroom opened, she tried to remove any traces of guilt from her face.

She looked up to meet her accusers. But it wasn't the mayor, or the Fairfields, or a firing squad.

"Costin?"

He leaned against the door, clad in black as usual, his glistening black hair falling over his shoulders. He wore a bowler hat with his lace shroud tucked into the brim.

"What are you doing here?" she asked, not sure whether to feel relieved or suspicious.

He pushed off the door, gliding toward her. "The door was unlocked. I tried knocking, but no one answered."

Westie glared at Jezebel, who'd been too infatuated with the dog to notice the intruder.

Costin looked at the dog. "I see you've picked up Nigel's affinity for strays."

"He was hurt."

"I see that."

Westie didn't know what to do with her hands, so she scrubbed the dog even though he was clean.

"What happened to your hand?" he asked.

The edges of the cuts caused by the bramble thorns had wrinkled from being in the water. They were deep and would probably need stitches. "I was helping in the garden."

He nodded but didn't look convinced.

Costin knelt beside the tub, his skin as white as curd next to hers. He grabbed the bucket of fresh water to rinse the suds from the dog's back. The dog instantly took to the vampire despite him being a predator, and wagged his tail, splashing Westie.

"Would you like to know what I was doing last night?" he asked.

"Not particularly."

He went on as if she hadn't spoken. "I was hired by the mayor to find evidence of foul play in the death of Olivia Fairfield."

Westie sucked in a breath. "Well," she said with a tremor in her voice she couldn't help, "don't leave me in suspense. Did you find anything?"

Costin looked like he was trying not to smile.

"What happened in the woods, Westie, with that little girl?" he asked.

She stopped breathing, mouth going dry.

"Can't say I know what you mean. I was at the docks yesterday morning."

"You know, the Native Americans get all the credit for their tracking abilities, but I'm an excellent hunter myself. I see things clumsy men wouldn't notice. That's why the mayor asked for my help. I'm good at reading people too, and you, my love, are hiding something."

Westie pressed her lips together to keep them from trembling. Twin tears raced down her cheeks.

Costin reached out, took her chin in his cold palm, and brushed away a tear with his thumb. The gesture was so foreign she forgot herself a moment and leaned into his touch. She nuzzled against his hand as Lucky had her leg—a wounded animal starved for affection.

He said, "I saw the hoofprints in the woods where Isabelle's body was found." Westie pulled away from him then. She leaned against the tub, mindlessly petting Lucky. "I also found a manzanita tree."

Her machine, rapidly tapping the tub, kept time with her heart. The gears had begun to grind after being in water. She'd need to oil it soon. "Ain't that something?" she said dumbly. "I thought all the manzanita in the forest burned up in the lightning fires. They burn hotter than other trees, you know."

He went on, ignoring her babbling. "So many dead animals, and fresh dog feces, yet no dog."

A miserable sound stumbled out of her mouth, barely audible. Her head swam with lies she could tell, but none that Costin would believe.

"I also found a bottle of Brave Maker at the scene. Your favorite brand—imagine that," he said. Her heart blasted at her ribs. He was playing with her, she knew, waiting for her to break. She had never been the type to balk under interrogation—and she had been interrogated a time or two in her day—but she was ready to break then. She wanted to tell Costin everything like she would a priest. "There was also a child's hair clip in the field, expensive by the looks of it, and right next to the bottle. I thought it a funny thing seeing those two items beside each other. A little girl out in the field getting drunk and killing animals." He shook his head. "Children these days."

Westie raised her head to look at him. He was smiling. A cruel, amused smile. He enjoyed watching her squirm.

His black eyes stayed on hers as he continued. "Then, when I saw two sets of footprints in the field heading toward the river, I realized the girl wasn't alone. Olivia's prints were easy. The other set was more confusing. Was the set of prints from an older child? Or were they from a little man? Imagine my surprise when I realized the larger set of prints had the boot heel of a woman's shoe. Once I was closer to the river, I picked up on a scent I knew very well. . . ." Costin looked down at Westie and smiled.

"It was an accident. She fell into the river and I tried to save her." The words tumbled out before she could stop them. "You have to believe me. As much as Olive deserved a good swat on the hide for what she did to those animals, I didn't kill her. I wouldn't do such a thing." She slapped the water with the flat of her hand, getting soap in her eye. "Why are you smiling? A little girl is dead. That seems mean even for you."

Costin tried to remove his smirk but failed. "Oh, I'm not smiling because a girl is dead. That really is tragic. But you humans, you think those who are different from you, those you call *creatures* as though we're some subspecies, are no better than animals. You think we kill for pleasure, that we are incapable of love. If I smile, it's only because I enjoy watching humans behave badly."

"I'm not behaving badly!"

He waved it off. "It's of no concern to me. You know I'll forgive you anything. But I doubt Nigel and Alistair will be as generous."

Costin stood. He reached toward Westie. She thought he would take her face into his hand again. She would have let him. Instead he took the towel from her lap and dried his hands.

She was on the verge of hysterics. "I'm in trouble, Costin. Nigel will think I killed Olive when the mayor tells him about the bottle and the set of prints from a woman's shoe. Once he learns the only thing missing from the store is the bottle of Brave Maker, my life is ruined."

Costin gently moved the hair from Westie's face. "They won't find that bottle or the prints, or the manzanita tree. I've dealt with the evidence. And besides, a bottle of Brave Maker wasn't the only thing missing from the store."

"What? But—"

"Turns out the thief took many things: horse grain, bedrolls, cigarette makings. Things an outlaw would take. What's peculiar is he left gold on the counter, enough to pay for the things he stole and the damage to the building." He dropped the towel beside her. "Oh, by the way, the investigation came to a close this morning, and Olive's death was ruled an accident," he said before walking out.

* * *

The first day of autumn fell on the same day as Olive's funeral service. Fall was a beautiful time of year in Rogue City, everything bright and full of color. The maple trees surrounding the church boneyard looked like paintings of fire.

The entire town—except for the creatures—showed up for the occasion, even though the Fairfields were strangers to most. Olive's death had somehow made her everyone's little girl.

Westie stood behind the crowd away from the others, observing. Nigel wore black. Alistair's soft leather dress coat fit snugly to his form, a rebellion when the current men's fashion could double as sacks to hold grain. He looked more handsome than she'd ever seen him before.

James and Lavina wore expensive clothes to mourn in, while Cain and Hubbard dressed as common as street folk.

James picked at his nails, staring at the ground. Hubbard fell apart, dissolved to tears, not caring what others might say. He made sucking noises, unable to catch his breath until eventually he dropped his head into his hands and buckled to his knees in the stinking mud.

Lavina was less theatrical, except for her dress, which was a production of its own, black lace ruffles and far more low-cut than most would find appropriate for a funeral. The tops of her breasts jiggled each time she moved, catching men's eyes all around. Her face was pale from powder, yet the skin of her chest and the tops of her breasts were golden brown and looked like the leather skulls of Siamese twins fighting for air.

Not a tear was shed by Lavina for her daughter while in the

public eye. In fact, it was the public that cried. Other than James, Nigel, Alistair, and Westie, there was not a dry eye to be found.

All the sniffling, breathing, whimpers—the sounds of mourning—filled Westie's ears. No one had cried for Westie's family. No one had cried for the little girl who'd lost her arm.

Her head throbbed, whether with guilt or annoyance she didn't know. What she did know was that she needed to leave before some mystery emotion spilled out of her in a public scene. She pulled the mourning lily the church had pinned to her bodice from her dress and stepped on it, twisting the toe of her boot until the white flower turned brown. No one noticed as she walked away.

# Thirty-One

The bright smells of autumn faded the moment Westie stepped into the Tight Ship. The barkeep saw her and immediately reached for the bottle of Brave Maker.

"I'll have a sarsaparilla," she said.

He looked at her as though her marbles had fallen onto the floor, his hand hovering over the bottle of whiskey.

"Is my hearing going?" he said.

"Don't give me sass, Heck. Not today," she said, dejected.

"Suit yourself." He poured her drink into a metal cup.

She sat at the bar. As she looked around, she noticed there were no creatures in the saloon except for a troll passed out on the floor.

"Where's everyone at?" she asked.

"Seems to be a bug going around," Heck said. His skin had a green tint to it. He didn't look too good himself.

She took small sips to draw out her time. There was to be a pot-luck after the service. Westie had no intention of going.

When someone sat down beside her, she didn't think anything of it until she heard the voice. Her back went as straight as if she'd been skewered.

"Red-eye," Lavina said to the barkeep.

"That's an awful strong drink for a proper lady," Heck said.

"Pour me one too, bar-dog. Make it a double," said Hubbard, his eyes still red and swollen from crying. He'd taken a seat on the other side of Westie while she'd been distracted by Lavina. Westie's gaze darted around the mirror behind the bar, looking for escape routes.

"Believe me," Lavina said, "I can handle it on a day like this one."

The barkeep poured Lavina's drink and slid it down the bar, where Lavina caught it before it bumped Westie's cup.

"You left early," she said to Westie.

Westie let go of her cup to find she'd dented the metal with her machine. She was suddenly in the mood for something stronger. "Didn't think anyone was aware."

"I'm very much aware of you, Westie."

The way Lavina said it, like she knew all of Westie's secrets, made her skin itch.

Hubbard made burping and hiccuping sounds beside her but didn't speak. He could've sat next to his wife, but they chose to box her in. Westie flexed her metal fingers, not sure who she should be more worried about.

Lavina gazed around the room, letting the silence between them simmer until it felt good and awkward before wrinkling her nose and saying, "It's nice to come in here without creatures around. I don't know how you can stomach sitting and drinking with all those filthy animals."

Westie thought about Costin. He'd risked everything to hide the evidence of her thievery and her possible link as a witness to Olive's death. Though Westie was guilty of prejudice herself when it came to creatures, it made her mad to hear it from Lavina.

Westie turned and looked Lavina straight in her flat brown eyes. "They're not filthy animals. They have the right to be on this earth just like the rest of us. They lived on this land for thousands of years, minding their own business, not hurting anyone. It belonged to them and the natives. Most folks never even knew they existed. Settlers saw an opportunity and took everything, killing anything or anyone that got in their way. Finally the creatures got sick of it and fought back."

Lavina took a sip of her whiskey and nodded slowly. "Yes, the creature war. But do you really think those beings are civilized?"

Westie wanted to hurl her drink at the woman. *Civilized.* Lavina didn't know the meaning of the word. Civilized people didn't hole up in cabins, preying on unsuspecting families in need.

"Banshees are so empathetic they can sense death before it ever happens, and they feel that pain so deep, so intense, that they can't help but cry out. Werewolf daddies never leave their children, not for any reason. They mate for life and take care of their families. And trolls"—she looked over at the troll, flies buzzing around him, so drunk he'd shit himself—"okay, I reckon trolls don't count. They're not much good for anything. But vampires, all they need is blood to survive. They don't even need to kill to feed. How's that for civilized? Can you say the same thing about yourself? If you ask me, the only real 'creatures' in this place are human."

Lavina squeezed her lips together. In the hazy light her face looked like a rumpled shirt, drooping and creased.

"I know what you think of me—of us." Lavina glanced at Hubbard. He had twisted in his chair to face Westie and was spinning the knife Heck had been using to cut limes on the bar. Westie kept her machine loose in case she needed to take it from him. "I was sad to hear such things, but you heard what the mayor said about Olivia finding those earrings in the forest where she played."

*Lies!* Westie wanted to shout, but Lavina couldn't know Olive had admitted the Fairfields were killers, or she'd have to admit she'd been with the girl before her death.

Lavina continued, "I do fear that accusation has tainted our reputation with the sheriff. He's been nosing about our business."

"Why don't you just go on and leave, then?"

"I've spent too much time with Emma. I want to see it through. Nigel may not like us, or even trust us, but he needs our money. I've seen that desperate hunger in his eyes."

Westie wondered how Lavina planned to invest without money. They must've discovered their missing fortune by now. Olive knew; she would've told them. Or maybe she'd been telling the truth when she said she hadn't told them. Westie couldn't be certain.

While she chewed it over in her head, Lavina said, "You remind me of someone I used to know. Doesn't she remind you of someone we used to know, Hubbard?"

"Can't say I remember her too much," he said.

Westie tensed, biting the inside of her cheek, tasting blood. Hubbard picked at his teeth with the knife.

Westie mashed her face into a scowl. "How exactly do I remind you of this person you used to know?" she asked Lavina.

Lavina chuckled, though her laughter quickly faded. "She was clever. She was a fighter, that girl." She reached out and touched Westie's hair. "The resemblance is astonishing. You even have the same color hair and eyes as her."

The muscles in Westie's neck tightened. She wanted to swat the woman's hand away. Instead she continued to crush her cup with her machine until liquid spilled out and it was no more than a twisted piece of metal.

The suspicion in Lavina's voice left no doubt that she knew exactly who Westie was. Westie looked into Lavina's eyes again and saw the recognition, though neither was willing to out herself. "What ended up happening to the girl you used to know?" Westie asked.

Lavina turned back to her drink. "Oh, I don't know. She'd lost her family, and her mind, I suppose. I'd like to think she found a new family . . . a better family." She slid a look at Westie from the corner of her eyes. "I'd like to think she moved on to enjoy the rest of her life and left the past behind her."

Westie tossed the metal remains of her cup over the bar into the trash bin. "Well, if the girl is anything like me, I imagine moving on with her life isn't likely." She stood and put her coin on the bar. "And anyone who crosses her ought to be scared," she said, and walked out.

Westie kicked at rocks as she headed toward the livery yard to get her horse, the conversation she'd just had with Lavina replaying in her head. The Fairfields obviously knew who she was, so there was no sense in pretending anymore. She could've told Lavina and Hubbard exactly what she thought about them, or maybe even asked questions. Being that her hands were tied and there was nothing she could've done to have them arrested, they might've even given her answers.

A knot of voices grew louder the closer she got to the livery yard. Turning the corner, she saw a line of creatures waiting outside Doc Flannigan's office. Fae were the only known healers in the creature world, but they were extinct, and since creatures and the Native Americans rarely got along, the doctor was their only option.

On the opposite side of the street, humans gathered in buildings, still in their mourning clothes, watching the creatures from windows.

Westie followed the line of creatures. Children wilted in their mothers' arms, the color drained from their faces. The sheriff was out there too, in the muck of it. She'd always heard him talk about how creatures and humans had no business living together, but there he was, helping an elderly warg lady to the front of the line.

Vampires milled around without their shrouds due to the overcast day. There was one in front of her bent at the waist, vomiting blood into the street. Westie recognized him as one of Costin's guards, the big vamp with the lazy eye who she'd choked with her machine.

"Hey," she said to him.

His eyes sprang open and he took a step backward.

She held her hands up. "I'm not here to hurt you. I'm just looking for Costin is all."

Tight-lipped and wary, he pointed toward the end of the line.

Westie headed in that direction but stopped when she saw the werewolf innkeeper, her pup draped across her arms like a wet shirt. When Westie approached, the wolf woman growled.

"It's all right," Westie said, slowly pulling her last gold coin from her pocket. "I just want to show him something."

The innkeeper's face was taut with suspicion, but her shoulders relaxed and she gave Westie a curt nod.

"Want to see a trick?" Westie said to the boy. His face was flushed, but his lips were pale as bone. He looked at her without turning his head.

Taking the coin in her machine, Westie began rolling it across the knuckles of her metal fingers, back and forth in both directions, faster and faster. The boy sat up, mesmerized by the trick, a smile forming on his dry, peeling lips.

Westie smiled too, smoothing down the sweaty hair that stuck out in all directions on his head, and handed the coin to him. She wasn't sure if there was magic left in the gold, or if that was even how it worked, but it was worth a try. "That's a lucky coin. Keep it close now, you hear? Don't ever let it go."

When Westie turned to go look for Costin, she found him only feet away, watching her.

"What's happening?" she asked as she approached him. His skin was the color of stone, his face and hair wet with perspiration.

"A brief illness. Creatures get sick too, you know." It was true, but they never got sick all at once. Every species of creature was built differently, and each had their own afflictions. Westie couldn't think of a single illness that affected them all the same—until now.

She looked up into the sky, her gaze sailing across the dome. There were several large holes in the membrane where the sky seemed to shine brighter.

"But there are rumors going around," Costin said, "about the Wintu spirits being angry and letting the dome collapse. Humans are afraid. One of my guards heard some men in the saloon talking about how they should start killing off creatures before we have the chance to kill them. Some of my fellow creatures believe the humans have found a way to poison us."

"That's ridiculous."

"Oh? Do you know something I don't?"

Westie didn't want to tell him the truth about magic disappearing. If that information found its way to the wrong ears, it could have devastating consequences. She had to make people believe the Wintu were still in control.

"Spread your own rumors. People already know that settlers once made a deal with the Wintu. Tell them as long as folks stayed out of the Wintu's sacred sites, the Wintu would protect this town from creatures." Costin rolled his eyes and started to speak, but Westie pressed on. "People aren't keeping up their end of the bargain.

Convince them to stop mining and leave Devil's Crag, and I'll make sure the Wintu keep the dome up."

"Is that the truth?" he asked.

*No*, she thought, *but it should buy enough time for Nigel to get Emma up and running before magic disappears for good.*

Westie tried to roll her emotions in a ball and put them away. If Costin saw the anguish she felt, he'd know she was hiding something. She pulled the handkerchief from her bodice to wipe his forehead. "Yes," she said.

"Careful." Costin took her by the hand, caressing her fingers before kissing her knuckles. "You don't want to get too close."

"I'm not worried about falling ill," she said.

Everything about him moved slowly from sickness, even his smile. "Perhaps not, but you should be worried about falling in love."

Westie laughed for a brief moment before sadness choked off the sound. "I need to go." She put a hand to his face and wiped a bead of sweat from his cheek. He was warm to the touch. "You take care now."

In front of Nigel's mansion, Wintu horses stood lipping at the tall grass in the yard. Their riders were clustered beneath trees. The Wintu were a stoic people, but their faces looked more serious than she'd ever seen them before.

They nodded as she passed. Bena and Big Fish stood with Nigel on the porch, deep in conversation. They stopped talking when they saw her.

"The magic, it's getting worse, isn't it?" she asked.

Bena touched Westie's hair, twisting at her locks. It was a tactic she'd used to soothe her as a child, but it wasn't working. "It's not as bad as it seems," Bena assured her.

Westie looked at Big Fish for a second opinion, but it was difficult to read her expression through her wrinkled flesh.

"It seems pretty damn bad to me," Westie said. "Have you seen the creatures lately? They're sick. And now rumors are being spread. There's talk of an attack. Folks might start killing off creatures first if magic doesn't get around to it. We need to find a way to fix the dome."

Nigel didn't look too good either, but Westie knew it was because of worry and lack of sleep. "With all the mining in the iron hills and the prospectors taking gold from Devil's Crag, magic is a little scarce in this area at the moment. We'll find a way to get it back," he said.

Panic filled Westie until she felt as if she might suffocate in it. "You need to use the Fairfields' gold to buy the parts you need to finish Emma."

Nigel shook his head. "Everyone selling copper knows that I'm broke. I've traded off everything I had of any value. And the authorities know the Fairfields' gold has been stolen. They'll be looking for anyone making large purchases with raw gold."

Westie thought about Costin's gray skin, the dark rings around his eyes. He'd saved her life more than once, and there was no way she would let him die over her vendetta against the Fairfields. If she hadn't taken their gold, Nigel might have already had the investment money and the parts he needed to complete Emma by now.

She held on to the back of a rocking chair on the porch to keep steady, but crushed it with her machine instead and stumbled backward. One of the Wintu men caught her before she could fall. It took all the fight in her to keep from crying.

"Then I'll sell myself to the blood brothel to get the money. I'll do anything. Just please save them."

Nigel grabbed her by the shoulders, shaking her until her eyes cleared. "You will do no such thing," he said. When he saw the shocked expression on her face, he took a step back. "I'm sorry. But please, Westie, don't go to the vampires. The Wintu have this under control. They plan to shorten the perimeters of the ward to exclude the lake and the crag. With the crag unprotected, people will stop mining. There are dwarves in those hills who were always attacking humans before the ward went up."

"It's too bad all the water creatures died off from pollutants," Westie said bitterly. "Folks never would've survived the boat trip it took to get to the crag in the first place."

"I don't want you to worry," Nigel said. "If things start looking dire, we'll move the creatures north where there's hardly any human presence and magic is dense. The north has a thriving creature population."

"These aren't wild creatures you're talking about transplanting, Nigel. Some have been in Rogue City since the ward went up. They're just as pampered as the rest of us. And what about the ones who can't survive the colder climate in the north? The vamps will be fine, but elves are cold-blooded. There's no way they'll make it through the winter. I doubt many would even survive the journey there. Have you seen how weak they are?"

Nigel said, "You know I won't let anything happen to the creatures. You leave their safety to me and leave the magic to the Wintu. Right now I just need you to stay out of the way. I don't need to be worrying about you too."

Westie tapped her foot, arms crossed over her chest, trying to hide the fact that it hurt her to know he thought of her as being in the way.

She nodded, tossing aside the remnants of the rocking chair still clutched in her metal grip, and walked away.

# Thirty-Two

Jezebel and Lucky tore through the house to meet Westie at the door. She gave them each a pat on the head in greeting and went straight to her room to pack, stuffing her clothes into a saddlebag as she prepared to leave with the Wintu.

She had almost finished packing, feeling confident about her decision to leave, when she heard the door creak open and then closed behind her.

"What are you doing?" Alistair's metal voice said.

Westie continued to pack garments while Alistair stood beside her, pulling clothes out of her bag and putting them back into her wardrobe.

"Stop that." She swatted his hand away, her face shades of red when he refused to let go of her knickers.

"I'll stop when you answer me."

She tossed her extra stockings to the bed. "I'm going to go stay with Bena."

"Why?" Alistair asked.

"That's none of your concern."

"Then I suppose you don't want these back."

He held her knickers to his front as if he were sizing them.

She let out a mortified squeal. "Give those back."

"No." He jumped onto her bed and over it, his boots landing hard on the wood floor.

"Alistair . . ." The metal in her knuckles ground together when she made a fist.

"An answer to my question would be lovely." He made her knickers dance, which only deepened her humiliation.

She sighed, finally giving in to his taunting. "I'm going to leave with the Wintu and say I'm staying with Bena."

"Where are you really going?"

"To keep an eye on the Fairfields. Nigel wants me to sit at home, doing nothing so he doesn't have to worry about me, but I can't do that. I need to be out from under his eye."

Alistair tossed her knickers into a corner. "How will I find you if I need you?"

"I'll check in from time to time." She lifted her saddlebag, hoisting it over her shoulder. If she left now, she could get to the Wintu before they left. Nigel wouldn't make a scene of her leaving in front of Bena and Big Fish.

His eyes were full of an emotion she couldn't place, the mask making a whistling sound when he took a breath. "Please don't go."

She'd imagined him saying those very words every time she left to go hunt cannibals. The power they held was almost enough to make her stay. But it was too late. Tears welled up in her eyes. "I'm sorry, Alley. I have to."

She turned her back on him and headed for the door. Just as she was about to grip the handle, something flashed in the corner of her eye, nearly missing her head as it struck the door. She yelped and jumped back, looking around at the floor to see what it was.

"Did you just throw something at—" Her voice snagged in her throat when she saw the metal mask at her feet. She took a step back and slowly turned to face him. Her steady heartbeat became a stutter.

Alistair stood before her barefaced. She stared, ogling him exactly the way he hated from others. She knew it was him and yet she had to focus, collecting his features and putting them together like puzzle pieces. When it all came together and she saw the Alley she remembered, the Alley she'd thought was gone forever, her heart started with a sudden wrench like one of Nigel's rusted inventions after being oiled.

He looked just as she remembered, as if he'd been kept frozen beneath the mask for the last three years. She dropped her bag and went to him, reached out with tentative fingers, touching his skin, his cheeks, chin, lips. No, he wasn't exactly the same, she realized. The line of his jaw was more pronounced. He'd lost that soft, childlike skin and replaced it with tougher adult skin. She could feel a hint of stubble. He was a man now.

He'd tried to grow a beard a time or two when he was younger, but it had looked more like molded tufts on a block of cheese. He could wear a proper beard if he wanted to now. She moved away from his whiskers to explore the rest of his face. She touched the lines of his scars, raised silver dots from stitch marks. He smiled, exposing his teeth. His mouth had been her favorite part of him. He had beautiful teeth, with the slightest overlap in the very front that made his lips look fuller.

"Alley!" She touched the scars on his neck, his jawbone, ears. He grabbed her wrists, holding her hands in front of him. She could've easily slipped out of his grip, but the way he looked at her, his lips parted, eyes focused, made her want to be exactly where she was. She thought he was trying to speak. Then the most unexpected thing happened.

He kissed her.

She had imagined what kissing Alistair would be like a million times since abandoning the notion that boys were wretched, smelly things. Nothing could've prepared her for the truth of it.

His touch on the side of her cheek was all the persuasion needed for her lips to fall apart and let him in. Her eyes melted shut as he twisted his fingers in her hair and the fabric of her dress, tugging and soothing with the violent tenderness of a long-awaited kiss. They took turns stealing the breath from each other and giving it back.

With each touch of his lips, her dead heart was galvanized as though being woken from centuries of black sleep. His kiss was alchemy, for she felt golden, illuminated. When they finally parted, she was left boneless and gasping.

She felt dizzy and half out of her mind. Her body swayed, and yet she wanted more. She wondered how she could ever have mistaken a vampire's bite for love.

He watched her, expecting something, so she said, "That's it? That's all you got?"

His smile was enough to knock her down. She was glad when he pulled her back into his arms, holding her up. She felt a difference in their second kiss, an urgency that hadn't been there before. She knew she could go too far. She wanted to go too far. But Alistair stopped her. She wasn't ready for it to be over when he finally pulled away.

She sighed when his eyes steadied on hers, and his lips flattened, becoming somber. She wanted to forget all seriousness and go back to kissing. She wanted to crack the safety barrier between them, claw at his chest, and crawl beneath his skin and wear him like a suit. It was only when they kissed that she could hear his true voice.

When Alistair lifted his right hand, folded his fingers, and put them on his heart, she realized some things were better than kissing.

*I love you,* his sign said. His hooded eyes, his loopy half smile with lips as soft as a puppy's tummy, matched the gesture.

"I love you too, Alley." A tear trickled down her cheek. She swatted at it like she would a fly. "I've always loved you."

She wanted to live in that moment with him for all eternity, away from the Fairfields, away from her memories. For the first time since arriving in the West, she felt like she could finally abandon the past and live for the day and even plan for the future.

Creaking floorboards outside her door roused her from her thoughts.

"Did you hear that?" she said.

Alistair nodded. *"I'm sure it was a maid,"* he signed.

"All the maids have left."

He crossed the room and reached for his mask, fussing with the clasps behind his head while she went to investigate.

Opening the door to an empty hallway, Westie looked both ways. There was no one.

# Thirty-Three

That night Westie sat beneath the stars on a flat patch of sand next to the river. It was one of the Wintu's most sacred sites. A bonfire was built, its flames reaching up toward the dome, pointing light at all its flaws. The men wore eagle-feather bustles, beaded breechclouts, and headpieces called roaches in the shape of Mohawks, made of porcupine quills and deer-tail hair.

There was drumming and singing. Some voices were a low chant, while others reached a high, desperate pitch, giving Westie chills down her arms. She watched in awe as beautiful broad faces and bronze bodies moved in ways steeped in thousands of years of tradition.

She'd been to only one other healing ceremony before, when Bena had found her in the woods after she'd escaped from the cabin. The stump of her arm had been infected, and she'd lost a lot of blood.

Big Fish, clad in full regalia, had used a fan made of feathers, blown smoke in her face, and used words Westie didn't understand to bless the ceremony. When the music had started, she'd felt the pain in her arm move into the center of her body. She'd screamed as it tried to force itself through her rib cage, as if something above her had reached into her chest to grab it.

The agony had caused her to pass out not long after, but the next day her fever had broken, the pain was gone, and her arm had started to mend. She had been welcomed into the tribe after that.

Other native tribes in the surrounding areas had joined tonight's ceremony. With magic disappearing, the Wintu needed all the help they could get. Big Fish was the only one who could control the amount of magic needed to build a ward, but such a concentrated amount of magic required a full tribe to lift her request to the spirits.

Several men from the other tribes walked past Westie wearing dangerous frowns. She fought the urge to give one right back. Instead she looked past them, at the fire, knowing how difficult it must be for them to see anything beyond her white skin; the same skin as those who'd cut their tribe numbers in half.

The dancing stopped and the song fizzled into a low murmur as Big Fish entered the circle. After blessing the ceremony, she began the ritual. Back before settlers brought their violence and illness to the Americas, magic had been limitless. It was said that early Wintu could read minds, conjure fire from the air, and even fly. Now that there were so few people left in the tribe and magic was weak, they could only perform smaller feats like bringing rain to a drought, creating wards, and healing, in addition to their individual talents of talking to the earth—which Westie realized they could no longer do after seeing the dead plant in the foyer of Nigel's house.

Others in the tribe began to chant their prayers. Westie prayed too. She prayed mostly for forgiveness in the hopes that the spirits wouldn't hold her being there against the Wintu.

After the prayer, Bena sat beside her. She wore a basket cap and a beaded tunic, but nothing as elaborate as the rest of her tribe. They watched the ceremony in silence until the dancing resumed.

"What is your next plan?" Bena asked her.

"Concerning the Fairfields? I don't know. For now I'm just going to keep an eye out, make sure they don't hurt anyone. Nigel told me to stay out of the way."

"You are going to listen to him?"

"Don't look so surprised," Westie said, folding her knees to her chin. Now that it was cold out, she wished she'd worn the hunting attire Bena had given her after all. She hadn't wanted to offend anyone from the other tribes, so she'd worn a simple dress instead. The breeze coming off the river had found its way beneath her skirts, making her shiver, and she was too far away from the fire to feel its warmth. "I've made a mess of things. Maybe it's time to let Nigel figure it out. He's a brilliant man. I'm sure whatever he comes up with won't end up blowing up our faces."

Bena nodded without conviction. "He doesn't have your fire. You may not make the best decisions all the time, but at least you make them." Westie smiled. It was no wonder she and Bena had become such good friends over the years. They both shared an impulsive mind. "Nigel thinks we should be patient and wait for the Fairfields to slip up, but we are out of time," Bena continued. "He says people with secrets can't keep them hidden forever."

Bena's words triggered a memory. "No, they can't, can they?" Westie said. She stood up, brushing the dirt off the back of her dress. "Not unless they're keeping those secrets in an iron safe with three locks on it."

Bena frowned. "What are you talking about? You have that look in your eye."

"What look?"

"That terrifying glow you get when you have a plan."

"I saw Lavina put something in a safe at the mayor's office when we had our meeting. The safe had three locks. Doesn't that seem strange to you?"

"No," Bena said. "This is wild country and bandits aren't unheard of."

"If folks have something valuable, they keep it at the bank— Lavina should know that better than anyone after having her gold stolen. When you have a safe with three locks, that means you're hiding something. I need to get into that office."

"That's more like it," Bena said with one of her rare smiles.

The next morning Westie stood with Alistair in the great room of Nigel's house. The clank of metal echoed off the walls as Alistair rifled though Nigel's tools looking for something that could pry a lock from a safe.

"You do realize it's schemes like these that get you into trouble," Alistair said.

"I don't see how I could possibly mess things up worse than I already have."

He tossed a hammer to the side. "None of these will work. I'll go check Nigel's office."

"I'll go get the horses ready."

Westie went down to the barn. She was glad for the chore, needing to spend some of her nervous energy. She didn't like keeping secrets from Nigel, especially after what had happened when she took the Fairfields' gold. Perhaps he would have approved of them breaking into the mayor's office and might've even offered to help. On the off chance that he would forbid it, she thought it best they go alone. Besides, his faulty leg would only slow them down. What really worried her most was the uncertainty of what they'd find in the safe. What if it were just money? She pushed the thought aside and tried not to get her hopes up. The disappointment of such a discovery might be the last thread to break her.

She was lost in her own head when she heard the shuffling of feet on the ground behind her. Old habits got their grip on her and she spun around, expecting to see the Undying at her back with their grabby hands and snappy teeth. She relaxed when she saw it was only James.

"What are you doing here?" she said, trying to keep the pity she felt for him from showing on her face.

He wore a sloppy grin and held a bottle of Heck's moonshine in his hand. His hair stuck out at all angles. She almost didn't recognize him without his slick hair and expensive suits. Instead, he wore brown trousers, a rancher's plaid shirt, and scuffed boots.

"I come to help with the chores." Each word slurred into the next until it became a jumbled heap of sounds.

"What are you talking about? Or better yet, what in blazes are you wearing?"

"Oh, this?" he said, pointing to his shirt. One of his eyelids was so heavy he looked as if he were winking. "Trying on poverty to see how it fits."

He spun around in a slow circle so she could get a better look, but lost his footing and stumbled into her. She caught him before they both took a tumble.

"Sit. You're drunk." If she hadn't known the pain he was in, she might've laughed at him.

"I can't sit. I don't have that sort of leisure time anymore," he said with dramatic flair as if he were on a stage. "I have to get a job!"

Westie wondered if the concept of work was so confusing that he had to get into character to make sense of it.

The act fell away and he looked at her with sad eyes.

"What's wrong with you?" she asked, even though she already knew.

"Haven't you heard?" He flopped down on a bale of hay. "I'm broke."

She sat beside him, taking his hand in hers. If he thought he suffered now, he had another think coming. Eventually James would learn that not only was he broke, but his entire family were cannibals.

"I hadn't heard," she lied. "What happened?"

He looked ready to cry. Westie hoped he wouldn't. She wouldn't know what to do with a crying man.

"I told Lavina not to keep our gold at the inn. There were all sorts of feral people going in and out of that place. It was only a matter of time before someone broke into our rooms and stole it."

Westie squeezed his hand. He looked so much like a young boy sitting there in his crumpled state. She wanted to tell him not to worry, that his money was safely hidden away beneath a loose floorboard under her bed and he would get it back soon.

"There anything I can do?" she asked.

He looked up at her through glassy eyes. "You can help me forget."

"All right. How?"

He leaned over and kissed her. She sat there a moment, her eyes wide, too stunned to move. She was afraid to push him away at first, afraid to crush his fragile heart. She used her machine to put an arm's length of distance between them, gently so as not to bruise his ego.

"I can't," she said.

He sighed, turning back into a sad boy. "Is it because I'm broke?"

"No, it's not because of stupid money. It's because I'm with Alistair."

"The mute?" he said with disgust.

Her eyes shrank into a glare. "And because you're an ass."

A smile pulled at the corner of his lips. "I *am* an ass and everyone knows it. You're the only one brave enough to say it." He leaned his head against her shoulder and promptly began snoring.

She laughed, nudging him awake.

"Come on, let's put you to bed." Westie helped him into the house and up the stairs to her bed. The oil from his hair made a black smear against her pillow.

Alistair stepped into her room, holding several glass bottles from the collection in Nigel's office.

"Are you—" His voice cut off when he saw James. "What's he doing here?"

"He's not feeling well. Just found out he's broke and went on a bender."

Alistair glanced ruefully at the boy before looking away. "Oh, I see."

"He's going need a safe place to stay."

"Yes, of course."

"What are those?" she asked, pointing at the bottles.

"Rust, aluminum powder, and magnesium strips" was all he said.

"Well, what are they for?"

His eyes turned to slivers when he smiled beneath the mask. "You'll see. We should be on our way."

They punched the breeze to get to town. Once they made it, they tied their horses up in front of the general store, slinking among the parade of vendors and prospectors to get to the mayor's office.

Alistair and Westie slipped into the alley behind the mayor's office and found a window. Alistair hoisted her onto his shoulders so she could look inside.

"He's gone," she said.

She tried to climb off his shoulders but got her foot caught up in his holsters and toppled to the ground with a grunt despite Alistair's best efforts to catch her.

Alistair's metallic laughter bit at her patience. He tried to help her stand, but she pushed him away.

She cleared the web of hair from her face. "Let's get on with it."

They snuck through the back door. Once inside Alistair busied himself with the bottles he'd brought with him while Westie kept vigil. She imagined the things they would find in the safe, perhaps keepsakes from victims. She was sure the mayor knew about the Fairfields' particular tastes. It was possible the mayor was also a cannibal. Maybe they would find the bones of victims, stuffed heads like the animals on his walls, or some macabre trophy inside—something they could take right to the sheriff.

They needed to find something to incriminate the Fairfields as well as the mayor. It wasn't just about revenge for Isabelle and the family Westie had lost in that cabin anymore. The fate of the Wintu and the creatures depended on getting Emma up and running. For that, they needed copper. To get copper, they needed to be able to spend that gold. When people realized the gold was stolen from cannibals, they'd stop looking for the thieves. She was certain it would all work out if only the Fairfields were behind bars.

There was a burst of light and a searing sound when Alistair ignited the powder mixture. Within seconds the locks were off. "I'm in," he said.

Westie rushed over to him, heart hitting her ribs like a bedpost in a brothel hitting the wall on payday. When she knelt beside Alistair and saw the single item inside, her excitement withered away.

"That can't be it," she said.

Alistair picked up the piece of paper with the list of names on it. Some of the names had been crossed out. "I'm afraid so."

"Well, what's it say?"

Alistair read the names to her. On the list were the Fairfields' and the entire Lovett family's names, written small and neat in black ink. Beside them were the names of Westie, Alistair, Nigel, and Amos Little, written in sloppy slashes of red.

"Amos Little?" she said.

"He's a banker in Sacramento. I recognize the name."

"I remember him," Westie said. "We met at the ball. There seemed to be some sort of grudge between him and the mayor."

She leaned over. "Why do you suppose the Fairfields' and Lovetts' names are crossed out?"

"I'm more concerned why *our* names are on this list."

"Maybe it's about Emma."

"Maybe. If it is, why hide it? And why are some of the names crossed out?"

"I don't know, but we should probably find out." Westie groaned. "We'll have to tell Nigel." She wasn't looking forward to telling him she'd been snooping around again behind his back.

"I'm afraid so. And I think we'll need to have a chat with Amos Little too."

"All right. Let's get on with it."

# Thirty-Four

While Bena was there, Alistair broke the news to Nigel about him and Westie leaving for Sacramento. Bena always knew exactly what to say to Nigel to calm him down.

Westie went to check on James. The floor creaked as she stepped up to the open door of her room. He continued his drunken snoring without pause.

He looked so young sleeping in her bed. She was tempted to touch his cheek, tell him things would get better. Instead she got on her hands and knees, wriggled beneath the bed, and lifted the board, revealing the stack of gold bars. They'd need money on their travels, money she didn't want to ask Nigel for. She pinched a piece of gold from one of the bars with her machine, put it in her pocket, then slid the board back into its place. It would be hard to find someone who would take raw gold as payment without alerting the authorities, but she was sure she could find some crook willing to make a trade in the city.

After tucking James in, she went downstairs to face Nigel.

He was in his office waiting for her. Alistair and Bena were leaving just as she walked in.

"I'll get our things," Alistair said on his way out.

Bena gave her a wink and a gentle squeeze on her shoulder. Westie wanted to stop her and ask about Nigel's mood, but couldn't without him hearing.

"Shut the door," Nigel said when she was in his office.

He was either nervous or angry, judging by the way he kept rearranging his desk.

"I seem to remember things going terribly wrong the last time you were in someone else's room without being invited—yet here we are again," he said, but he didn't sound upset.

Westie sat down in the chair opposite Nigel, propping her boots up on his desk. "And I seem to recall someone saying they'd help take the Fairfields down no matter what scheming had to be done."

Nigel's lips twitched but didn't quite turn into a smile. "I did say that, didn't I?"

"Are you angry?" she asked.

Nigel leaned back in his chair, looking up at the sepia-painted Vitruvian Man on the ceiling that used to give Westie a touch of the giggles when she was younger. "No, but I am concerned about your healing process should your travels not yield the results you want."

"You're talking about me drinking."

He nodded. "I just want you to be all right."

"You don't need to worry about that anymore—trust me on that one."

He opened his mouth to say more, but she interrupted him, wanting to escape the subject. "James is upstairs in my room. Take care of him while we're gone. He's in a bad way now that all his money's gone."

"I'll be happy to have him. While Alistair's away, I'll need the extra pair of hands to help me move Emma into the mine. I plan to attach the engine, and once I do, it'll be too big for the great room.."

"Take care of yourself too. Both your names are on that list we found," Westie said.

Nigel stood and forced Westie into a hug. Once the awkwardness of the embrace wore off, she settled in and leaned her head against his shoulder.

"Don't worry about us," he said. "I'll take care of James. And we have Jezebel and Lucky looking out."

"We'll be back day after tomorrow," Westie said.

With a final squeeze, she let go of Nigel and went to meet Alistair.

They left soon after Westie's conversation with Nigel and rode through the night without stopping, and without sleep. Westie had forgotten how peaceful the road could be away from the clicking of so many inventions. Even with the silence and tired eyes, she couldn't turn off the sound in her mind.

It was morning. An overcast sky threatened rain. Autumn was beginning to show in all corners, but the cold gusts made it feel more like winter. Crisp air stung Westie's nose with the scent of pine. The closer they got to the city, the more maples they encountered until they were swallowed up by them, enchanting splashes of color in an otherwise dreary landscape. Deep orange, scarlet, and purple leaves fell from the sky like embers from a burning airship. Westie raised her parasol to keep the sugar sap of the leaves from sticking to her hair.

She'd stayed quiet during the ride, but there was a question that had been nagging at her ever since their kiss.

"I want you to tell me something, and I need you to be honest," she said through chattering teeth. In her haste to leave, she'd forgotten her duster. Her fingers and toes had gone completely numb.

Alistair looked at her, raising his brows. "Of course. What is it?"

Now that she had his full attention, her courage leaked away. She opened her mouth and closed it. After three more tries, she finally found the right words. "Three years ago, at my birthday party, you put on your mask and never showed me your face again. Why?"

He looked down, face going red, mask humming loudly. "Oh, that," he said.

"Yes, *that*. It's hard for me to believe, after all those years of you hating me and avoiding my very existence, that you love me all of a sudden."

He shook his head and made a sound she thought was laughter. "I never hated you. The opposite, in fact."

"You could've fooled me—and everyone else around for that matter. Everyone saw it. Even Isabelle."

She choked on Isabelle's name. It was still difficult for her to say out loud.

He took a breath and let it slowly whistle out through the mask's air filter. "I'd never seen the way others treated you prior to that party. Once you left school, it was just me and you. I'd assumed they were afraid of you like they were of me—especially after you crushed Isabelle's hand."

He chuckled at the memory, but when Westie didn't join in, his laughter trailed off into a hum. "I was happy that you had friends, and I enjoyed watching you interact with them and be a normal girl for a change." He sighed, a long hissing sound. "While I watched, I saw how the boys looked at you. I recognized the stares because I'd caught myself doing the very same thing."

She looked at him, surprised.

"Just one year earlier you were thirteen, all bones and skinned knees, climbing trees and crying when I wouldn't play stickball with you because you could hit the ball so much farther than I. You seemed like a child then, while I was a man of sixteen. Then suddenly, at fourteen, you didn't seem so young anymore." The redness in his face deepened. "I was terrified by the way I'd started to feel about you. I knew that I'd always loved you, but it had changed into a . . . mature kind of love."

His words floated in the air above her. Just letters and sounds she couldn't make sense of. When they finally fit together, all piled up and heavy, they came crashing down on her. For the first time in her life she was speechless.

He hung his head. "After seeing how those boys were with you at your party, I knew it wouldn't be long before there were more. With all those admirers, why would you choose a mute with scars on his face when you could have the James Lovetts of the world?"

Sadness welled up inside, burning her nose and chest as if she'd breathed ammonia. The pain of it grew and grew until she was drowning in tears. She was overwhelmed with—she wasn't sure with what, joy, confusion, an anger as strong as dark whiskey.

"You are a coward!" Things would've been so different had she known his true feelings. Maybe she would never have left Rogue City to hunt cannibals, or fallen prey to the bottle. She wouldn't have felt as used up and poisoned as she had.

When she spoke again, it was with a sad lilt. "You broke my heart, Alley."

His eyes were wide and glittering. "I know. And I'll spend every day of my life trying to make it up to you."

Gentle rain tapped against Westie's parasol. It was just a few drops at first, and then the sky opened and rain spit out like sharpened spears. She could hardly see what was right in front of her face. The lace of her parasol wilted, useless. She folded it up and attached it to her saddle.

The valley was known for its flashes of rain and quick floods. The storm turned the road to glue, and the horses struggled to move in the mush collecting beneath their hooves. Then the hail came.

"We need to get off the road," Alistair shouted.

The hail chased them into the maple forest, beneath the canopy of leaves where the beating was less abrasive. Westie's clothes soaked up the wet, chilling her to her core.

Henry stumbled in the muck. She fell but managed to grab hold of the saddle horn with her machine before hitting the ground. Spooked by the sudden shift of weight, Henry took off at a full run, dragging Westie through the brush, knocking her against trees. Branches reached out like clawed hands scratching at her skin until she finally let go and fell into a pile of leaves.

"Westie!" Alistair slid from his saddle and rushed toward her.

He helped her to her feet and led her below a sturdy tree. Nothing hurt more than a bruise. The scratches weren't deep enough to draw blood. She knew there were no broken bones, but the cold she felt was just as crippling. Alistair grabbed his pack from his horse. He used a large sheet of hide to make a shelter and laid out his bedroll and wool blankets.

Westie had started to peel off her clothes when she noticed Alistair frozen in place. The exposed skin around his mask made him look like a child who had gotten into his mother's rouge.

"What?" she said. "I'm freezing and I'm not getting under blankets in these wet clothes."

He looked at the ground. "Of course not. I'll go find Henry."

While Alistair was looking for Henry, Westie stripped down to her underclothes, desperate to get warm. She found flint in Alistair's pack and built a fire beneath a tree just outside the shelter with the driest wood she could find, then wrapped herself up in his blankets, trying to stave off hypothermia.

Alistair returned after a while, but the feeling in Westie's limbs had not.

"Henry wouldn't come to me," Alistair said, warming his hands by the fire.

Westie's muscles were wound tight, and she shook so violently she could barely get words through her clenched jaw. "Give him time to settle his nerves. He'll come back."

"I couldn't get your bedroll—" His eyes grew when he glanced back at her. "Your lips are blue."

"No shit?" she tried to say, but her words were broken by the clack of her teeth.

"We'll have to share," he said.

He started to move beneath the covers, but she stopped him.

"Not with those wet clothes you're not."

With a bashful tilt of his eyes, he shed his clothes down to his underwear, which were mostly dry, and got beneath the blankets with her.

Westie felt some reprieve from the cold when she saw Alistair without his shirt. The skin of his chest was smooth on top of layers of muscle, far more than she remembered from when they were kids. He was built much better than she'd imagined in her dreams where he was scantily clothed.

"What are you smiling about?" he asked.

"What? I wasn't smiling," she said, clamping her lips together.

Alistair's teeth chattered when his skin touched hers. His shivering moved the blanket off her shoulders, and she huddled closer to steal his heat.

"Your skin is freezing!" he said.

He wrapped his arms around her without permission, without thought. She knew it was out of concern rather than an excuse to touch her while her clothes were off.

His skin was hot like fever against hers, almost painfully so, but each time she tried to pull away he gripped her tighter, winding his limbs with hers like two trees that had grown together until becoming one. The rain stopped as suddenly as it had started, but still he held her.

Her eyes closed as her body warmed, exhaustion taking over.

Sleep had just crept over her when she felt the tips of Alistair's fingers move across her back. Her eyes opened to the wall of his chest, panic and dizziness making her head float. It was a different kind of touch than what she knew from him. And though his fingers remained only on her back, this particular touch she felt all over.

She looked at his face. His eyes met hers, blue and illuminated against the grayness around them. Being there alone with Alistair in the woods, she realized she'd wasted their years together, avoiding her true feelings. If the loss of her family and Alistair's near death had taught her anything, it was that time with loved ones moved faster than wild horses burning the breeze.

His pupils dilated when she reached out to him. With two snaps she undid his mask and pulled it off. Stubble dotted his jaw around the silver map of scars. Everything seemed to stop. Leaves paused on their way to the ground, birds silenced. It was as though the world held its breath.

She moved to kiss his scars, but he recoiled before her lips could touch them. Fear wrinkled the skin between his eyes. The fold smoothed in an instant.

She pulled back, wondering what she'd done wrong. They'd kissed before, so why in blazes . . .

Then it hit her. She'd tried to kiss his scars. Last time anyone had put their mouth to his cheek, it was to eat his flesh.

"Balls," she cursed. She leaned away from him, put her hand to her mouth, and talked between her fingers. "I'm so stupid. I should've known—"

He put his finger to her mouth to keep her quiet.

She pressed her lips together, tried really hard, but just couldn't do it. "You know I'd never do anything to hurt you, don't you?" she said.

He took her hand, put her palm against his cheek, and nodded. She ran her finger along the raised lines of his scars, read his heart-breaking story down to his neck, and stopped when she reached his breastbone. His body quivered beneath her touch. She felt the *bomp-bomp* of his heart racing against her own, both rushing to the finish line to connect to each other once more. She breathed him in, the sweat, the rain.

Leaning forward, she put her lips to his chest, tasted the salt of his skin. His breathing became more labored, and his muscles began to twitch.

A confidence like nothing she'd known prior to that moment led her actions. She let her hands slip down to his narrow waist, where she grasped his hips and pulled him toward her. She smiled when she felt the evidence of him wanting her too.

He pressed against her, none too gently. She didn't want gentle. She wanted the anguish that had been building up inside her for so long to be decimated. His hands moved across her skin and knew exactly where to touch. Each perfect landing made her body shiver.

Westie drew in a sharp breath as he rolled on top of her. She wrapped her arms around his neck while their lips consumed each other. They kissed until Westie felt like she would detonate. She grabbed hold of his arm with her machine and flipped him onto his back, where she shredded the rest of his underclothes. An animated smile split his face in two and made Westie laugh, but as soon as she removed her own underclothes, his smile melted away.

Her confidence fell apart when he looked at the part of her arm where the pins of her machine had been drilled into skin and bone, latched on like some metal parasite. Westie had always kept that place hidden, even as a child. She started to wrap the blanket around her shoulders to hide herself, but he stopped her and reached out, touching the raised scars around the pins where Nigel had attached two other machines that hadn't worked.

The teasing and stares from strangers had formed a callus around her heart over the years, but being there, exposed to Alistair, Westie felt soft and pliable. Like one disappointed frown could shatter her world.

His finger traveled from the edge of her skin to her machine, caressing the gears, cogs, the copper wire, down to the metal fingers. The muscles in Alistair's jaw rippled when he touched the bare skin of her leg. There was a long pause before his hand moved again. He pulled away, and Westie watched his fingers fold into the sign for *beautiful*. For once she felt it was true.

Alistair rolled her slowly onto her back. She blew out a shaking breath and worried at her bottom lip with her teeth. He propped himself on his elbows, cradled her face in his hands, and looked at her in a way she'd never seen before, a way that needed no words. She knew then that she would give him a gift she could never get back. It made no matter. That gift was always meant for Alistair and no one else. With a kiss and an arch of her back, it was his forever.

# Thirty-Five

They slept for a couple of hours. By the time they woke up, Henry had settled down enough for them to ride. They arrived in Sacramento by noon, Westie on the verge of bashful and Alistair with eyes squinting in a permanent smile.

Fleets of aeroskiffs flew over the city, the sky tinted brown from the smoke exhaling from their stacks. Most of the coaches on the road were the walking kind, just like the one Isabelle's parents had bought her. They struggled to move as their sharp metal legs sank into the softened mud of the streets.

"Are you ready for this?" Alistair asked her when they reached the bank. His hair was wet and had turned to soft waves.

"Ready as I'm likely to get."

They climbed down from their horses. Alistair held her hand, a gesture that would've felt foreign only days ago. She wrapped her fingers around his, taking comfort in the strength of his grip.

When they stepped through the doors of the bank, everyone inside stopped what they were doing to stare. Some gasped, others shied away upon seeing the pair's mechanics. Westie noticed Alistair's eyes shift to the ground as they did whenever people stared.

"Is it my dress?" Westie said, loud enough for all to hear.

Her clothes were wet and splattered with mud. Most of the folks in the bank wore fancy clothes to ask for loans or beg for extensions. Westie used her machine to shake out her dress, slinging mud onto everyone else's silk and velvet.

"That better?" she asked.

Alistair chuckled beneath his mask, a sound that was as familiar to her ears as her own voice but spooked others. No one moved or spoke, just stared.

An older gentleman with a strangely sculpted beard that split in the middle and curled up at both ends stepped out from behind the counter. "May I help you?"

"We're here to see Amos Little," Alistair said.

The man's face rolled from smile to sadness in one swift motion. "I'm sorry—you must not have heard."

"We don't hear much about the outside world in Rogue City," Westie said.

He braided his fingers protectively in front of his chest the way some folks did when they were about to tell someone something sad enough to flail their arms at. Westie's heart sank lower each second he prolonged the silence.

With eyes lowered and a tremor in his voice, he said, "I regret to inform you that Amos Little has passed on, but I'll be happy to help you with any of your banking needs."

The hope Westie had felt earlier dissipated, its remains carried away on the wind like a dandelion. She leaned against a wall covered in Wanted posters. *Dead?* But he'd just been at her party not that long ago.

"How did he die?" she asked.

"House fire—a terrible accident."

"Accident my ass," she mumbled low enough to keep the banker from hearing.

Even after closing her eyes and slowing her breathing, the malevolent thing knotting in her chest grew until it was painful. She put her copper hand to her heart. They'd come all this way for nothing. Whatever rivalry there'd been between Amos and the mayor, now she'd never know.

Deciding there would be no hysterics, the banker dropped his hands to his sides and asked, "Is there anything *I* can help you with?"

Alistair hung his head. "No, thank you," he said. "We're here conducting business for my employer. He asked us to speak directly to Amos."

As Westie and Alistair turned to leave, the banker said, "Your employer is Nigel Butler, correct?" Westie looked over her shoulder. Alistair twisted on his heels to face the man. When he saw their quizzical looks, the banker said to Alistair, "I've seen you here before. I was Amos's assistant and helped with most of his dealings with your employer. I assure you Nigel won't mind me helping you."

"I'm afraid it's nothing you can help with," Alistair said, making up the story on a whim. "Nigel's going into a business venture with Mayor Chambers and the Fairfields. We're here to check on their references. Amos was one of them."

The man looked skeptical. "I can't imagine the Fairfields venturing from their home, let alone into business. And I highly doubt Amos would give the mayor a reference after the investigation."

"What investigation?" Westie said, taking a step forward.

The banker hesitated and looked around the room before saying, "Amos was looking into the mayor's past dealings when he was still a property lawyer. I'm sorry, but I can't go into further details regarding bank business."

"What did you mean about the Fairfields not venturing from their home?" Alistair asked.

The banker's mouth opened, looking confused. "Everyone knows the Fairfields are recluses. No one has seen them in years—oh," he said, looking embarrassed, "that's right. I keep forgetting you're not from around here. It's difficult to believe a distinguished man such as Nigel Butler would live in a town like Rogue City."

Westie and Alistair looked at each other, brows curling in question marks. The last thing Westie would've called the Fairfields was reclusive. After all, they were in Rogue City making friends with anyone who gave a damn about Nigel's machine. And Lavina, with those flashy dresses and low-cut bodices, gliding from store to store spending James's inheritance . . . it seemed impossible.

"Is there anyone else who might be able to tell us about Amos's investigation into the mayor, *unofficially*, that is?" Westie said.

The banker looked around the room as if he were being watched. Finally he said, "If anyone knew about the goings-on with the investigation, it was Amos's wife, Lucy Little. He did most of his work from home. You'll want to give her a few days, though. Poor thing barely escaped with her life, but it seems she's doing much better; I talked to her nurse at the hospital just this morning."

Westie sighed. They didn't have a few days.

"Thank you for your help," she said.

As they rode through town, Westie's stomach felt sick with dread. Though she couldn't prove it, she was certain that Amos Little's death and the list of names she'd found in the mayor's safe were connected somehow.

She pulled at Henry's reins when they came across the blackened remains of a burned-up house. It looked like the carcass of some giant black mythical beast, with shards of brittle framework sticking out like rib bones.

The smell of scorched wet wood hung thick in the air. Piles of rubble continued to steam after the rain. The fire had taken everything. All evidence of the life Amos and his wife had built together was gone.

Alistair stared at the burned rubble, eyes glazed over with worry. "If burning someone in their home is what the mayor does to those who investigate him, imagine what he'd do to those who accuse his friends of cannibalism."

Westie put a hand to her stomach. "I'm trying not to think about that." She climbed off her horse, kicking at the rubble to see if there was anything to be salvaged from the ruins. She made her way to a charcoaled support beam, where she sat and wondered which room she was sitting in. As she looked up at the sky, a drop of rain landed on her lashes. She blinked it away, trying not to let the hopeless feeling inside consume her. If nothing came of their trip to Sacramento, all would be lost. The Fairfields' gold was useless without Hubbard and Lavina being in jail, and it was doubtful Westie could find a crook brave enough to trade eight gold bars for enough money to allow Nigel to finish his machine.

Alistair sat beside her on the beam and leaned his head against her shoulder. His hair smelled like earth and macassar, and she was reminded of the connection they'd made beneath the maples. Closing her eyes, she tried to hold on to that moment of happiness. "I have to fix this, Alley," she said, voice barely a whisper. "Of all the plans I've messed up, this can't be one of them."

"We'll fix this, I promise. We won't stop until we do." He moved his hand to her hair, pulling out a maple leaf. "Let's start by talking to Amos's widow."

Alistair stood and reached out a hand to help her up. When he took a step back, Westie noticed something under his foot, a piece of paper. Picking it up and dusting the soot off, she realized it was a photo.

"Look at this," she said, holding the photo toward him. It was a picture of Amos and a man shaking hands. Behind him was a family of four, no one she'd ever seen before except for Amos.

"What about it?" Alistair asked.

In the photo a young girl with coal-black curly hair held a doll wearing a dress with a distinct crisscross pattern. "That's the same doll Olive was holding when the Fairfields first stepped off the airship in Rogue City. She threw a fit and tore its head off."

Alistair took the photo from her to study it closer. The edges were burned and curled, and the paper was brittle. He was careful only to touch the border so as not to smear the wet image. "I don't think that's Olive in the picture, unless she's wearing a wig," he said. "Perhaps their families bought the dolls at the same store."

Westie shook her head. "That's no store-bought doll. I know a handmade doll when I see one. My momma was always making them for me. That's the same doll. We need to find out who these people are."

Alistair nodded, handing back the photo. "But first let's talk to Amos's widow."

# Thirty-Six

The hospital was a long, flat building with a cross on its east-facing wall. It looked bigger on the inside than out, about two thousand square feet of beds to accommodate the sick and injured. The workings of the machines in the room filled the place with a concert of sound, as if there were thirty Alistairs sitting around just breathing.

Westie recognized the machines as being inventions of Nigel's. He had his own signature way of twisting and combining various metals to make the simplest machines look like they had taken years to assemble.

A nurse sat at a desk in the entryway, checking off boxes on a piece of paper. She held a clumsily rolled cigarette pinched between her fingers, the smoke curling up her arm. When she looked up and saw Westie and Alistair standing there, she stubbed it out in a metal ashtray.

"Are you in need of medical assistance?" she asked as she studied Alistair's mask and Westie's metal hand without any hint of fear or curiosity.

"We're here to see a patient," Westie said. "Lucy Little."

Flecks of ash from the cigarette speckled the front of the nurse's dark-colored dress. She dusted them off, leaving white smears, and checked the patient roster. "Last bed on the left."

Even though the place was full of strange machines, folks looked at Alistair as if he were the grim reaper come to steal them from their beds. Luckily, he was too distracted by Westie's quick pace to pay much attention.

At the end of the row, Lucy Little was sitting up in her bed. She was small like her husband, with a head full of wavy, fading yellow hair that was white at the roots. Her arms were wrapped in bandages from her burns, and she held copper tubing in her mouth.

When she saw Westie and Alistair, she pulled out the tubing and reached for the spectacles on the table beside her bed.

"Westie Butler," Lucy said with a hint of surprise in her singed voice.

Westie paused, cocking her head. "You know who I am?"

Lucy nodded, smoothing the blankets on her lap. "Amos talked about you after the ball. There aren't many girls around here with metal arms."

"No, I reckon not." Westie sat on the unoccupied bed beside Lucy's. So did Alistair.

Lucy said, "If you're looking for Amos, he's—" Her words were closed off by a choking sound. Tears trickled down her cheeks, following the lines around her mouth.

"We heard," Westie said, chest tightening when she saw the woman's sadness.

With a shaky breath, Lucy collected herself enough to speak again. "What can I help you with?"

Westie hesitated. Clearly the woman was in no shape to be talking, but what choice did she have?

"I wouldn't be coming to you if the situation weren't dire." Westie paused, trying to come up with the right words, then just decided blunt and honest was the quickest way to the answers she needed. "I'd like to know why Amos was investigating the mayor."

Lucy's open expression shut down. She closed her mouth, leaned back against her pillow, looking out the window beside her bed. "I don't know anything about that."

Westie could tell by Lucy's wavering jaw that the woman was lying. If someone had set Westie's house on fire with her inside, she'd be afraid to speak too. But Westie wouldn't let it go. She needed to know what Lucy knew.

"Do you know my father, Nigel?" Westie asked, brushing the hair out of her eyes. Lucy didn't answer, or even look at her. "He's a surgeon. Surgeons are like doctors; they take an oath not to talk about their patients without permission. I'm sure Amos was under similar regulations when it came to bank business." Still no response from Lucy. "Anyway, that oath never stopped Nigel from coming home and wanting to vent after a long day at work. I'm his daughter, so of course he could trust me, just like I'm sure Amos trusted you. Some days I wished Nigel hadn't trusted me so much. You wouldn't believe some of the things folks needed to have surgically removed from—well, I'm sure you can imagine."

Westie waited for Lucy to crack a smile, or at least relax, but her attempt at humor had failed.

"Look," Westie said, lowering her voice and using her flesh hand to touch Lucy's, "I know you're scared. Believe me, I'm terrified too. When the mayor finds out I'm conducting an investigation of my own, he'll come after me—and the people I love. That's why I need to know what Amos had on him. I want to take that bastard down once and for all so he can't hurt anyone else. None of us are safe until I do. Please, Lucy, I need your help."

Lucy's lips began to tremble. When she closed her eyes, a river of tears escaped. She nodded her head.

"Yes?" Westie sounded far too eager. Others in the beds nearby looked over at her.

Lucy made a shushing motion with her hand. She looked around, hesitating before saying, "Amos believed Ben Chambers was responsible for the airship explosion that killed our former mayor seven years ago."

"Why would he do that?" Westie asked.

"To become mayor himself, of course. He was the president of the board of supervisors, the next in line in case the current mayor was unable to perform his duties. He has big political plans. First mayor, then governor, senator, and one day president. He might've succeeded by now had he been more likable. He will do anything for that kind of power." She wiped the tears from her eyes and took a shallow breath that made her cough. "Amos had recently found an old receipt in the county budget for explosives signed out by Ben Chambers only a day before the airship crash. Ben was a property lawyer back then and attended demolitions, only there weren't any demolitions planned, and the explosives were never returned."

Westie picked at her lip as she listened to Lucy speak. If the mayor was willing to kill an entire airship of people to get to just one, he was more devious than she'd thought.

"But none of that matters now," Lucy said. "All the evidence burned up in the fire."

As soon as the last word left her mouth, Lucy began to cough, the kind of violent hacking that sounded like she might cough up her spine. Westie reached over, cranked the machine to start it up, and handed Lucy the copper tube. It made chugging sounds as it pulled the debris from her lungs. When the coughing stopped, Westie pulled the photo she'd found in the rubble out of her coat pocket.

"Do you recognize any of these people?" she asked.

Lucy nodded, pulling the tube from her mouth and touching the face of her late husband. Her lips eased into a soft smile. "I don't know who that family is behind them, but that's Amos shaking hands with James Lovett after he won the mayoralty for the third time in a row. That photo was taken for the newspaper. Amos kept it in a frame in his office." Her smile fell. "That was just days before James Lovett and his wife were killed."

Westie squeezed Lucy's hand once more. "You've been a big help. I promise we'll get the mayor. You won't have to be afraid anymore."

Lucy tugged at Westie's hand when she tried to leave and looked deep into her eyes with a ferociousness that hadn't been there before. "When you take the mayor down, you be sure to tell him I hope he rots in hell."

Westie nodded. "You bet I will."

As they walked away, Alistair said, "That's a hefty promise to make."

Westie looked up at him. "And one I intend to keep. Even if I have to kill the man myself."

# Thirty-Seven

Westie and Alistair left their horses under an awning out of the rain and walked against the wind into the center of town.

"Where are we going?" Alistair asked, the tail of his duster snapping in the wind behind him.

Westie put her head down, charging into the storm. "The library keeps records of old newspapers, right?" she said above the howling wind.

"I believe so."

"That's where we're going. This picture was for the newspaper, and since we know James Lovett Senior was killed only a few days after, that gives me a date to look. The name of the family with the little girl holding the doll should be in that article. I need to know who they are and how Olive got that doll. If they're still alive, perhaps they can tell us more about the Fairfields."

Just as the clouds started spewing sideways rain, they slipped inside the library, their wet clothes dripping on the floor.

The Sacramento library was an empire of knowledge tucked into the most perfect, ornate building Westie had ever seen. It smelled dusty and old, but in a good way.

They found a shelf of scrapbooks of old newspapers, hundreds of them. There were four different books from the year she was looking for. Pulling them from the shelf, she plopped them down on the table, hearing people shush her from dark corners.

She cracked open one of them. Alistair took another. Reading made her eyes dry and her lids heavy. She yawned and scratched her head, fingers tangling in her dirty locks, wishing she were conducting her research from a tub full of hot water and freesia-scented bubbles instead.

"I think Sacramento may be cursed," Westie said. "Listen to this." She began reading the headline on the front page. "Tailor Harvey Mull died after falling on his own scissors. And this one: Milkman David Kinsey swallowed an entire chicken leg and choked."

"I saw a couple of those too," Alistair said. "A housemaid named Sugar Babineaux fell from the deck of an airship." He flipped a page. "A paperboy named Maximilian MacPhee was mowed down by a runaway coach."

"Jesus," Westie said, "sounds like it's safer to live in Rogue City. I'd rather take my chances with bandits and creatures."

As Westie scrolled through the various stories, she came upon the article about the airship explosion that had killed James's parents.

"Here's the article about the airship explosion, but—" She turned back several pages. "There're stories missing, all the front pages of the news that happened the days leading to it." Westie leaned back, rubbing her flesh hand across her face, vision blurred from reading. "Including the one that would've had the photo of the girl and her doll in it."

"Well, this was a waste of time. What now?" Alistair asked, wiping his eyes.

Westie pressed her lips together, fighting the sense of defeat that made her want to get on her horse, ride back to Rogue City, and just give up.

"I reckon now we go to the Fairfield house, see what we can find."

"This is insane—you know that, right?" Alistair said as they rode down a long, twisting path.

"Yes."

Alistair rolled his eyes. "At least you're aware."

"Relax, Alley. The Fairfields are in Rogue City. No one will be there to catch us snooping."

After they'd ridden a half mile on the narrow road, a house came into view. It had taken some nosing around to get the address, but finally, after Westie had convinced the postman she was a long-lost relative of the Fairfields, he gave in.

The house was in the country surrounded by unfarmed acreage, a modest colonial that might've been beautiful once. It was run-down now, the yard overgrown, crabgrass reaching through the cracks in the walkway. Two pillars held up a sagging porch like old sentries, their white paint peeling.

"This is it?" Alistair said. "I imagined a mansion and stables with exotic Arabian horses. I can't imagine James living in filth like this."

Westie didn't think so either, but it was out of the way. Privacy seemed beneficial for a family of cannibals.

Westie left Henry to graze while she climbed the steps to the porch. Dozens of weathered doll heads looked up at her from the ground. She shivered, kicking one of the more morbid-looking ones away.

Alistair nudged a bottle of milk next to the front door with the toe of his boot. The goop inside barely moved. The door opened as soon as Westie touched it. She took a breath and walked across the threshold.

Leaves scattered across the wood floors, following them inside. The living space was expansive, with a fireplace big enough to fill it with warmth. There was a brick of wet newspaper beside it, the ink melted away long ago and the pages stuck together. Wind moaned as it funneled through the chimney, causing a draft.

Alistair ran a finger across a ceramic figurine of a faery, then wiped the dust on his trousers. "Looks like the maid took a day off."

To Westie's surprise, the Fairfields lived humbly. The furniture was handmade of roughly carved oak; the wallpaper was an outdated floral print that bubbled and folded in the corners. There were hooks on the walls, but all the pictures had been taken down. Only four circular plaster molds of handprints remained. Westie stepped up to get a closer look.

Below each hand was the name of the person it belonged to carved into the plaster.

Westie scowled at the molds. "Put your hand up to Hubbard's print."

Alistair studied the shapes a moment before pressing his hand to the mold, his fingers reaching the tips of Hubbard's. "Does that look like the hand of Hubbard Fairfield?"

Westie thought back to the ball, the way Hubbard's hand had swallowed up Nigel's when Nigel had helped Hubbard to stand after Westie nearly crushed his fingers. Nigel was not a little man with little hands, but Hubbard had made it look that way.

"Not at all. Maybe the plaster shrank when it dried."

It was possible, Westie thought, though she doubted it. "Yeah, maybe," she said, and continued to poke around.

"Looks like they left in a hurry," Alistair said, pointing to the open cabinets still full of the family's personal effects.

"Let's go see their rooms," Westie said.

There were six rooms on the top floor of the house. They went to the master bedroom, which must have belonged to the married couple. Alistair was right. It did seem as though they'd been in a great hurry to leave. The bed hadn't been made, and there were clothes strewn about. Alistair went into the closet while Westie checked a stack of shoe boxes in a corner. There were a lot of things tucked away in the boxes, but nothing personal, nothing that could teach her anything new about the Fairfields other than the fact that they lived like slobs.

Westie then squeezed into the closet with him to look. All the clothes were still in their tailoring bags. She opened one with a dress inside. Like their little prints, it seemed the Fairfields had little bodies as well.

She lifted a brow. "I don't suppose their clothes shrank too when they dried."

Alistair shrugged, looking at the dress. "It's possible. Perhaps the tailor washed the clothes after making them, or maybe he just took the wrong measurements."

"Or perhaps the dress wasn't meant for Lavina at all. Look at the name on the bag," Westie said, remembering the name from one of the articles she'd read.

"'Harvey Mull's Tailoring,'" Alistair read aloud. "Why does that name sound familiar?"

"Harvey Mull was one of the people who died seven years ago when he fell on his scissors, remember?"

"Right, of course."

Westie's mind began to spin. "There's a stack of old newspapers next to the fireplace, so old they've practically turned into a block of wood. And the milk next to the door; the milkman dropped it off but never came back to pick it up, and you said it yourself, the place is in need of a maid."

Alistair straightened, face opening up with comprehension. "All those people died around the same time. You think the Fairfields killed them—but why would they do that?"

A theory was slowly forming in Westie's head. She talked slowly to keep from getting ahead of herself. "Seven years ago, seven years go," she kept repeating as the pieces came together. "I don't think the Fairfields we know are really the Fairfields at all. The people who killed my family—seven years ago—obviously made their way to Sacramento. They were murderers, no doubt looking for a fresh start." Westie edged past Alistair out of the closet and began pacing the room. "The banker said the real Fairfields were hermits. Perhaps the family we know saw this as an opportunity. All they'd have to do was kill off the real Fairfields and a handful of people who knew them."

"But how would the killers of your family know the Fairfields were hermits? And how would they know who the Fairfields knew and didn't know?"

Westie looked up at the ceiling in thought. An ugly brown water stain stretched from one corner of the room to the other. "They wouldn't. But the mayor would. Ben Chambers took Mayor Lovett's seat after he died. Ben would've known about the Lovetts' ailing son and their fortune, as well as the family of recluses who stood to inherit all of it."

"All right then," Alistair said, sitting on the bed. As soon as something moved beneath the covers he hopped back up, a screeching metal sound coming from his mask. When a little brown field mouse scurried out, he let out a long breath that whistled through the sound box. After gathering his nerves, he said, "How would a bunch of vagabonds know someone as important as Ben Chambers?"

"Will you stop that?" Westie said with a scowl.

Alistair chuckled. "These are questions Nigel will ask you when you go to him with this theory of yours."

She sighed. "I know. I'm missing something, I'm just not sure what yet. The answers have to be in this house somewhere."

Frustrated, Westie began digging through drawers.

Alistair leaned against the closet door. He looked as tired as she felt. "The Fairfields we know are crazy, not stupid. They won't leave evidence of their crimes lying around for anyone to find, especially while they're out of town."

Westie's hand hovered over a pair of knickers too small to fit Lavina, her thoughts spinning back to the day they'd broken into the Fairfields' room at the inn and she'd found Olive's box of souvenirs from murder victims under the bed. Westie also recollected the conversation with the little girl by the manzanita tree, when Olive had said that she kept trophies even though her mother told her not to.

"No," Westie said, her voice rising, heart filling dangerously with hope. "Lavina and Hubbard wouldn't keep evidence of their crimes, but I know who would. We've been searching the wrong room."

"What are you talking about?"

Westie stood in front of Alistair, smiling so wide it felt like the corners of her mouth would split. "You're a genius, Alley, a goddamned genius." She grabbed him by the face, kissing his forehead.

He stood proudly. "Am I?"

Westie laughed. "Yes, you are!"

"All a genius gets is a kiss on the head?" he said with a playful look that turned his eyes to slivers.

"If I find what I think I might, you'll earn much more than a kiss."

Alistair made a choking sound beneath his mask, his face flaring pink.

All Westie had to do was follow the trail of doll parts to find Olive's room. Inside was a bed with a dirty pink canopy, a rocking horse, wicker furniture, and ruffles covering everything—

"The curtains," Westie said, pulling the photo from her pocket.

She studied the crisscross pattern of the doll's dress. It was a perfect match to the curtains.

A nagging feeling, a mix of hope and sorrow, shivered beneath her skin. "I think the people in this photo might be the real Fairfields. The doll's dress was made from the same fabric as these curtains."

Alistair did his own comparison, putting the picture right up to the curtains, his mask whirring. "I think you might be right." Though she couldn't tell by the sound his mask made, she saw excitement in his eyes.

As she brushed aside the clutter on the floor, Westie tried not to think about what might've happened to the little girl holding that doll. Alistair bent down to help.

"Yes!" Westie shouted, and began to laugh as she caught sight of the box beneath the bed. Even little girls had their habits.

She sat in front of the box a moment, just looking at it. It was painted pink with white stripes and the word *TOYS* in block letters. After a while she closed her eyes and prayed to the Wintu creator, the spirits, to Nigel's god, and to anyone else who might've been listening, to please not let her fail.

With a shaking flesh hand and her machine, she pulled the box out from beneath the bed.

She lifted the lid. On top was a quilt of various colored fabrics stitched together. Beneath it were picture books, pretty and neat and unassuming. Westie took each thing out, one at a time, so she wouldn't miss any clues. When she got close to the bottom, she cried out.

"Is that—" She covered her mouth with the back of her hand. "Oh God, it is."

Several scalps with the hair still attached lay in a crumpled heap beneath the books. Though most of the hair was stained with blood, she could tell the hair had once been dark and curly, like that of the family in the photo with Amos and Mayor Lovett. There were five scalps all together. Olive had braided the ones with long hair and added bows. Over time, they'd turned to leather, but they still held a mild stench of decay.

"My God," Alistair said beside her.

Westie pinched her nose against the smell and picked up the clusters of hair with her machine, setting them aside, revealing newspaper beneath, crusted in dried blood.

"It's the missing newspapers from the library," she said, carefully unfolding the pages, which had stuck together. To her disappointment, the first was the same picture she had, but there were no names mentioned. Fortunately, on the next page was a picture of Ben

Chambers, his hands tied in front of him.

"Listen to this," she said, and started to read. "'Property advocate Ben Chambers, arrested for public intoxication and harassment after his third loss to James Lovett Senior in the race for position of mayor for the county of Sacramento.'"

When she turned the page over to read the next story, she sucked in a startled breath.

"What is it?" Alistair said.

Westie blinked several times to make sure that what she was seeing wasn't something she'd conjured in her own mind. "'Festus and Birdie O'Brian, arrested for thievery, their children taken into temporary custody by the state.'"

"Who are Festus and Birdie O'Brian?" Alistair asked, taking the paper from her. When he saw the picture beside the article, he said, "Oh!"

The picture was of the Lavina and Hubbard they knew, wearing the same clothes Westie remembered them wearing at the cabin when they'd killed her family.

"They must have met the mayor when they were in jail together." Westie looked at the dates on the different stories. The O'Brians and Ben Chambers had been arrested on the same day. "It all makes sense now. Ben Chambers wanted to be mayor more than anything, but he had to get James Lovett Senior out of the way first. Only his greed didn't stop there. He wanted the Lovett fortune as well. He couldn't steal it—that amount of gold is too difficult to move without raising suspicion. An agreement must have been made between the mayor and the O'Brians to share the fortune. That's why he's so protective of them. He's protecting his investment."

Alistair folded the paper neatly and handed it back to Westie to put in a satchel she found nearby to keep dry. "But why would they stay in Rogue City for Emma after we've already accused them of cannibalism? It seems like too great a risk."

Westie grabbed her satchel. "It does seem that way, but it doesn't matter. This photo proves they're imposters." She took Alistair by the face, her smile bursting from somewhere deep within, and kissed the part of his mask where his lips would be. "We finally have them, Alley! Let's get home. We've got a necktie social to plan for."

# Thirty-Eight

Standing outside the Fairfield home, Westie imagined the ghosts of the O'Brians' victims wandering the empty rooms, looking for escape. How many horrifying, unspeakable things had those walls witnessed?

"We should burn it down," Westie said.

Alistair pushed the wet hair from his eyes, the voice box of his mask flooded from the rain and gurgling when he spoke. "The authorities will want to see inside."

Westie frowned, knowing he was right. "Should we send Nigel a telegraph bird, tell him what we found?"

"Too easy to intercept."

She filled her lungs and blew the air out. "If we leave now, we'll make it home by morning."

Alistair put a hand on her shoulder, kneading the taut muscles just below the skin. "We'll never make it if we run our horses into the ground. Let's get food and some sleep. We'll stay at an inn here and leave first thing in the morning and be there by sundown tomorrow like we promised Nigel."

Westie's arms and legs itched with nervous energy. There was no way she'd be able to sleep, but he was right about the horses.

Nodding, she took one last look at the house, then tried to erase it from her mind forever.

They left before the sun was up the next morning. Henry was a fast horse, and so was Alistair's mare, but for Westie it felt like they were standing still. No matter how much distance they chewed up, there was always more ahead.

They reached the mansion before sundown. Westie didn't wait for Henry to stop before sliding off his back and landing like a cat on all fours. She sprang toward the steps despite her aching backside and numb feet. She couldn't wait to tell Nigel the news.

Inside, Lucky's barks, Jezebel's howls, and the sound of claws scratching at a door came from somewhere upstairs.

"Nigel!" she shouted.

Alistair's calls echoed behind hers.

The clamor of footfalls woke the quiet house as she took two steps at a time. She found Jezebel and Lucky locked up in the library. After letting them out and checking the other rooms, she met Alistair in the great room.

"Emma is gone," he said. "I remember Nigel mentioning before we left that he was going to have James help him move it into the mine."

Westie's heart felt like there was an orchestra in her chest, building to its crescendo.

"I have a bad feeling about this, Alley."

The look in his eyes told her he felt it too, but his body stayed straight, unwavering. He was trying to be strong, she realized.

"I'm sure everything is fine. Nigel and James are together, and Nigel knows the threat of the Fairfields. No one could've gotten into this mansion uninvited."

"No, not with Lucky and Jezebel in the house, but they're shut away in a room. Why would Nigel do something like that when he knows the Fairfields are gunning for us?"

Alistair tossed his hat to the side and pulled his fingers through his hair. "I don't know. I mean he wouldn't, I don't think. But before we panic, let's go look for him. He may be in the mine, perfectly safe, and we're worrying about nothing."

"Let's get over there before it gets too dark to see where we're going."

Westie grabbed a telegraph bird from Nigel's office on her way to the foyer.

"What's that for?" Alistair asked when Westie bent over a table to scribble a note.

"I'm letting the sheriff know we have the evidence we need against the Fairfields as well as against the mayor. He's closer to the mine than we are. We can meet there and form a plan."

She rolled the note and stuffed it into the bird's metal beak and sent it on its way. As she was about to head out the door, she saw a spot of red on the edge of the table.

"Is that blood?" she asked, voice cracking.

Alistair stared down at the spot warily, touched the red, tacky substance, rubbed it between his fingers, and sniffed. "I believe so."

Dread filled her. "What if they hurt him?" She gathered her skirt in her fist.

Alistair took her hand, soothing her. "Look at me." She met his gaze and let the fiery determination in his eyes curb her anxiety. "Nigel will be fine. He's a smart man—a brilliant man. He can take care of himself. Besides, there's barely enough blood there for a paper cut. You've seen the scars on his hands. The man always has an open wound after working with rough metal."

Westie nodded. Her resolve felt like a glass vase on a shelf during an earthquake, so close to shattering. "I suppose you're right. Let's get on while the sun's still with us."

Westie and Alistair took Nigel's steam carriage to give their horses time to rest. Alistair drove while Westie fed the fire. The more coal she gave it, the faster it wanted to go until Alistair was begging her to slow down. Finding the road flooded, they had to double back and take the longer route through town. It took thirty minutes to get to the mine on the other side of Nigel's property. The sun had just settled behind the mountains when they arrived. The weak light coated everything in a dull gray haze. The buggy and draft horses used to tow Emma were out front, as well as the sheriff's horse and James's lazy city pony.

"See, there was nothing to worry about after all," Alistair said as he secured the brake.

Westie had to admit it was a relief seeing the others' horses. She grabbed her parasol off her seat. Just in case.

The darkness of the mine's entrance looked like a solid thing, as if it could break a bone were someone to step too quickly into it.

"It's awfully dark in there," Westie said. "Why aren't there any torches lit?"

Alistair took her hand. She detected, for a moment, the slightest tremble in his touch.

"They might be too far inside the mine to see any light."

"Nigel!" Westie called.

Only her echo answered back.

Before they'd left the mansion, Westie had dumped her bags, bringing only the newspaper clippings with her, not even thinking she might need the lantern.

"They'll have a torch inside. We'll just keep walking till we see light," Alistair said, his mind on the same track as hers.

Westie heard the tinny clink of Nigel's machine somewhere in the dark and felt the weight of the world on her shoulders lighten. Perhaps Nigel and James were too deep in the mine to hear her calling them. As she walked farther in, she heard a noise like a hiss—but not the same kind as Alistair's mask—that made her stop. A light flickered a short distance in front of her.

"Did you see that?" she said.

Alistair made a sound beside her that would have almost sounded like a yelp had his mechanics been capable of making such a sound. She heard his feet kicking at the rocky ground and felt his hand tug at hers until they were yanked apart. The cold emptiness of his absence filled her palm.

"Alley!" she cried.

Something brushed against her arm in the dark. Not Alistair, she knew, and not Nigel or the sheriff, for they would've revealed themselves.

The sound came again, that same scratching hiss, only this time she recognized it as flint being struck. A spark in front of her turned into a drop of light at the tip of a candle's wick. Westie sucked down a startled breath when she saw Lavina's face illuminated above the flame, a floating head in a black sea.

"Finally," Lavina said calmly. "Did the two of you walk back from Sacramento?"

Every muscle in Westie's body was wound tight enough to crush her bones. "I swear if you hurt him, I'll blow your lamp out once and for all."

She pulled the parasol from the scabbard behind her back and held it at her side.

There was another hiss and then another as torches ignited, stripping the wide cave of its mysteries. Westie squinted as her vision adjusted to the light, and when it finally did, what she saw brought a new and improved kind of fear, bigger and more special than anything she'd ever experienced before.

They stood like a morbid family portrait, with Emma as their backdrop: Lavina and Hubbard in the middle, Cain to the right with his arm around Alistair and a blade to his neck, the mayor and James to the left, Nigel gagged and tied to a chair, beaten but otherwise unharmed. Then there was the sheriff's mutilated body lying on the ground in front, naked from the waist up, his arms, half his face, and his belly all eaten clear down to the bone. When Westie opened her mouth, it wasn't a scream that came out, but a sob.

She closed her eyes, brought her hands to her mouth, and told herself she wouldn't panic. She was a wild thing. Wild things didn't fear other predators. She took several more breaths, and when she was sure she wouldn't lose her mind, she dropped her hands.

"Hello, Westie," James said, his carefree smile dazzling. As the shock wore off, she noticed more and more details. The bloodstains down the front of James's and the Fairfields' clothes but not the mayor's, and the bag of gold beside James that she'd hidden under the loose floorboards beneath her bed. He must not have been asleep after all when she'd crawled under the bed to take the gold for the trip to Sacramento.

"Alistair was right about you all along," Westie said in a strangled voice. "You won't get away with this."

"Oh, I don't know," James said with a dismissive shrug. "I might."

Westie shook her head. "No. I won't let you."

"Now, Westie," Lavina said, walking toward her, careful to avoid her machine, "this doesn't have to get ugly. We just want to talk."

"I don't want to talk. You've got your gold, so why don't you just go on and leave us be?"

"It's not about gold or money. Never was."

"It's about Emma, isn't it?" Westie said. She knew Lavina was desperate to get the machine, but she still hadn't figured out why. "I don't understand why you want that machine if not for the investment. Without the aid of magic, it's not worth a damn thing except for the copper it's made of."

"Why don't we go outside? I'd like to show you something," Lavina said.

Westie didn't want to go outside, but when Lavina raised the point of a knife in her direction, Westie gathered it wasn't a question needing her answer. She led the way, with Lavina's blade pointed at the middle of her spine. The others followed. Westie glanced back to see if Nigel would be left unattended in his chair and felt a spark of hope for the man with a million gadgets hidden on his person. But Hubbard grabbed the back of the chair, easily dragging Nigel's weight along with him.

It was still light enough out to see by, but that wouldn't last long. There was a strong wind kicking up. Westie thought maybe, when it was dark enough, there was a chance the torches would blow out and she could make a move. Until then she would mind her manners. There was no sense putting her family at risk if the situation weren't absolutely dire.

"The blue trees," Lavina said, pointing at a line of them beside the cave. "That's the edge of the Wintu magic ward, correct?"

"Yeah, what about it?" Westie said.

Lavina handed her lamp to Hubbard and walked up to the line of trees. Westie could just barely see the shimmering surface of the magic dome. Lavina took a visible breath, shoulders rising and falling, before stepping through the watery membrane. Nothing happened at first, just Lavina standing there, looking at Westie from the other side. Then, after a few seconds, the color drained from Lavina's face. She bent to vomit. Her back arched like a hissing cat and she vomited black liquid that gathered into an oily pond at her feet. When she looked up, making eye contact, Westie saw that Lavina's pupils were a murky white color, like pearls set in pools of mud.

Westie gasped and took a step back. "What the hell . . ."

Hubbard rushed to his wife's side, helping her to stand. Once they were back in the confines of the magic ward, the symptoms quickly subsided.

Westie's heart clenched. "You're turning into the Undying?" She recognized the signs immediately, remembering all those people back in Kansas when they'd first gotten sick, the look in their eyes, the black vomit.

Lavina struggled to catch her breath. "Such a nasty affliction," she said through coughing bouts.

"But how? Everyone knows eating creatures of magic will turn you into the Undying." She wanted to ask if Lavina was as dumb as she was ugly but let that dog lie.

"Yes, well, it turns out young werewolves in human form don't give off a musk like their adult companions."

Westie laughed. She couldn't help it. "You ate a werewolf?"

Lavina coughed and spit gray mucus onto the ground. "Someone likes them young," she said, turning her glare on James.

James smiled unapologetically. "The meat is much more tender that way."

The amusement drained from Westie when she thought about them killing and eating Isabelle.

"There's no cure for the illness," Lavina said, "But there's a suppressant if caught in the early stages."

"Magic," Westie said, remembering the stories from her childhood.

"Luckily, the illness is gradual. James, after his time in Kansas, recognized the symptoms right away. Everyone knows about Rogue City's magic ward and do-good Indians, and their special friendship with Nigel here," she said, patting him on the shoulder. He looked exhausted. Westie ached seeing him sitting there tied up and beaten. She wondered how long they'd held him captive while waiting for her to return.

"We knew we only had a few days, so we hurriedly packed our things and made arrangments to leave Sacramento. Our plan," Lavina continued, "was to move to this horrid little town before we completely turned, and live among its disgusting creatures. Then we heard about Emma. With a machine like that casting magic wards in every American town, we could live anywhere, hunt anywhere. We had the Lovett fortune and Nigel needed investors. It seemed too good to be true. Once we arrived in Rogue City"—Lavina narrowed her eyes at Westie—"I saw that it was."

"Because of me," Westie said, a touch of obnoxious pride twisting her lips into a smirk.

"Yes, because of you. James recognized you first and tried to warn us, but by then it was too late."

"James?" Westie looked at him, watched his entire face transform beautifully with his cocksure grin. "But how did you recognize me unless you were there at the cabin with—"

Something about his lips, the small white scar through the bottom lip that was invisible until he smiled, brought back a memory so sharp it severed her words. It was a memory nearly covered and forgotten beneath the layers of time: Westie having a tea party with her Clementine doll on the porch of their home in Kansas, Tripp slopping through the mud in the yard. She hadn't been paying attention to him until she heard his screams and looked up just in time to see one of the Undying grab hold of his foot. Westie had leaped from the porch and played tug-of-war with the prairie-sick man for her brother's life until he lost his grip, flinging Westie and Tripp into the steps, where her brother busted his lip clean open.

The humor drained from his smile. "I'm hurt it took you this long to recognize your own brother."

# Thirty-Nine

"No. No. You're not Tripp." The circus of emotions cartwheeling through her made it hard to stand still. She didn't know if she would laugh or cry or simply implode. "Tripp had red hair, not black. That's not something you just grow out of."

"Come on, haven't you noticed the grease in my hair? Cain wears it too. Surely you've noticed his hair change colors."

She had, but she hadn't put too much thought into it. Westie rubbed her eyes with her flesh hand, trying to push away the pressure building behind them. With her machine arm she tapped her parasol against her leg.

"Tripp's dead," she said, blinking back the tears that blurred her vision. "I saw his leg on the butcher block next to a pot of stew."

Lavina said, "That was the last of the stragglers from your caravan. Tripp was locked up in the back."

Westie tugged at a strand of her hair to keep from reaching over and ripping Lavina's throat out.

"But how, and why?" Westie turned to Lavina. "Why would you kill my folks and try to kill me, but keep Tripp alive?"

If Lavina felt any remorse at all, she did a good job of hiding it. "I never planned to keep your brother alive, but at the time he was too sick to feed us. Hubbard wanted to kill him and throw him out to the chupacabras, but I felt it was in our best interest to nurse him back to health just in case we needed to feed on our way to the valley."

Westie looked at James, but he remained unperturbed by Lavina's admission. "Then Olivia got attached to him. He was so frail and weak. I think he reminded her of one of her dolls. We decided to keep him and raise him as one of our own. It's a good thing, or we would've had to keep the real James Lovett Junior alive. I'd never been around such an annoying child in all my life."

Westie continued to stare at James, his green eyes, the spatter of freckles on his slim nose and cheeks, and watched as Tripp's features slowly leaked through James's cocky facade. Part of her wanted to take him in her arms and hold the boy she'd loved so dearly as a child. It wasn't his fault he was a monster. His mind had been twisted by Lavina's deception.

A tear slipped down her cheek. Whether it was his fault or not, he was already ruined, she knew. Once you kill your own kind and eat their flesh, there's no going back.

Westie shook her head. "God, Tripp, how could you stay with these people? They killed our parents."

His smile wavered, then fell from his lips. "We do what we need to do to survive. You should know that better than anyone, since it was you who left me back at the cabin to be eaten."

The more Westie looked at James, the more he took on the features of her brother. But he didn't look exactly as she remembered. What she saw in his eyes was not the kindhearted little boy she had once loved, but something else, something dark and evil.

"This isn't you, Tripp. You were a good boy, a sweet, loving—" Her voice got trapped behind the wall of emotion building in her throat.

"I'm not Tripp any longer. I'm James now."

"So everything you've told me about your life has been a lie."

"For the most part, yes."

"Enough of this." The mayor's voice exploded in the night, startling everyone. "You've had your family reunion, now let's find some copper and get on with the business at hand. That machine won't finish building itself."

Lavina nodded. Westie felt her fear and desperation rise up again when she looked at Cain with his knife at Alistair's jugular.

"What do you care about Emma?" Westie asked the mayor, hoping to keep him talking while she thought of something, anything, to get them out of the mess they were in. She was sure when Emma was up and running there would be no need for the Fairfields to keep her family around. "I know you're not a cannibal. I saw you in the mine—by the way your face turned green when you looked at the sheriff, your last meal was fixing to come back up for a greeting."

"Heavens no, I'm not a cannibal," the mayor said, flexing his face into a cringe. "I'm just in it for the money. Co-inheriting the Lovett fortune has helped my station plenty, but selling a machine like Emma will help build my empire."

"Aren't you forgetting you need magic for that? There's no way the Wintu will help the likes of you."

"The Wintu aren't the only ones with magic. I know a fine shaman in the valley willing to help us out. He has a taste for the firewater, you see, and has made some poor choices in life that only a mayor can help him with—for a favor, of course," he said with a grin.

Westie looked at Nigel. The sadness in his eyes bled into her heart.

Their situation was bleak, and it was all up to her to fix it. Her reputation for mangling past endeavors didn't leave much space for hope to set up camp, but she refused to give up.

"Enough chewing the fat already," James said. "Let's deal with this machine so we can be on our way."

"That's it?" Westie said. "After the machine is built, you'll just let us go?"

His smirk said that wasn't the plan. They had no intention of leaving witnesses behind.

Westie's voice sounded more frightened than she wanted it to when she said, "If you plan to kill us anyway, there's no point in Nigel finishing it now, is there?"

"There is, actually. You have two options. Either Nigel can finish the machine, and you can all die together quick and painless as a family, or Nigel can sit there while I kill you and Alistair, slowly and painfully." His eyes grew big and so did his smile.

A string of curses erupted from Westie so foul even James blushed.

"Cain," James said. A look passed between the false cousins that Westie understood enough to spew apologies.

"No, please. Whatever you're about to do, don't," she begged. "I won't say another word, honest I won't."

Nigel roared beneath his gag, thrashing in his chair, trying to rid himself of his restraints when Cain pressed his knife against Alistair's neck, hard enough to draw out a line of small blood droplets.

"No!" Westie cried. She tilted her parasol so the tip of her gun faced Cain. It wouldn't misfire again, for Alistair had fixed it and he didn't make guns that failed.

The cut on Alistair's throat wouldn't kill him, but just a few more pounds of pressure would mean his life.

"You don't think I'll have Cain do it, do you?" James said in a teasing voice.

"I do." Tears poured down Westie's face. "Don't hurt him, please. I believe you."

James brought his finger to his chin, twisted his face in thought. "No," he said, drawing the word out, "I don't think you do. Cain, please do the honors. I'd like to show Nigel we mean business so he will see what I can do to his precious daughter if he fails to provide our machine." James winked at Westie. "And I've been wanting to watch that prick bleed since I arrived. After all, he's not good enough for my big sister."

Westie screamed when more blood spilled from Alistair's

wound. She pulled the trigger. The gun Alistair had fixed for her didn't fail. Unfortunately, her aim did. With a painful howl Cain dropped the knife on the ground and brought his hand to the side of his face, where blood leaked down his cheek and onto his shoulder. Everyone was frozen, waiting for something to happen, to see how badly he was hurt. Westie looked at Alistair. He was wild-eyed and stiff, but alive.

When Cain moved his hand, part of his ear was missing. He screamed, a loud and ferocious siren that sent chills up Westie's spine. Cain bent for his knife again and put it to Alistair's neck, but before he could do anything further, he was yanked off his feet. Westie gasped. She was in too much shock to scream, or move, or do anything at all. It took a moment to register what had happened, but when it finally did, she wept.

Costin held Cain against a tree by his neck with one hand. No one had seen or heard his approach. Thunder cracked from above, and the wind rustled the trees. Costin's long hair whipped like a horse's tail behind him. He was slight compared to Cain, but vampires were stronger than humans and faster than they had any right to be. Cain clawed at Costin's gloved hands. For the first time since Westie had met Costin, she saw his aloof mask crack to reveal the threat that he was. He was more snake than bear in his predatory ways, tall and poised to strike.

No one spoke or made a sound at first. Cain's eyes had bloomed with fear, but they soon creased and a smile moved his lips. "What are you going to do?" he taunted. "Oh, right, nothing. If you kill me, you'll melt under the Wintu spell."

Westie looked at Lavina and Hubbard. Their frightened stares and slack mouths showed they weren't as confident in their son's safety as he was. The vein protruding from Costin's forehead led Westie to the same conclusion.

Westie finally found her voice through the confusion. "Don't do it," she shouted at Costin above a crack of thunder. He whirled around to face her, fangs bared. She reeled back. Though she knew he wouldn't hurt her, the look on his face frightened her all the same. "If you kill him, you're as good as dead."

The malice in Costin's eyes softened only a little.

"I don't get it," Cain said, his teasing tone warring with the nervous twitching of his lips. "Here I was, about to cut Alistair's throat. It's obvious how you feel about Westie. You could've had her all to yourself." Cain's grin fell flat. "And now you have nothing."

Costin looked back at Cain, considering the young man a moment. "Which, I suppose, means I have nothing to live for."

Costin opened his mouth, lips curling away from his fangs.

"Costin, no!" Westie yelled at him.

Cain screamed. His mother and father joined in to form a trio. Costin sank his teeth into Cain's neck in a frenzy of violence, slashing at skin, snapping vessels, tearing tendons, crushing bone, exposing the inner workings of his neck.

Cain fell from Costin's grip and crumpled on the ground, eyes open but vacant.

Westie watched Costin through a glimmering fall of tears. He stood proud, looking back at her, his chest out, chin up, lips pinched together, but he couldn't hold it for long. As the skin of his face began to smoke and bubble, a scream punctured his lips. He fell to the ground and writhed in the dirt, kicking at the rocks around him.

Westie was screaming, frantic. The Fairfields, the mayor, and her long-lost brother were temporarily forgotten as she ran to Costin and dropped to her knees beside him. She tried to soothe him, but his pain had gone beyond hearing words. In her desperation she looked for Alistair. He'd been helping in Nigel's surgical rooms for years. Maybe he could tell her a way to stop Costin's agony. She knew, of course, the only way to do that was to put him out of his misery. But she also knew, after being in the same position before with Alistair, that she didn't have what it took to be humane.

She found Alistair right where he'd been standing when Cain had nearly cut his throat, also staring at Costin. He had the same bewildered look she'd had moments before, as if trying to comprehend what had happened.

"Alistair," she called to him. His eyes met hers when he heard her voice. "We need to—"

Her words stopped when Lavina stepped up behind him, knife in hand. "Look out!" Westie shouted.

Lavina raised the knife, the blade catching the last of the day's light, underscoring its sharpness. Without thinking, without breathing, Westie reached for her sword, heard the hiss as she unsheathed it from her scabbard. Using all the strength of her machine, she flung it sideways, letting go when her arm was extended. The sword spun two full revolutions before it reached Lavina, severing her head from her shoulders. The head hit the ground and rolled to a stop at Hubbard's feet, looking up at him. Lavina's body swayed a moment before it fell.

Hubbard Fairfield looked at his dead wife's head. He didn't fall to his knees or sob like he had at Olive's funeral. Instead he turned to Westie and calmly picked up the knife that had belonged to Lavina.

Alistair saw Hubbard heading toward Westie. Alistair jumped onto Hubbard's back, but he was no match for the giant man. Hubbard flicked him off like a stubborn bug and continued his path of rage.

Westie felt a rush of fear sweep her away, back to her childhood, into the cabin in the woods where she had first come face-to-face with the emotional void of Hubbard's stare. She had been a scared child back then, but she wasn't that helpless little girl any longer. No matter how frightened she was, she would not run from him again.

He charged toward her, the knife ready to strike. She lifted her arm just as she once had to defend herself, but before the blade could meet her machine, an arrow with bright-red feathers at its end pierced his eye and sank into his skull, killing him instantly.

Westie gasped and whipped around to see Bena still poised with bow in hand. Alistair came up beside Westie, worrying over her.

"Are you all right?" he asked.

He had a deep gash above his eye after being thrown from Hubbard's back. She should've been asking him the same thing. "I'm fine." After a quick study of her surroundings, she decided all threats had been eliminated. The mayor was gone. She looked over just in time to see James and the torch he was carrying disappear into the woods. "You have to help Costin," she said to Alistair. "Whatever it takes to stop his pain, you have to do it, you hear?"

She wanted to stay with Costin, to say good-bye, but she couldn't let James escape. She had seen the evil inside him and knew there was more to come.

Alistair nodded. Westie started to leave, but he grabbed her arm. "Where are you going?"

"To get James."

"No, Westie, please."

She reached out, touched his hair, remembering the silky feel of it. "I have to. You know I do."

He looked ready to protest further but sighed and let her go.

Despite Nigel's frantic mumbling beneath his gag when she walked past him, Westie took off after James, leaving Bena and Alistair to help Costin and untie Nigel. Westie chased the sphere of light through the forest. Even with fresh mud on the ground, she had gained on him far quicker than she imagined until she was right on him. The light stopped behind a copse of trees. Her mouth was dry and it was hard to breathe, but there was no time to rest.

Perhaps James thought he was far enough away that he was safe. She snuck up to the gathering of trees, treading as lightly as possible. Turning the corner, she found his torch abandoned on the ground and coughed the last of her breath from her lungs.

The scent of spiced cologne reached her before the sound of crackling branches behind her. That was when she knew she'd been duped. Turning, she came face-to-face with her brother. Seeing him standing there was no surprise, but the sadness wrinkling his mouth was. He was out of breath and holding a branch the size of a club in his hand. She'd been disarmed by the expression on his face, and so the danger hadn't registered until it was too late. James swung the weapon toward her, its breeze whispering against her skin before hitting the side of her cheek with a crunch.

Something in her jaw gave. She fell to the ground. Pain flared red before her eyes while flashes of light snapped in her peripheral vision. Her breath left her in gushes. James stepped forward until he stood above her. She looked at his feathered edges, struggling to bring his features into focus.

"Ouch," he said wryly, studying her. "That looks like it hurts." There was a playful ring to his voice.

Westie reached up to touch her face. Her skin felt tight and achy underneath all the pain. It felt somehow *off*. She tried to talk, but it was difficult. Not only because of the pain it caused, but because her lips didn't match up.

James knelt down beside her. "It's too bad it had to end this way. I really didn't want to hurt you. The old part of me, the boy who was Tripp, secretly hoped we could run away together and go on adventures like we had in the cornfields in Kansas. Do you remember that?"

She would've spit curses at him had she been able to move her mouth. Every memory of her childhood would be tainted because of what Tripp had become. Her happy childhood before the journey west felt like a lie.

James tapped the branch against his leg. "I looked up to you, you know. You were so funny, always full of mischief. When we were kids, I wanted to be just like you. I really am sorry for what I have to do. I want to let you go, really I do, but you're too hardheaded for that. I know you would never stop searching until you found me. If I'm to find a cure for this blasted prairie sickness, I can't have you on my trail."

The pain in her jaw bellowed as she opened her mouth to speak. "Are you going to eat me?" The words came out squishy but were easy enough to understand.

His eyes darted between her face and her machine, always on the watch. If her vision had steadied, even only a little, she would've battered him with it.

"I thought about it. Some native tribes believe that by eating the heart of one's enemy they gain his strength. With your heart I could be invincible. But I can't imagine, even in death, you going down without a fight." He winked at her. "You'd probably give me a wicked case of indigestion."

As he stood, Westie could see the regret on his face. He really was sorry. However, that didn't stop him from lifting the heavy branch above his head.

Tears stung Westie's eyes. Her little brother, whom she'd spent seven years mourning, had been resurrected and was going to kill her. She doubted she'd survive the attack, but if she did, she really would hunt him down the rest of her years. And even if she didn't survive, she planned to haunt the little shit.

James's face was crushed into a look of molten aggression as he brought the branch down. Westie rolled away, hearing the splash of mud when it hit the spot where she'd just been lying. With what little strength Westie had left, she sprang to her feet and swung her machine at him with enough force to kill a vampire. The damage it did to James's beautiful face left him unrecognizable.

*So much for postmortem photographs,* she thought before falling to her knees.

Alistair yelled out her name, but she couldn't call back. She couldn't even stay upright. Rolling onto her back, she closed her eyes to fight the nausea she felt. When she opened them again, Alistair's face floated above her, his head framed with stars.

Westie tried to speak, but all that came out were wet gurgles. She wanted to reach out and hold him, rejoice in their victory. But she couldn't move. Her eyes couldn't focus. She felt as if she were on the wrong end of a bola being twirled in the air. Looking at the sky for something solid and unmoving to focus on, she didn't see any stars. With a sick feeling, she realized it wasn't just the sky that had gone dark, but her vision too, and then suddenly there was nothing.

# Forty

Westie opened her eyes in spasms. She was in her room, on her bed. There was a clatter of chairs and shuffling feet as Nigel, Alistair, and Bena swarmed her. She blinked. The first clear memory that came to her was drinking Costin's blood and the cramping in her stomach. But no, that wasn't right. That had happened a while back, and her stomach felt fine. It was her jaw that hurt.

Another memory flashed in front of her, as crisp and startling as a slap in the face: Cain with his knife to Alistair's neck, about to spill his blood until Costin came to his rescue, tearing out Cain's throat. And then...

Westie looked up at the ceiling, at the different patterns in the wood, the knots that looked like screaming mouths. She wanted to join them. It was hard for her to believe that such a short time ago she'd thought of creatures as nothing more than vicious talking animals put on the earth for her amusement. Never imagined one could be as selfless as Costin. She never could have pictured herself calling one a friend. He had been a friend, though, the best kind, the kind who was there for her even when she didn't deserve it.

Westie tried to sit up, but the throbbing in her head knocked her back onto her pillow. She tried to speak but couldn't open her mouth, and all that came out were incoherent mumblings.

"Relax," Nigel said, peeling a damp cloth from her head. "Don't move your mouth. Your jaw is broken. I had to wire it shut."

Had it been any other time, she was sure Alistair would have had something smart to say about that. Instead he stared down at her with open worry, a bandage covering one of his eyes.

Without a voice she had to sign. *Is James dead?* she asked.

Everything had been a blur in those last moments. She wanted to make sure her memories weren't skewed by the hit she'd taken to the head.

Nigel's brows came together. "Is James . . . I'm sorry, I don't know what you're trying to say."

Nigel's signing was adequate enough, though not fluent, which turned out to be tiresome.

"Dead," Alistair translated for her. "She wants to know if James is dead."

"Oh, yes. I'm afraid so," Nigel said.

Westie closed her eyes and sighed. It was over, finally. James and the Fairfields were dead. She had her revenge, but the loss of Isabelle and Costin made it bittersweet. She opened her eyes and felt a tear slide down her cheek.

"It must be hard to learn that James was the brother you'd mourned for so long," Nigel said, confusing the reason for her tears.

She moved her hands in lazy arcs.

"She doesn't care about James," Alistair said for her.

It was true. She didn't care about James. She cared about Tripp, but the real Tripp had died a long time ago, and the man who'd almost killed her was a demon who had possessed her brother's body. She had already mourned her brother. That time was over, and now she had someone else to grieve for.

She took a breath that whistled through her teeth and tried to gather her emotions. She would mourn Costin on her own time, when there was space to weep without making everyone around her feel uncomfortable.

She signed again, and again Alistair spoke for her. "At least you have the money to finish your machine. Something good has to come from all this madness."

Optimism hadn't quite settled in yet, but it didn't stand a chance once she saw the miserable look on Nigel's face.

He said, "I'm sad to say the gold is gone."

*What?* she signed in an explosive hand movement that needed no translation. She sprang into a sitting position, ignoring the pain, even though it felt like someone was mining for gold fillings in her teeth.

"Relax before you pop your stitches," Nigel said.

*What happened?* she signed.

It was Bena who answered. "The mayor took the sheriff's horse and slipped away with the gold during the chaos. He was the least of our concerns."

Nigel finished by saying, "We haven't been able to find him. With that amount of gold, it's doubtful we ever will."

Westie wanted to crawl under the covers and scream. She didn't want to believe that her epic search for justice would conclude with the last of the bad guys getting away with the gold meant to save magic.

Her hands felt like clumps of lead as she began to move them. *So that's it—it's over?*

With slower and more deliberate hand signs, Nigel seemed to understand well enough without Alistair's help.

"Well, no, not exactly," Nigel said.

*What do you mean?*

"I mean I found another investor for my machine."

*What?* Westie didn't want to get excited for fear of being let down, but she couldn't help herself. *Who?*

She watched Nigel's mouth, waiting for his lips to open and a miracle to slide out, so when she heard the smooth, rich voice come from the doorway opposite him, she started.

"I've been looking for investments," Costin said. He leaned against the door frame, not a scratch on him. He smiled his arrogant grin when he saw the shocked confusion muddying her features. "What's the point of being disgustingly wealthy if you can't brag about all the little people you've helped along the way?"

Westie jumped up from her bed, nearly tripping over her sheets, and threw herself into his arms. His body was cold and stiff and more comforting than she could ever have imagined possible. She held on to him like a vise, with her face against his neck. His cold skin brought some comfort to her aching jaw. After a few minutes in his embrace, she suddenly remembered everyone else in the room and stepped away.

*I thought you were dead,* she signed.

"Oh, this is delightful," he said with a full body laugh. "I don't suppose it's permanent?" He pointed to one of the metal wires that stuck out of her mouth and curled around her bottom lip in a decorative loop.

She hit him in the chest with her machine, nearly knocking him to the ground, unperturbed by his teasing.

Alistair laughed too until she turned her glare on him. He cleared his throat. "She wants to know how you survived."

Costin's laughter trailed off, but his smile remained. "I'm not exactly sure, but I believe Bena had something to do with it."

Westie looked curiously over at Bena, whose cheeks were the color of overripe peaches. *Embarrassed,* Westie thought with some amusement. The only other time she'd seen her friend that ruffled was when Bena had let it slip that she had feelings for Nigel.

Bena raised her chin as if that might drain the blush from her cheeks. "Big Fish has informed me that I will succeed her as chief when the time comes. She has been helping me to talk to the spirits. I was able to reverse the effect the protection ward had on the vampire before it was too late."

Westie didn't ask Bena why she had kept such important news about becoming the next chief from her. It didn't matter. All Westie cared about was that her family was with her.

*I don't have to tell you how glad I am the two of you saved us, and that Costin is alive,* Westie signed, *but how did you find us out there?*

Alistair translated for her.

Bena said, "The sheriff sent for us as backup when he received your telegraph bird. Unfortunately, he was closer to the mine than we were and went in without us."

Westie pulled her fingers through her hair with a trembling hand. Nothing had gone according to plan, but it could've gone so much worse. A heavy fog of relief settled over her. Her family was safe and Costin was alive. That was all she wanted to think about.

Westie had Jezebel and Lucky on leashes standing between Alistair and Nigel in a large gathering in front of the mayor's mansion in Sacramento. There was a slight breeze, but not a cloud in the sky. Folks from all over had flooded into the north valley to hear Costin, the new mayor of the Sacramento Valley—and first creature to ever become an elected official—speak.

Costin wore his authority well. He stood on a platform with Bena and Emma, hands clasped behind his back. The Wintu made up a large portion of the crowd. Now that the old mayor had been replaced, there was no one to keep the the tribe out of the city. Once folks had learned it was the Wintu who were responsible for the magic ward that would keep their town safe, they didn't seem to mind the tribe's presence—even if they did stand feet away.

Westie laced her fingers with Alistair's and leaned into his ear so she could whisper.

"Isn't it something to have a creature as our new mayor?"

It had been six months since her broken jaw, yet it still clicked every time she opened her mouth. She didn't care about that, though, and was just thankful to have kept all her teeth.

Alistair touched the small of her back and rubbed slow circles as he spoke, a new habit of his that Westie adored.

"Something indeed," he said. "It's too bad what happened to the old one."

A smile grazed Westie's lips. "Sure is. Bandits can be mean ol' suckers, can't they? I do wonder who will change his diapers while he's convalescing."

Costin went on to finish his speech about the machine, about mankind and creaturekind coming together, and how Nigel's invention was a symbol of hope and tolerance. He told the people it was a step closer to a united America, where humans and creatures might one day live in a world without the need of wards.

Westie thought he was full of shit, but it was a nice speech nonetheless. When Costin finished speaking, he stepped back and let Bena take center stage. She took a nugget of gold the size of a marble and placed it inside the machine's amplifying compartment, then began to speak the words of the Wintu incantation.

Westie squeezed Alistair's hand. It was Emma's first time out.

When Bena was finished, she stepped back. Westie held her

breath. At first nothing happened, and worried murmurs skittered across the crowd, but then the trees around them started to turn blue, the color starting from the base and rising up to fill the leaves. Westie looked up when the sky took on an opalescent skin as the magic dome materialized over the town. Laughter and applause broke out all around her, and finally, for the first time in a long time, Westie could breathe again.

# Acknowledgments

First I want to thank my agent, John M. Cusick. I couldn't have asked for a better champion for my book. I also want to thank my editor, Kristin Rens, and assistant editor, Kelsey Murphy, two very smart and insightful women. I've learned so much from working with both of you, and it's been an absolute pleasure. I also want to thank Caroline Sun, Nellie Kurtzman, Renée Cafiero, Alison Donalty, and Jenna Stempel for my beautiful cover and Nim Ben-Reuven for the lovely hand-painted title. Next is Jerry Gannon and my dauntless mother, who's always supportive even when I'm a nightmare to be around; my daughter, Haydn, who skipped fireworks with friends to talk characters; and my son, Xander, who only complained a little when I turned his closet into my writing space. You two delightful turds own my heart. Next I want to thank my best friend, Alena Clark, my first reader and my loudest foul-mouthed cheerleader. My critique partner, Heather Roetto, and her husband, Nick Roetto, for moral and technical support. Our weekly gatherings keep me sane. Also, Sam Snoek-Brown and Bonnie Cox for our early discussions about craft. This long journey began with you. Last but not least, I want to thank Xanax. Because stress.